The Wild Folk

D1522503

FLORA KENNEDY

To Laura
with love,
Flora

^ Mountain Thunder ^

Mountain Thunder

First Edition, 2014

ISBN: 978-1500687984

PRAISE FOR THE WILD FOLK

"Nature writing with juicy bits." *John Beswick*

∧

"Kennedy makes words dance a wild jig. Her writing is pleasantly pungent and rustic. The Wild Folk is a quiet story of family, the choices we make and what we choose to believe in." *Stella Stedman*

∧

Vigorous and enchanting, earthy and surreal." *Owen Luckey*

∧

"Compelling, well-written, haunting. I loved it. Stays with you long after reading. *Stacy Pond*

To my mother, and my daughter

- 1 -

LORNA

The fairytale-teller told me to write it all down which in itself is strange. Here it is, for the descendants:

Lachie didn't drown. I knew that right away even though everyone else thought he had.

Always on an island everything is to do with the water. Here I am with the damn dam of it all broken. Water lashing, making landslides and pouring out rushing through my fingers, wrapping my whole body and me tilting my head back and away from the splash of it but not closing my mouth.

No, he did not drown in the washing grey Atlantic waves off Struan shore. They may have found this body lying too dry - wrecked like sea wrack and with dry sand blown into the creases of his stiff jeans and the darker sand of where the waves broke over him clogging his checked shirt, streaking his hair into bleached sandy-brown ruffles like a lace murex seashell - but this body they have found does not belong to my Lachie, not really.

Ah, so many times he, and I, could easily have drowned here at Struan, taken quickly by the ocean drifts that came all the way from America. There have been decades of time for that to happen. This place was our playground. The whole East End of the Isle of Coll from the Fishing Gate to Sorasdal was our territory and Struan our head quarters.

I, for example, could easily have slipped on the big rocks that took the hard breakers far out. But I would make my soles bleed clinging like a limpet, skin sucking to the sharp rocks, so as not to be sucked down by the love of a wave that wanted to take me out. I always preferred blood over water.

Lachie had slipped, often. I never knew did he slip or did he slide and jump because always he was fine. Even in those massive, tsunami-seeming swells of powerful water surging towards us, mountains on the move, aqua lava spill, I would instinctively jump backwards from the edge even when I was not even close to it. But Lachie never did. Off he would go, grabbed by the sea, hugged tight by her he was.

Bobbing in the water around the rocks the waves pushing him on, sometimes under, with only his head showing like a seal. He'd slither through the seaweed, its flowing, feeling, fingers of fronds fondling and tangling and he would point to the place he was going to land himself, always a different place, with a bony pale white finger at the end of his lanky arm and I would race over to that spot of his choosing and wait and watch. Me on the grounded shore. Lachie in the flowing water. Separated.

No, Lachie did not drown.

Why did we never feel the cold? Now, as a mother

myself, I think of towels and the drying of the sea-skin and the need to prevent chills and fevers. I wonder must it not have stung when my soles bled, salt water in my veins? And was it not agony walking back through the machair with pre-cut feet? Did Lachie never shiver?

I remember no pain. Back then Lachie and me were children and we were wild then and had no need of towels and fussing and moaning. It was 1974, the year we knew we were the firmest of friends; better even than brother and sister. We were nine years of age. I was born in the autumn of 1964 and he came in the spring of the following year. He was a rush of flowers after barren winter, I was always on the wane, a leaf falling, whispering to the dark part of the year. We had never seen a television nor heard a telephone ring. How tender and so wise were we then.

Now it is summer 2005 and they are taking the body to the doctor's in the village in the back of Jordan's Landrover. The doctor is here, of course, standing over the body and murmuring to John-Mac the special constable, but the body is to go to be laid out on a stainless steel bench just like the one at my own veterinary surgery in Glasgow. No, it definitely cannot be Lachie because I know Lachie would not like that. Smooth man-made metal against his bare skin. Precision-sharpened knives. Latex-gloved hands. Scientists looking at him objectively, logically, rationally. Machinery and tools made in factories. A space controlled by man and yet with nature held back.

People will need to come from the mainland to look at this body; the police and other curious parties. I hear voices shouting over the wind, 'shouldn't we not take photos of him here?' 'does anyone have a camera?', 'who's got a camera on their phone?', 'the tide's coming in', 'when's full tide?'...

I am standing away from them and alone. I am seeing that body in my mind's eye and the way the tidal waters flowing away from it have left beautiful patterns of long feathers in the sand, all around the sides. The body seems to have angel wings, folded. Inside of me everything is crushed as I stand alone on the seashell sand. I am glad I have neither camera nor cell phone.

Thousands of years of sand and my ancestors wailing and I feel a primal urge swelling from my belly to blast apart this stupid tiny crowd and lift that too-too-heavy body with its fullness and white greyness and dripping, abandoned flotsam feeling and take it into the sea and let it go or bob, go or bob.

It cannot be my Lachie because I am just on my way now to see him at Elleraig. I have only just got off the boat. I am on my way to see him. It is not Lachie here because Lachie would not drown.

Another seagull flies down to settle with the group of them on the rocks above, not far. I wonder are they the same ones that follow my father's small fishing boat, catching fish guts before they land in the water.

I look out to sea and frown. On the skerry island in the middle of the bay the seals watch us from the rocks; not one of them bobbing in the water, and they do not move at all.

- 2 -

Summer, maybe 1973? Me and Lachie have decided it's a better idea to drink from the burn up past the bridge because of the sheep shit just before the bridge where they drink and have worn away the clover-covered soil with their cloven hooves.

We don't want to eat shit so we run up over the tough grass and the tiny purple orchid flowers are bent under our ripped sandshoes.

The water is the colour of tea. Sunshine shows us the sandy sides and smooth glistening bottom of the burn and here and there the spin of tiny fish in the sand, flounders and baby trout perhaps, and the peat water lingers pale brown and golden in this pool before splashing over the lichen to pitch downwards pouring sure and true to the bridge.

It tastes warm in my mouth and when I think of it now and try to re-capture the taste I cannot. A mineral-rich liquid of metamorphic rock and ancient botany, organic dragonfly wings and meadow pipit tongues.

We are just wiping our lips with the backs of our hands when I hear a jangle of strange sounds coming from the road. The road is two tracks of shell shale with tussocks of wild grass in between. A few fortunate men on the island are charged by the Council with the task of cutting this grass for a part-time wage and it is a long, slow process that never ends. The undersides of all the vehicles are brushed clean here. Over the curved road on the hill come a troupe of summer swallows; people from the mainland come for their holidays.

I put my hand against my forehead to shield the sun and see that there are four men, three have a Tennents lager beer can in their right hand, one has his hand in the pocket of his waterproof jacket. They all have fishing rods, long and springy that are dancing in the air ahead of them. Maybe they are fly fishing rods which are always grand with round reels and lithe whipping wood.

Lachie waves to them and two of them wave back. The others haven't seen us yet. We run to meet them and Lachie is clamouring with questions; where are they going? are they fishing for trout? what kind of bait are they using? do they want us to collect worms – there is a good collection of cow pats and sheep shit over there, he could have a look under them now for the worms if they like …

The men are going to Loch Fada which is in the opposite direction to our beaches and away to the south eastern side of the island where there is no road and nobody ever goes now except at the gathering. There will be plenty of trout in Loch Fada. No doubt they will elude the strange pretend feather flies of the fly fishermen. All the rods are long ones I see. All the men are related to me one way or another. 'Hello Lorna! Where's your dad today? Out in the boat?'

How would I know?

They tell us we are not to come with them. We tag along behind them nonetheless. It is not that we want their company or that we want to go fly fishing. It is that they have invaded our territory and like little spiders with flies exploring their web, Lachie and I watch them.

It's not long before we lag behind so far we cannot see their backs. We are so used to our ambling ways, leisurely exploring and examining grasses and flower heads, twisting long grasses into pleats and chewing them, picking at rock lichens and pulling off mossy tufts, wading through bog waters and putting our hands into the clefts of dark peat that overhang the burn. The burn must run out of Loch Fada I think to myself but there are so many lochans out this way, joined by peat bog that I have no idea. Just the same as neither me nor Lachie know the names of plants or birds, we have no idea what names are printed in books for people to label every kind of soil or rock or bird or flower; label fragments of the whole.

We just know what to eat and what not to and so it is that as we put our right hands through the next cleft of peat and fish around in the darkened still water beneath it we scoop up the tiny plankton freshwater shrimps and whatever is there and spill the mix into our mouths, checking our fingertips for any wrigglies left over to lick at with our tongues.

The sun weighs down on the backs of our necks and I can see that Lachie's is red, a firey blush so mine must be too and I check it with my palm and it is bonfire hot.

We lie down in a nook of heather and avoid the gnarly branches that are like miniature trees by shuffling our backs and buttocks about to flatten it all out underneath leaving edges of pink and lilac and purple heather bells around us, comforting and cosy and bees zinging. We cannot hear the sea and that feels odd. I close my eyes. I say 'tell me again Lachie' and he says 'OK'. And he tells me again about how he came to be my friend.

Lachie wakes up first and 'Lorna' he says 'wake up!' It is like a different day altogether. The sky is full of cloud and the light is dim. I have goosebumps on my arms. When I stretch I can see ahead of me storm clouds over where the sea is. My heart goes all fluttery like there is a bird in there, trapped, flapping its wings against cage wire.

It's not the storm but what it means that makes me jumpy. It means my father might already be home and me not there like I am supposed to be.

Lachie puts his hand out to push himself up and it's a hard metal than digs into his palm; a can of Tennents lager with a bare-breasted woman on it that one of the day fishermen have left next to him. They've been back this way already then.

Together we hurtle back the way we came. My stomach feels empty and I am light-headed already. It is miles to the caravan at Struan or it feels like it.

A hundred years later I am running down the grassy slope towards home. The caravan gas lights are on and I can see him moving about inside, hulking. Yes, he is staggering. Where could I hide? He's seen me. Here he is flinging the door open so it slams metal against painted metal making the rounded pebble groove where the handle hits the caravan side another millimetre deeper. The door handle is a wave crashing and smoothing a rock of metal little by little over time, wearing it down, deepening its impact.

'I see you! Get in here! You've been with him again'.

Why do I go inside? Why do I not run to Auntie Ruby all the way along the winding rocky road to the village? I am eleven and it seems now that I was always doing what I was told at the wrong times.

He smells of salty, brine fish bait, pungent and repellent, and lager and whisky, maybe just a dram or two, and his own smell as well which is rank and foreign. His sour breath blasts my face as his finger jabs at my nose and his words are just a rush of fury that blurs the moment. It hits my ears and I see out of the tiny grey window that the sky is clearing over the water, clearing almost at the same rhythm of his storm building and so I focus on the sky and the frame of outside that I can see.

He must have met Big Brodie and the others on their way back along the road to the village swinging their trout and rods and half-cut on cans of lager drunk in the summer sun on the sides of a faraway lochan that nobody but they ever visit and them only once a year. Look at that now. If the weather hadn't turned he would have still been out in the boat and they would have passed and he wouldn't have seen their fish nor heard their news and I would not be getting shouted at here in this wee space and feeling so very tiny.

We were in the boat the next day, me and my father. It took me years to realise that he did this to torment me. For so long I imagined he was wanting to be with me, show me the work he did, make me part of his life.

No, he knew how much I hated to see what he did on that boat. He loved to see me trying not to weep for what he would do.

It would begin well and with promise. Out on the sea in a little wooden boat, oars painted green nestled in their rollicks, dipping in and out of the velvet Atlantic waters with that beautiful slurping sound, gentle as a heartbeat and the little waves kissing the bow of the boat and us at almost sea level. My father rowing us along the narrow channel of Bousd harbour, rocks protecting us on either side, water a hand span away and me with my hand over the side and the ocean between my fingers, caressing and holding my hand and then he's say 'keep your hands inside the boat and out of the water'. I thought because he was worried I would have my fingers bitten off by a shark but now I think it was a different reason entirely.

And how would it have been instead if we had maybe got the Seagull outboard, a simple thing of wonder to me with its coiled and knotted rope starter, if we'd got it going at the head of the channel and puttered over to Eilean Mhor, me and my father, just to see the seals. The wind blowing our hair like a mother tucking loose curls behind our ears and us smiling at one another. The seals would come near our boat just to feel our contentment. They might stare at us with huge round eyes and perhaps we would clap our hands and the ones lying on the rocks would slap their flippers that have finger bones inside and this communication and this connection would fill our hearts with a sense of belonging. And the fish would jump from the sea into the boat and we would sing a song of thanks when there were only as many as we would need to eat …

'Hold that' he says, 'No! Not like that! Like this. And hold it tight. *Tight* now. Don't let it go or it'll rip your hand open'

Here am I with my too-small hand trying to grip a slippery nylon rope with ragged, sharp bits coming off it and attached to this rope I am holding is a lobster creel, leagues under, and the weight of the sea on top of it and I am not strong enough.

My fingers are jammed between the taut rope and the side of the boat and even with my determination and the leverage I have of the boat's side working with me we cannot take the giant swell of the water not wanting to let go the creel.

He's smiling, trying to light a cigarette with his petrol lighter and his oilskins are dripping water into his cupped hands. Any second now I am going to let go. And through some miracle I happen to look down and lift my feet up and away from the tangle of rope they were in and just then a big wave rolls under us lifting the boat high, first crushing my fingers, oh the exquisite pain, between the rope and the side of the boat then releasing tension on the come-down swell and away the rope flies from the bottom of the boat so fast it seems to go slow and God forgive me I am hoping his feet are not free of it and even when he turns towards me furious I see him fly over the water and down with his creel to the bottom, tangled in his nylon rope and hanging for the fish to eat, the best of bait.

I've to sit in the bow where the spray soaks me quickly nursing my crippled hand that's too sore to hold in my other but I feel safer here. He is swearing when the creel comes in and there are crabs in it, some of them babies, and he takes his boat hook and smashes the handle of it through the nylon rope cage through the crabs shells and their legs twitch and oftentimes when he does this he doesn't finish them off, just reloads the bait of salt fish into the loop of rope in the middle of the creel and throws the creel back into the depths and I pray to myself that nothing enters that creel and that the crabs die quickly.

The next creel has an eel in it and this is his mortal enemy so out comes the knife and the slashing and writhing and next one is a lobster, small, which he takes out, of course, why wait for it to grow or breed when he can get the money for it now? Next more crabs and they scuttle frantic and he smashes them with the end of boat hook and it seems to me that it is the crab creels and eel creels he appreciates the most and the murderous rampage goes on all day because the sea is a land of rolling blue-grey hills.

Once he spared a conger eel the knife and instead put it in the back of his car where it lived squirming in petrol spill and green nylon rope and old tools for three baking summer days, each day less noise from its movement, before being macheted, ripe, for the bait barrel.

As we are coming back into Bousd harbour where he keeps his boat and the silver black herringbone streaked shimmering mackerel are flipping and the saith curling their fins and me with my hands slippery with their blood and guts as I gut them from hole to the 'V' under their gills and scrape out their insides with seagulls screeching MORE! MOARE! MOARE! and I throw the guts over the side and wipe my fingers on my yellow oilskins that are man-sized so difficult to work in, I feel him. First and furtive I look to the side and there he is with his hand raised knowing I can't wave back but he smiles and he knows I'm glad to see him. He'll have waited for a while at our pool – the big rock pool at this side of Struan beach – for me.

I've worked out that if I do certain things – make him porridge in the morning – no milk but with plenty of salt in the water, collect freshwater from the burn near the road and drag the container back across the machair to the caravan using the jetsam rope and fish box sled I've made, and get the kettle going for his coffee with six teaspoons of instant coffee in his stained mug that he is less likely to notice me. If I do these things and others; tidy the kitchen and wash any dishes, hang the tea towel out on the barbed wire fence to dry in the fresh sea wind, collect driftwood off the beach at Cornaig to store at the side of the caravan for bonfire wood in the winter, I am likely to hear his car roar into life while I am peeing for the longest time in the toilet which only I use which has spiders hanging from the fishing box wood ceiling.

I do a lot of domestic chores.

- 3 -

Me and Lachie have a signal for when it's safe. I am at home, reading books borrowed from school before the end of term, a stack of them high next to my bench bed like a wall. I have a much smaller stack at Auntie Ruby's in the village, those books borrowed from Mrs Cuddy's library. She calls it her library but it is really a collection of books her grown-up children have left behind. The two ancient Bunty Annuals are my favourites.

Our signal is a scarlet handkerchief of my mother's that I wrap around a round grey stone on the roof. The stone is there on the corner to stop the tarred roofing material curling off in the heat. Lachie can see the roof of the caravan, the big caravan that is, not the small one perched on the side of it like a wee fluffy fledgling tucked into its mother's breast. Lachie can see the red from the hill at the end of Struan beach between his place and ours and knows it's safe for him to come.

Sometimes I put the hanky in the back pocket of my jeans and start walking to Elleraig where Lachie lives with his mother. She is also probably related to me though I hardly ever see her, maybe at the Agricultural Show or outside the village hall or sometimes near the school if her 'lodger', as she calls him with a smile, is working on the roads that day, and maybe Lachie is related to me too but nobody has ever mentioned it. I long before stopped pestering Auntie Ruby to tell me what our connection was. Everyone is related to everyone on Coll in one way or another. Even most of the summer swallows. It is not that way so much today.

What roots survive? On the machair where we live, sand displacing under our caravan with imperceptible, grand slowness, you would think it is only the tough, sharp long grasses whose roots can remain close-grained in the sand. And it is true they hold somehow the tiny shell fragments in place, slowing their unsettling, letting them rest in giant sand dune heaps above the beach. But in between the sturdy strong long rooted grass there are pretty and delicate yet hardy tiny flowers with leaves flattened against the surface of the machair and these flowers with tiny petals and flat leaves lie low, hugging the land, and they survive, protected by the tall grasses.

I meet him almost exactly half-way near the sea ravine where cars are dumped, dragged by the tractor and let go into it. We think there are four rusting hulks of cars in there and an engine or two but we don't like the place and so we are not sure.

'Are you well in yourself?' says Lachie his blond hair parted in the middle and falling into his wide face. His grey eyes are keen beneath the weight of long, bleached eyelashes.

I nod once, quickly.

'Want to go see Bob?' he says.

'I wanted to see the cats' I'm talking about the wild cats at Sorasdal and I am keen to see if there are any kittens left, the water rats steal them away. Or so I am told by old Seumus who lives there alone.

'Bob is still in the byre'

That settles it and we turn back my way towards Cornaig Farm. It only takes about fifteen minutes easy walk on the crumbling tar of the two-track road and each of us take a track and I am on right track and Lachie on the left.

We make ourselves invisible when we pass the turning to Bousd harbour which even today still has a bad smell maybe because of the peat coming so close to the sea water and all the creatures that have died there. Fish caught and gutted. Before that seals. Before that whales. Since then sheep, breaking their legs under mounds of fleece negotiating hooves through sand mud and rock, falling over and unable to get up and the tide coming in. There seemed to always be one or other sheep's skull near the head of the harbour, ghostly wisps of matted wool sticking fast to melting grey skin. I hated running over a gentle hillock and trying to stop before the mess of fleece on heather in the dip, a wide cage of ribs like a basket.

But my father won't see us I always think when we pass by because it is hard to see anything when you've the mouth of a half bottle of whisky pressed to your cold lips and your eyes almost closed for squinting in the sun.

It is quiet on the road and our feet march with our heartbeats in time with one another. A hedgehog strolls across the road in front of us, spindly spider legs stretched long and gangly, it doesn't look at us though we stop to watch it. 'Mr McMurchie says they're sick when they're out during the day' I say. Mr McMurchie is our teacher at the school. Me and Lachie are two of the twelve pupils and we are the oldest and the only ones to walk to school from the East End. They say in the old days there were enough children that in the East End the low riding house with the red roof at Struan was a schoolhouse, organised by something called the Ladies Association.

Wild children just like we were would have sat in the dark there, candlelight flickering out of the wind, no light from the small windows without glass and learned, I suppose from a bible, all they needed to know which was not much and far less than they would have learned if they were with the men and women watching and listening.

Me and Lachie, or 'LachieLorna' our other name people called us, our names run together like we ran together, were taught to read and write, at least I was, in a bright grey pre-fab modern building in the village with pale yellow walls and maps stuck on them in our classroom, the only classroom. The school sat halfway up a slow hill looking down on everyone, and most especially the Manse where the Minister, Mr McAdam, lived.

'What does he know?' says Lachlan. 'I do not like him.' Of course I know this, Lachie and Mr McMurchie have never got on even when Lachie was five and hardly spoke a word. But I like him. I like him a lot and it annoys me that I hesitate to mention his name when there are so many things I've learned from him.

Mr McMurchie is away back to the mainland where he is from for the summer holidays and I have worried every year that he will not come back. But this year it's me not coming back to school. I'll be off to the high school in Oban and so will Lachie, of course. I'll be staying with my Auntie Peggy and Uncle Charlie who are childless but nice. Uncle Charlie is my dead grandfather's brother. Auntie Peggy bakes empire biscuits that melt on your tongue and make you feel you'll never eat anything so good in your whole life again as her empire biscuits. Two perfect circles of plain shortcake biscuit with her own homemade strawberry jam between them, a rush of white icing and a jelly tot sweetie on top.

Lachie will be going to the hostel with the other island children who don't have relatives in Oban. I am excited. Lachie is silent on the subject.

We creep across the rattling cattle grid at Cornaig Farm, LachieLorna is very good at not making noise so as not to be interrupted. There is still a sweet smell of milk curds and wholesomeness wafting from the dairy, an old silver metal railway container. My heart always lifts here. I remember being tiny and taught how to milk a cow, perched on a little wooden stool, with a giant, heaving balloon of cowhide in my face, resting my forehead on it, I feel the hairs now, and me unable to see, only feel for, the massive, dangling pale pink teats with so much skin so that the folds rolled and rolled and creased. Even when the teats were dripping milk my fingers were not yet nimble enough to squeeze and pull like Uncle Niall did. When he milked his cows he was a virtuoso orchestral musician and the sound of the milk squirting into the metal pail, changing tone as the pail filled up so that you could tell how full the pail was by the key of the squirting stream of milk on milk, was as captivating and moving in its own simple way as any piece of music, was it pentatonic I wonder now, as any I have ever heard.

And his cows are in good hands, hands that are warm and firm and experienced and most of all, hands that are kind. They were beautiful cows Uncle Niall's, so deep their eyes, so long their lashes, so unpredictable their flicking tails and they seemed wise to me these old ladies with their strong knobbly legs and chunky hooves with chipped cow shit nail varnish that sometimes slipped on the cobblestones of the byre and my Uncle Niall would say in a voice rich with Gaelic 'take your time, my old lass, take your time'. They would move in as one cow of many parts, Buddhist monks, when the sun was up awake in the sky and when the sun felt tired and was heading for bed and the little herd would make their pilgrimage to the byre and Uncle Niall filing in without command or call and stand happily, knowing their place in their allotted booth, crouching white ceramic walls separating them but letting them smell one another and as I saw it, talk.

They would chew thoroughly and slowly the straw they tugged from the hessian netting. Steam would mysteriously rise from their backs. The byre would fill with contented grunts and scrapes of cow hooves on stone. Best of all it would fill with a smell that made you fill your lungs deep with it so it would enter your body and live there forever. A smell of new milk and straw, cow sweat and hide, my Uncle Niall's flat cap hat that was only ever washed when it rained, the sea salt white like chalk in ripples on the cows backs from when they'd been down to the beach. This smell. The slap, slap of a cow relaxed and shitting into the slough trough directly under their arses and even that smell too, fresh shit from sturdy cattle who were as free as we to eat wildflowers and lichen, even that smell was like a happy thought.

If I got so much as a dribble of milk in my metal pail I would smile and smile and my Uncle Niall who died when I was nine would come to me and smile and nudge me off the stool that was worn to the shape of his skinny buttocks but I would not go far enough and would lean against him in his denim overalls and breathe in his smell and close my eyes to the sound of the music of the milking. Often would I fall asleep. A moment or two.

It was an honour I thought to be shown a half-full pail of milk and nodded at. This would mean I was to carry it to the dairy. The curved metal handle would nestle in my palm but I would need two hands because even empty the metal pails were heavy. We would slop to the dairy where my Auntie Bessie was already washing the bottles in hot water, later she would have waxed cardboard cartons and less to do except unfold them and set them, made up on the counter but what I remember is her getting ready with the foil cap press to go on the tops of the bottles, slicking a smear of oil in its hinge each day. The farm cats would trickle behind us licking at the milk and my uncle knew fine that I was spilling some on purpose and he did not mind at all.

Once he got out of his bed their son Ruarhi who was ten years older than me would drive the milk around the island, delivering milk to the doors of those who wanted it. Milk that was potent with nourishment, fresh from the teat that morning and thick double cream settling on top, a food in itself and no need of cereal. He would do it in a little, black

Morris Minor van that he was able to fix himself if it broke down anywhere but nonetheless would one day find itself sandwiched in the rock-jawed ravine at the shore.

You could see how the farm had grown from a single black house; a house of rocks piled together and small spaces for windows, a door in the middle, thatch on the roof and rocks hanging from string from the netting over the thatch. Not long before, in my father's time, the family would live in one straw and mud-floored room and 'the beasts', the cows or sheep, in the other, sheltering together and the beasts creating heat too as well as milk and meat later.

This single bothy was ruined even then and next to it, close, another the same but less ruined and next to that one another, less old again and another that was used as a store and more. And then the new farmhouse that sat proud and sudden further up the slope. You could see how the fertile land here had grown houses and people and as some people died and others remained those who lived prospered.

Me and Lachie had explored these old ruins and even managed to get the padlock off the newest house, for years a byre. It was in there we discovered the huge harness of leather and metal and realised the story of my Uncle Niall's horse was true, that he had had a horse and the plough this horse pulled did indeed sit rotting outside. They said my Uncle Niall could put his hands on any animal and heal it, and I believed them. They said that his horse, the animal he loved more than any other, the one he went all the way to the Borders of Scotland to buy as a foal, a fine Clydesdale horse, had faded from him and the grief of it changed my Uncle Niall and no-one mentioned the horse again.

I sniffed the inside of the harness and there was a foreign, heady smell of horse, a bit like cow but fierce with it. I had never seen a real, live horse. When I asked Auntie Bessie about Uncle Niall's horse she put her fingers to her lips and told me not to touch the harness again. It was then I remembered seeing scuff marks on the floor of that padlocked byre and realised that was where Uncle Niall would sit and smoke when he went 'to think'. And I have no doubt now that he took draughts of horse scent from that harness too.

I would love to touch that harness now. I have not seen it since then. Did they bury that harness with my Uncle Niall I wonder? When he died of tuberculosis and my Auntie Bessie of throat cancer six months later.

Today, as me and Lachie sneak across to the new, tall, metal byre that makes such a racket in the wind, and slide back the metal bolt that's stiff, we know Ruarhi is away, his Landrover is gone from the front of the house. He is probably down the village at the boat doing his pier-master. We both jump when Bob barks suddenly but we are inside and the big border collie with his wide head and massive paws whines and howls and rolls on his back, pathetically submissive, and wees all down his back legs regressing to puppyhood with the joy of seeing us. I take a too-fast breath and my eyes fill with tears that I push back down my throat.

'Bob' we say, 'hey Bob, good boy' and we go to him and I hold his head and Lachie pats him good and firm on his back and flanks for Bob is up on his feet now and his tail could not wag with more spirit.

His brown eyes are wise and make you want to stare and stare into them. I unclip his chain which has become tangled. It was never long in the first place but now it is so short he has not been able to move away to take a shit and there is a pile a good foot high that he has just kicked over.

I get the mucking out spade and scoop his shit into the wide bin at the far end which has more shit in there that has gone mouldy and blooms with white fur.

The food bag is not far from Bob, he can see it from where he is chained and I can estimate from the shit pile that it has been maybe 3 days he's been chained. Bob stretches and stretches some more and yawns and looks at us expectantly.

Lachie is already pouring his food into the caked and chipped enamel dish and adding water from the big tap and me adding my left-over fish from last night's dinner and Bob is starving for all his shit. 'Could it be longer do you think?' says Lachie and I nod. 'If he's not eaten he wouldn't shit. The shit was dry and didn't smell. Maybe a week then?' Lachie shrugs in reply, 'let's go' he says.

Bob is at the byre door already, nose pressed against the metal and we slide it open and he is off and runs under the high metal gate and into the field that ends at the shore but we know he'll go full-pelt, fast as he can, a rush of freedom filling him 'til half-way and be back on his own and here he is, tongue lolling and happy.

He comes with us on our rounds and his company makes everything different and it is nice. Bob doesn't chase the blackface sheep he's been trained to herd by someone on another island and he ignores the cows and he is altogether the best dog in the world.

We wander about parallel to the road but we can't see it for the tall grasses and poppies heading towards the Fishing Gate which is the border of our land and we drink from the burn that has been cut out of the peat near the barbed wire fence and Bob jumps in and we laugh when he is drookit and shakes himself and the drops lash our faces and 'how can his coat take on so much water?' I say, wiping my cheeks and running my wet hands through Bob's thick coat and shaking the fur between my fingers. We check out the quarry – I am looking for fossils because Mr McMurchie has shown us some from the south coast of England. Ammonites they were called and I love those ones with their layered shape in the same way I love mushrooms when I first see them in the shops in Oban.

We find no fossils and it is too dry in the scoop of a quarry bowl so we head back towards Cornaig Farm and go past and head towards Cornaig beach through the sand dunes and crossing the burn twice because of the way it winds and the way the fence has been placed, this fence newer so we have to lift Bob over it in a tumble and climb it ladder fashion ourselves – first me and then Bob, Lachie holding him high and me scooping his wet sandiness into my chest, his legs straight out and in the way. We are strong with things like that me and Lachie.

The tide is in at Cornaig beach but we walk along the fence on top of the rocks all the same and it doesn't matter that we can't walk the tidal sands to the small island. I never like doing that anyway, it is Lachie who always want to do it and I think he hopes we would be stranded there with the sea deep and full tidal around us, spending the night there. It fills me with dread and I am always checking whether the waves are dying towards the sea or dying closer to land to know if the tide is coming in or going out.

Who drilled holes in these sea rocks and cemented metal fence poles here and why would they do it? As far as we could see LachieLorna was the only visitor and even the sheep don't stray down these sea rocks. So many tiny mysteries here.

Lachie slaps his arms around his body and hugs himself when he comes out of the water that's thick with the spaghetti of dark, leathery seaweed. 'Does it not try to drag you down to the bottom?' I say.

'No, sure it's like being stroked by mermaids' says Lachie. I would never ever go into that part of the sea jammed between the rocks of the island and the pincushion of rocks and metal poles of the shore. The seaweed breaks the surface in curls of blackness. It scissors the waves, snipping and pinking and the seaweed frightens me with its unpredictable movements pushed and pulled as it is by the tidal waters.

There is a wooden fishing box stamped "Mallin Fisheries" in faded blue stuck in a crevice around the big rock and we slump because we know we should take that back with us but it is always a nuisance to lug stuff about when you are on a wander but you cannot turn your back on flotsam and jetsam on an island where sometimes the boat, the ferry from Oban via Tiree and sometimes Barra that is, doesn't call.

We look around for fishing rope, there is always nylon rope on the shores cast loose or torn away from the fishing nets of the Russian trawlers off the coast, and until we find it we carry the fishing box between us. We have learned from previous skelf incidents to carry the raw splinter-filled wood lightly.

We take turns dragging the box once we've tied the knotted orange fishing rope caught in the machair to it. Once we are further inland I begin to unfurl the tufts of sheep's wool combed from the blackface's fine fleeces from the wire on the fences where they have been rubbing or best of all the pot of gold places where they go under the fence and have made a dip there from passing through and have left tons of wool as they struggled on the bottom wire spindle. I know where all these dips are with their sheep wool bunting and maybe tomorrow I will go around and collect more wool.

'Auntie Ruby told me that if I collect enough sheep's wool I can use it stuff a cushion and maybe she'll give me one of her old summer dresses to use as a cover' I say and Lachie smiles and nods 'tha sin uabhasach math' that's very good he says, will you make one for me too?'

Over the sand dune we see a figure at the pool of deep water at the bridge of the road that we call the Gloumac. It is a bottomless pool. You need to be careful at the edge on the tussocky side which is where it's best to fish from otherwise the sun casts your shadow over the pool with your rod end and the fish will not come to you.

I recognise him right away even though he is taller this year because he was here at the Gloumac last year too. My cousin Murdo. They are all cousins of mine, as if my grandfather had no end of brothers and sisters. He is a year or two younger than us a city boy who lives in Glasgow and is scared of dogs and the bull and everything really. The Gloumac is ours and he's from the village, having not even made his own way here; instead dropped off in a car by his father no doubt and he will be here all the day taking our trout.

Even Bob is not interested in him and stays by our sides. We don't wave but just walk the way we were going before. We put Bob back in the byre. We dream of a free Bob who lives with either of us but everyone has said no to that idea before. If we don't put him back in the byre someone will shoot him for roaming. He has had a good day. What more could any of us want?

We make sure the chain has plenty of length and move the old stool and plastic fishing box away so the chain is less likely to tangle and he has more space. I plump up his bed and he curls up on it, tail patting slowly, ears flat. Lachie's got his food and we leave him with a bowl of it and plenty of it too and fill his water dish and he is settled and tired and we are all happy.

We, jailers too, slide the byre door over, push the bolt back. Ruarhi shouts, 'hey! what are you doing?!'. His hobnail boots make his feet circle up at the toes so he seems to roll up to us. 'Did you let him out?!' his face is red but mostly from the wind and sun. He pushes his black-framed spectacles back up his nose, 'well did ya?'

'No, I did not' says Lachie taking the question to mean did we take Bob out this very second when we slid open the door. 'I only just fed him.'

'You fed him did ya? Well that's very good of you now.' A hen screeches from near the farmhouse and another joins her, a squabble of clucks. A feather, unrelated, drifts down from where it had clung to the runner of the byre door. 'A good day today' he says looking at the still blue sky.

We nod, shuffling our feet about in the grey shale, staring down at each others footwear. His hobnail giant's shoes next to our tatty, sandy sandshoes. Lachie pretending I'm not here so Ruarhi can too and not say anything to my father.

'You want a job for day after tomorrow?' Ruarhi asks and we look up and it's both of us he's asking.

'What job is that?' says Lachie.

'Gathering.' We know that everyone is asked to help gather the sheep from the remote back lands to the south west but never as far as the sea on that side.

'Sure you'll come' he pauses, 'Bob'll be there. He'll need you to look after him.' He huffs and hawks something out of his throat and spits. 'Aye, I better get on. You behave yourselves.' Ruarhi takes off his cap, there is a stark line of white skin on his forehead before his hairline and his hair falls out all greasy with Brylcreem and he pushes it back off his red and white face with his cap, puts his cap back on again, adjusts it, pushes up his spectacles and walks away up toward the house. We watch him until he goes in through the shed door that leads to the scullery that leads to the kitchen.

'Will you go?' I ask Lachie.

'Aye.'

Whenever I ask Lachie will he do a particular thing it's a given that I am meaning the two of us.

But that day I am in two minds. I hate the shouting and yelling about where to stand and when and not running fast enough and being blamed and bellowed at and have fists scrunched up at you from a distance as though you're getting a beating later when the sheep separate over a hillock and Ruarhi screaming commands that don't make any sense to me never mind Bob, changing every second and whistles that don't mean a thing and swearing and shouting and quarter bottles and glugs of drinking and it is the longest day of the year for everyone and walking the full day through the bog and cotton top grasses, seeing at last the white water lilies on the lochans out there and irises enveloped in brown paper bag sheaths and pulling ticks out of your skin the next day.

I could easily get off the tramping and gathering itself just by being a girl but I never thought of myself as a girl or any less able that any of them, except for Lachie, but he gives me the confidence to do most anything.

I decided next day to meet them coming back in the late afternoon and do the last home stretch to Cornaigmore with them. The climax was in the flat field there, so barren all the rest of the year, but now there blossomed in a spilling stampede white tufts of cotton grass that were as they came closer not cotton tufts but thousands of white-fleeced black-faced sheep. What a sound; masses of sheep, close-packed baaaing and scurrying and moving in currents like fish shoals in water until some were pressed hard against the barbed wire fence, panting and eyes rolling.

A few of the sheep were like yaks with two coats on – ones that had missed last year's gathering and they must have suffered bad those ones with not just the weight of their bi-fleeces hanging in rags of so much wool Auntie Ruby could make a mattress out of one sheep but the ticks and hunger and broken hooves and horns and all the rest and then two years of wildness in their hearts suddenly coming to this.

There are plenty of summer swallows helping out, exhilarated and fluttery at being so close to sheep sweat and primal fear. A flock of wives have arrived from the village in Hughie's transit van, their wide floral-patterned collars blowing up in the wind and their flared trousers flapping. They have cakes and cameras, shop-bought thick white bread sandwiches with sliced ham and tinned salmon, pancakes with butter and jam, huge plastic bags full of hundreds of miniature packets of cheese and onion, ready salted and salt and vinegar crisps, bulging plastic bottles of cola and lemonade that say "pppsssssttttt!" and explode when their tops are unscrewed 'for the kids' and there is much posturing and posing, as much as there is with the sheep.

But after the cans of lager and Sweetheart Stout are crunched empty in raw-knuckled hands and thrown in a pile in the corner of the fank with dings of musicality and the counting of the sheep and the wiping of brows, it was too hot that day but better than that pouring rain, after all that ritual for the longest time when they all leave it will be quiet and still and very little would move. You could hear the flies at last and the bees always humming and Ruarhi would smile as he looked at his flock. 'Very shi-fine ma tha' the men folk would say in mock-Gaelic and shake his hand one by one as they left, piling into Hughie's blue transit, a green Hillman Imp and a black Austin Maxi to head back to the village or 'the big smoke' as they called it.

Tomorrow will be worse for the sheep. My father will be here tomorrow for the dipping and the hitting as the sheep go through the runs to the deep trough where their feet go out from under them and if Ruarhi has his way their heads too for a moment or else they will be pushed under the chemical water with a byre brush. There is always a boy like Lachie ready to haul them off the bristles tangled in their fleeces should they not come back up again and drag them back into the maze.

Before that though the shearers will be here from New Zealand, away across the whole world these huge Maori men who are just like our folk except that they speak little, drink less, giggle like small children and shear fast and well. Their simple shears are like big snippers, a single piece of honed metal with an almost circular bend at one end and two sharp edges at the other pointed, snip, snip, snip they go. Precise. Perfect. When I have watched them I am reminded of my Uncle Niall and there is a mesmerising quality to their work. There was no buzz of electricity back then, of course, or wires hanging from ceilings. There were not even ceilings. The Maori boys have just clippers and a duffle bag and a pocket full of pound notes as they traverse the Hebrides of Scotland shearing sheep and sleeping wherever there is a free bed and a welcome.

Later in Oban there was a girl at my school who was eerily beautiful with her brown skin and black curls. We were friends for a few weeks and she said she had been told she was a throw-back to the Spanish invaders centuries ago. I told her she looked Maori to me and how I wished I looked like her and I told her of the Maori shearers who slept where they were welcomed. She had not known and it was not long after that we drifted apart. I wondered should I not have mentioned the handsome shearers.

Me and two others will stand at the end of this ramshackle production line with ancient horsehair brushes, bristles glued with years of layers of red paint ready to mark the sheep as they come from the shearers with a smear across their purest-white-I-ever-saw backs as near to the tail as we can get. When they come through I will see as before where the shears have nicked them and sometimes the nicks are deep and near where I have to mark them.

Mark them. Mark them as belonging to someone.

- 4 -

It's Friday and we're off to the dance. He is off to the dance at the village hall. I am staying the night at Auntie Ruby's.

I have to sit in the back of the jalopy that is my father's car. I think it used to be a Ford Cortina. His .22 rifle is propped against the front seat. There are rips in the vinyl of the back seat. The springs inside make it bouncy and I trampoline until the windy gap. The windy gap is where the two tracks of road reach a tight valley between high hills and you have to pause at the sharp zenith in case there is a vehicle coming the other way as fast uphill at you. My father never pauses.

Rabbits scatter as we race down the other side. He pulls over at the bottom of the hill and grabbing the rifle is out with his back resting against the frame of the open car door and muttering. The sound of his shot is like a cannon in the green and golden sands foothills. I rest my forehead against my window on the opposite side thinking, 'run rabbit! run away!'. On this side the grey brown rabbits sit on their back legs, front paws against their chests like little old women in fright. Their ears are raised up in wonder at the noise and what it is.

I know what they look like under their fur. Pale meat and veined. My father showed me long ago the art of skinning a rabbit. It's like pulling a jersey inside-out. While the technique is nearly the same, the gutting of rabbits is not like the gutting of fish. Not for me anyway.

It is rare for him to go collect a carcass now. Maybe he just doesn't bother. But always he says when he gets back in, 'think I nicked that one. Damn mixy'.

Mixymatosis he says makes the rabbits sit bulging eyed on the road wanting to be run over and put out of their misery. They need to be shot because of the mixy. I've seen them bulgy-eyed on the road caught in headlights bright in the darkness but it is fear not the mixy that makes their eyes so wide.

I dread the bump-bump of a rabbit under a front and then a back wheel. It is a long time since I looked back to see if it was dead or not. Now I don't want to see the dragging, useless back legs.

Past Gallanach Farm and its old tulip fields of the 1950's the land lies flatter and it's a winding but lowering stretch to the Crossroads. He swings the grunting car to the left between two rocks, the cattle are near the road, a calf is on it. I see the heifer thinking of suckling; rubbing her head against her mother's side and I slide down the vinyl backseat so the front headrest is a barrier to my view as he roars past.

The flat of the estuary runs a long way parallel to

the road, brown and muddy and peaty. A dog barks from the backyard of Archie's house at my father's car. And now the road rises up to the skyline plateauing and there is the old schoolhouse on the right and the sea away on the left, almost always catching the sun or moon and twinkling with light and just before the two-tracks decline to a triangle and the shore there is the sign, "Arinagour".

He'll take me straight to Auntie Ruby's. He always does. She is out in the garden across the few metres of road from her doorstep. Her garden is splendid with red roses, pink gladioli, a magnificent young pampas grass in the middle and a little metal seat to sit upon and admire it all.

It is fenced off to stop the free-grazing sheep eating her pansies and peonies. The land drops suddenly from her wee patch of flowers to the shore, all gritty mud and lapping, quiet waves when the tide is in.

Her house is called Rose Tree due to her mother's rose tree that used to curl over the jamb of the red door. Auntie Ruby is my real auntie. She is my father's much older sister and I love my Auntie Ruby.

She is unmarried having been brought suddenly home from her nurse's training to nurse my grandfather and here she has stranded like a magnificent minke whale; too late for the finding of a man on the mainland, too late to finish her training. I heard Mrs Rohane telling Jessie that she should have just missed the boat that day they made her come home and she would have not missed the boat altogether.

'Hullo a gradh' my love, she says to me, her wide bosom swelling and making her floral apron strain.

'Come to me a gradh' she says when I am already unclipping the front seat catch on the car floor and pushing it forward to get out. The rifle bangs against the dashboard. 'Watch what you're doing for Christ's sake!' The smell of Old Spice aftershave sharpens in my nostrils.

'Did I put the safety on?' he gropes at the rifle. 'Get out of my sight!' He spits it at me. 'You'll be the ruin of me so you will.'

I see him wipe his palm across his face like a flannel as I propel myself out and into Auntie Ruby's big arms and swirling mist of rose-scented cold cream. She swaps me to her right side, her arm around my waist like I am a toddler being carried on her hip. The world of Arinagour village, or at least her house which I can see, tips with my head as she leans down to see her brother in the car.

'So we'll see you tomorrow some time? Or will you be back tonight?' she says.

'Sure I'll be back tonight.'

'Are you not going to leave the car here then?'

'Chan eil', I am not, he says, 'I've to go up and see Fergus'

'Tha sin gle mhath, mo bhràthair' that's very good, my brother, she says.

She shuts the passenger door and slaps the top of the Cortina hard twice with the flat of her palm. 'Away you go then you rascal you' she says knowing he can't hear her and smiles at me a melty smile of sponge cake and jam.

'Sure you'll have had nothing to eat a gradh? See how there's not a pick on you. Does he not feed you at all? Och you come in now and see what I've got for you here.'

I wipe my mouth up the sleeve of my blouse, which is one Auntie Ruby made for me last year. She shakes her head seeing it and puts her hand down inside the neckline of her apron and under her dress and takes a tissue from somewhere deep in her bosom and wipes my whole face and not just my mouth. 'Ocht. No wonder you're drooling a gradh'. No wonder indeed. You're still not filling that blouse now a gradh' she says as she pulls the side seam and shakes her head.

She waves at Wullie who is sitting in his wee garden next door to hers. He is mending his fishing nets, sitting amongst his darrow feathers that flicker in the wind around him hanging off his fence. He lifts his arm, pipe in hand as if to finish a conversation he was having with her.

A front door and a dark room either side of the tiny hallway which is cluttered with oilskins and wellies. The sitting room is on the right. The table is laid with the good tablecloth, it's broderie anglais from Glasgow, and there is so much food I cannot see hardly any of the design. In the middle a sponge cake the height of which makes it too tall to fit in my hand, there are scones and a glass dish of butter, bright yellow, and bread with a crust you could live on and shortbread and soft biscuits with icing and slices of something with wild apples in it and a big jug of milk with a picture of purple and yellow flowers on the side.

I stand as I always do, as I did every Friday night of the summer and I just eat the smell of it all. 'I've something in the oven for now' says Auntie Ruby and away she goes to the dark coolness of the back scullery.

I lift Miss Bonny the fluffy tabby cat from the 'visitor's chair' next to the stove and put her on my lap where I stroke her and stroke her purring engine and run her giant feathery tail through my hand again and again. I close my eyes as her claws gently pull at the fabric of my old jeans near my knees.

'Why do you always make so much food Auntie Ruby?' I say as she comes down the two worn stone steps from the scullery with a dishcloth-wrapped pie dish that is steaming.

'Here's a ling pie for you, a gradh. You start on that right away my darling. Come now to the table and sit down.' She clasps her hands together for a moment over the abundance of the table. 'Wheesht. Are we not expecting company? The selkie? Is he not coming tonight?'

She looks out of the tiny window towards the bay, 'have the seals taken him already?' she says.

'You shouldn't call him that Auntie Ruby. He doesn't like it.'

'Well maybe not but he is a selkie so what's the harm in it a gradh? You know I wouldn't say it in front of him.'

She nods at me to start eating the plate loaded with a quarter of the ling fish pie she has served up for me at the table.

Miss Bonny smells the fish and jumps down and towards the table. 'No, Miss Bonny. Don't you try to steal Lorna's food off her plate. See here, I'll put some in your dish in a minute.'

I pull the hard wooden chair out from the table and sit on it at an angle. And Auntie Ruby pulls the other chair closer to me, dragging the burgundy-patterned rug forward with its feet.

'But he is odd Lorna' she whispers it to me. 'Odd in a good way I mean' she sits back and lifts the chair to rearrange the rug. She swipes a duster rag over the bottom rungs of the chair.

'There's no sense denying your nature. God preserve us if I don't know that for the truth of it.' She pats the gold heart-shaped locket at her neck. 'You wheesht now and eat it up before it gets cold.'

'Where's yours Auntie Ruby?'

'I had something earlier.'

For all her pretty plumpness I hardly ever see Auntie Ruby eat. But she drinks a lot of tea.

The fish disappears off my tongue before I swallow it. The creamy sauce is like ambrosia (I have just learned that word in class) and I am just tingling all over.

'Well I hope he manages it' says Auntie Ruby.

'Manages what?'

She breaks from a haze of thought that is a mystery to me, ' … something to eat. I mean makes it here for something to eat.'

She glances at the tiny gold watch face on her wrist that is heart-shaped to match her locket. The Roman numerals are so tiny and squashed together I don't know how she reads the time at all.

'It's a while 'til the dance starts yet. They'll all be at the hotel first anyway having a few drams.'

The mantelpiece clock thuds its seconds.

'Did you see his mammy on the road at all?' she says.

'No.' I slurp the word making sure not to lose any ling and cream sauce from my mouth so I tip my chin up too.

'I think her Bill Travers is getting a motorbike.

Supposed to be arriving on the boat tomorrow.'

'Lachie says his name is Alfie and that he's a famous artist' I say. 'Who is Bill Travers?'

'Humph. Alfie is it you say? Och, you know, Bill Travers the film star. You won't know it. It's a grand film. The Bridal Path. He's a Englishman playing a Scotsman looking for a wife. I saw it when I was training in Glasgow. He's a fine looking man. I can see why they call him Bill. Sure and she's lovely herself that Kirsty. Oh, and do you remember now me talking about Ring of Bright Water that I saw in Oban, och, you were only about four years old. Bonny wee Lorna a gradh'

'Why do you say Lachie's a selkie Auntie Ruby? Nobody else thinks so. It's only you.'

'Nooooo. That's not true. There's others like me. They just don't let on is all. I told you she told me herself. And I believe her so I do.'

I stand up to reach for the milk jug and take the muslin off it. The cowrie shells sewn to the edges hold it taut over the top to stop flies drowning in the milk. They tinkle. 'Did you make this Auntie Ruby?' I ask fingering the stitches worked in soft creamy thread. 'Ha' she nods, distantly. She comes back, 'will I show you how to do it?'

'That would be grand' I say. 'All right then.' she says. 'Aye, it's all alright.'

In the quiet I can hear the seagulls screeching and calling to one another. They are very sociable creatures the seagulls. They are always talking to each other and being sure to be heard.

Lachie always knows what it is they are saying. 'What was it she said Auntie Ruby I mean *exactly*.'

Auntie Ruby takes her seat at the fire. I call it her

'talking seat'.

Immediately I get up. 'Can I poke the fire?' I love that dull iron black stick of a poker and shoving it into the red coals and stirring everything up, wee sparks flying and a rush of hotter heat.

'No, it's fine. Just leave it now. I don't want another loose coal burning the rug. See here from the last time you did it?' There are quite a few burned-out scoops on the rug.

Her talking chair is a modern rocker that only rocks a tiny bit. A 'visitor' left it with her several summers ago and it suits her just fine. The armrests are narrow, shiny wood, far too narrow for her to rest her huge cake-batter-beating arms upon and they get in the way of her long knitting needles which is why, she says, she prefers the thin four double-pointed needles and the knitting of woollen socks.

There's a scrape of feet at the back door. Only the intimate are allowed to use the exit door to come in.

'Och, it's yourself Lachie' says Auntie Ruby, lifting her knitting from the basket on her right hand side. 'How are you today?'

'I'm fine. Mammy says I've to go and see auld Jessie. Something is going for the hens. The new ones. She thinks it's an otter so I have to go.'

I stare up at Lachie and I say nothing at all. There's no need for words.

'Will you not have something to eat before you go?'

Lachie hesitates. Me and Auntie Ruby know fine he's going to take something, and something for the hens too. He's already glanced at the shortcake biscuits. Several are bundled into his deep short trouser pockets and he flattens his woollen jumper over the pocket opening. With a free hand he takes a slice of sponge cake. It is at least twice the width of his palm. 'Tapadh leat' he says, thank you very much and Auntie Ruby smiles quietly to herself. 'Aye, very good laddie' she says. 'We'll maybe see you later then?'

'Maybe. Glè mhath, very good, I'll away then.' He steps up the first back step in reverse, his foot finding the step easily from habit. He turns around at the top step and the back door bangs shut behind him.

He leaves us a sweet scent of sea air in the cosy, stuffy dark room and me and Auntie Ruby are the better for it.

'Mr McMurchie says we've not to listen to fairytales and stories about the island. That they're all superstitious nonsense he says.'

'Does he now? What makes him say that do you think?'

'He's educated Auntie Ruby. He knows all about India and Australia and everywhere, in fact. Remember that project we just did on South America?'

'Oh yes, and you did so well a gradh. And you agree with Mr McMurchie do you Lorna? An incomer like himself?'

I know I should say I don't but the simple fact is I do. I feel in my blood it is not right to agree with an incomer, no matter how educated but Mr McMurchie knows such a lot.

'I think he's a good teacher Auntie Ruby.'

'Aye, well, sometimes the best teachers are the ones that don't call themselves teachers at all.'

'Can I have another of that slice, Auntie Ruby?'

'Of course! You help yourself now.' She's knitting

and rocking and with such a full stomach and the dimness and the flickering of the gas light and its mellow buzzing and breathing and the fire crackling low and hot and me thinking of all the things I did that day I feel my limbs heavy and my eyes too.

'Don't you fall asleep in that chair!'

'I was just thinking about Lachie. He's not wanting to go to Oban.'

'No, of course he isn't. What is there for him there? And in the hostel too. It's all right for you at your Auntie Peggy's. It's a right shame they couldn't take him too. Your father would have none of it. I didn't even ask him. Humph.'

Humph means Aunty Ruby is very annoyed about a thing.

'Why does he not like Lachie Auntie Ruby?' It's not the first time I've asked this question but I'm hoping that with me leaving for the mainland and high school and this being a well-known rite of passage to adulthood, as Mr McMurchie said, or at least, teenager times, I might now get an answer.

'I don't rightly know now. Some things we're better off not-knowing. I know you love your learning Lorna.'

She stops rocking. 'It's good you're going away to Oban. you make sure you make the most of it now. Don't be like me.'

I see she's dropped a stitch in her knitting and is holding the work close to her eyes to pick it up. 'We're all just like snow on seawater so we are'. She smooths the grey hair at the side of her head which swishes up into a tight bun at the back.

'Aye. So it is. We're here but a moment and away - as if we never existed at all. You make sure once you make it to the mainland and finish school you don't let them pull you back to the island.'

I wait and don't breathe at all. I know if I just wait one, two, three, four and count, five, six, that she'll continue. But if I make a noise there'll be nothing but the seagulls squawking and landing with flapping feet on the corrugated iron roof.

'I don't suppose Mr McMurchie goes to the shore much does he now?' she says.

'He wouldn't have been able to spend a lot of time there now would he, with the seals and the otters and the oyster catchers what with his marking of papers and reading about the big, wide world outside of Coll?'

'He thinks we should know all about the world so we can go and get good jobs. He's not interested in boring things like the shore.'

'Boring you say?'

I blush lightly under her glaring eyes. I should just be quiet.

'So he's taught you nothing at all about your island home? It's all India and Australia is it? Well, yes, now I suppose it *is* very important to know about kangaroos and koala bears when you live on the west coast of Scotland.'

A tractor trundles past the window. We feel its huge wheels coming before we see the flash of the red Massey Ferguson. We know it's my Uncle James from the west end. He'll be heading to the pier to collect supplies the boat has left in the storage area.

'The story about Lachie isn't boring Auntie Ruby…' I give her my best all-ears-and-innocent-eyes look.

'Och, your mammy would be so proud of you

Lorna a gradh. If only she were here to see how lovely you are. You look so like her …' Her eyes are wet and pooling. I hate that.

'You were going to tell about Lachie being of the seal folk Auntie Ruby.'

'Was I now?' she checks her knitting and smooths her work, checking for any previous mistakes.

'Your mother was brought here by your father but Lachie's mother came on her own.' Her bosom plumps out and deflates.

'She came in an old van all on her own, Kirsty did. Packed to the gunnels with stuff and she came because her people were from the East End. She hadn't known that, of course, until just before she came. But when she knew, she came. She came back.

'Your great-great-great- let me see now, yes, your great-great-great-great-great grandmother married her great-great-great-great- is that right now?' her fingers are splayed, counting generations. She folds them like cards. 'Anyway, they were married.

'So she came, Lachie's mother, and made straight for the ruin of her ancestors at Elleraig. What a lonely place for a young woman. She came here first for her tea, of course. I saw her in the shop so I did and told her to come to me for her tea. She didn't look pregnant to me.

'Away she went and in no time at all, her house was built. In the old style, you know - with the men from the East End and some from the village building it for her. But not like the old days, she had to pay them to do it!'

Auntie Ruby gets up and pours out the tea from the teapot and swirls water from the single tap in the sink by the front window looking straight ahead through the lace curtains to her little garden, checking for sheep, and letting the tea leaves catch in the muslin she'd left in the sink, for the roses, not the telling of fortunes today, she likes to say.

Scoops of fresh dried tea leaves are delivered to the dull silver-coloured teapot with its intricate filigree engraving. She takes a thick wad of fabric from the rail above the fire and uses it to lift the kettle off the heat of the stove and pours it in the teapot as it is heating its bottom on the hotplate.

'We'll just leave that there a minute.' And it is these comforting rituals of tea-making and the knitting of socks and the wooden spoon beating of cake batter in a giant ceramic bowl that I will awake to the following day, those domestic details that made me so frustrated with impatience back then, today as I think of them there is harmony and rightness and a sense of all as it is meant to be and nothing more.

'Every man working on the house swears he didn't touch her. And yet, nearly ten months to the day from when she arrived she arrives in the village with a baby!

Such a bonny, big baby he was, your Lachie. Och! The big red cheeks, the massive fat legs of him, blubber all over. And when she pulled back the swaddling from his head – I remember it was a cream Shetland wool style blanket, lacy and tiny stitches you know, must have been a family heirloom – Did you bring the wool?

'Oh no! I left it in the car. I've got quite a lot though, what with the shearing too.'

'That's all right a gradh. You can get it later and we'll do your wee cushion. I've looked out some fabric for it.' She pauses looking to the back bedroom and then in the middle distance where there is nothing but perhaps a memory of a thing.

'The eyes! Och the eyes! Huge!' she tilts back her head. '*Just* like a seal's they were. *Just* exactly like a seal's. Big rock pools of blackness on his face. Slipping down a bit at the sides; sad-looking you know.

'So strange. They're not so bad now right enough, at least there's a bit more white there than there was. But then he's got those whiskers now … Anyway, me and Jessie just stared at him, sucking our lips at him right outside the door here. I bustled her and himself in and Jessie went off to spread the news, or 'gossip' as she likes to call it.

'I was fair bamboozled, I don't mind saying. There had been no sign of a pregnancy at all. Not a word and no big belly neither. I know because I saw her regularly, she was in the village every week at least and would come here for her tea.

'Ruby!' she says to me, all breathless. 'I found him! I found him on the shore!'

'I fell into my chair, it was the old armchair, do you remember? Before this one?'

I'm having a feeling that Auntie Ruby thinks she's talking to my mother because I have never had this amount of detail before.

'What do you mean you found him on the shore?' I say to her and I'm thinking has she gone mad, alone out there at Elleraig where everyone know spirits march up that stony wee shore every evening at dusk just as they did as real men years ago from the boats they tied off to the iron rings in the rocks after the seal hunts? I have heard those spirits myself so I have.'

She puts down her knitting, tidily in the basket.

She pushes herself out of the talking chair using the narrow arms as levers, takes the smaller piece of wadding for the teapot handle and carries the teapot to the table where she swirls it in circles and pours its peat burn-coloured water into a bone china cup, absent-mindedly upturning a second cup so it's ready to take the tea but remembers herself, stops, and sits down in her chair with her cup of tea steaming and fragrant.

I hear the rain suddenly hammering on the roof. Damn it to hell I think; I won't be able to hear her and will she stop talking altogether?

'That'll sort them' she chortles, all round laughter. I know she means the men drinking out the back of the village hall, not dancing yet, but nursing half bottles. Me and Lachie have spied on the goings-on at the dances many times.

For a moment I remember my father crying on the road outside the hall, falling in the ditch there and crying because Uncle James had punched him. I had never seen my father cry before. Or since. LachieLorna did not know what to say or do. And, of course, we stayed hidden behind the gorse bushes, scratching at our grazes from their thorns.

The rain has gone and all that's left is the gurgling sounds of its quickness lashing down the slope at the back of the house and slurping down the roof pipe to the rain barrel and flowing out of it.

'Where else could he have come from but where she said she found him?' she says with tight lips.

'There was no-one pregnant that summer though it was a good year for lambs. No-one at all. So it wasn't someone else's given to her, you know, like we used to do you know, in the olden days, when it worked out well to do such a thing?

'I believed her. It was her face. So entranced. No. So *enchanted* she was. She was just as you would be if you went down to the shore of a morning and found a big baby brought in by the sea and left when the tide went out.

'She said she saw it first from her kitchen window and thought it was a seal pup. But she heard no sound of a seal mother calling to her young and she said she looked right away at the seal rocks in the bay straight ahead of her and they were all just looking at the house.

'So she went out and she said to me it was like she was taken-over with something as soon as she walked out the door and she walked down to where the sea had gone out and the sand was still wet.

'As she got closer she could see already fat legs and arms and that it was no seal pup. She said to me as she passed the babe to me to hold for her arms were aching from carrying such a weight, she said, and I had a sense the whole of her was aching for something, "It was a baby Ruby! This baby! Whatever will I do?'

'At *this* the wee fella started to howl and the wildest sound you ever heard in your whole life and we; me and Lachie's mammy, we froze there like two eejits. It was the sound you see, Lorna, a gradh, it was not the sound of a human baby at all. It was like a bark of a wail. We were afraid someone would come and what would we say?'

There's a timid knock at the door "Thig a steach, Agnes, come in!' Auntie Ruby raises her voice. It is her next-door neighbour, Agnes Dunbrae from Glasgow, though she's lived here for years, 'have you a mantle Ruby dear? I thought I had plenty under the sink but Jack's used the last one and not told me.'

Auntie Ruby gets her a spare gas mantle from the box under the sink.

'Hullo Lorna-dear. How are you tonight?'

'Very well, thank you Mrs Dunbrae.'

'It'll no be long 'til you're at the dance, will it, hen? Lovely wee lassie like you, hen'

'Yes, Mrs Dunbrae'

Mrs Dunbrae takes the delicate moth-weave mantle holding it with her fingertips by the plastic edge and cups her hand around it as she makes for the door because even the wind can tear it. 'See you later Ruby, thank you.'

'Thanks Agnes' says Auntie Ruby.

They are all like that in the village; always nipping in and out of each other's houses for the want of a thing. It's just an excuse for seeing who is where and what's going on. My Auntie Ruby doesn't do it. Or so I like to think to myself when I'm eleven years old and about to go off to high school in Oban.

'Did Agnes see the baby Auntie Ruby?'

'Oh aye, of course she did, she misses nothing does Agnes. It was Agnes had the orphan milk we gave him but he wouldn't take it at all. And that when his mother – see, even then she was always his mother, even him a selkie fairy man – had the thought to put some fish oil in the milk.

'We mashed up a mackerel Wullie had just brought me, it was lying in the sink. We didn't even cook it, and bones and all, mashed up good and with the mortar and pestle too and in with the orphan milk and he was perfect.

'That was the solid proof of it for me. I knew then

for definite he was a selkie.'

I have a fierce knot inside me. How can I believe such a thing when I know from school that all of this stuff is nonsense. Lies people tell children to stop them asking questions.

Mr McMurchie doesn't do that. It's all facts with him and you know where you are. But then Auntie Ruby is not a liar either. I suppose she is just mis-guided.

'They say it's just one of her fairy stories like the ones she sells.'

'By 'they' you mean the ones who think she's mad?'

I am squirming inside. 'But it makes sense doesn't it Auntie Ruby? That she would make up a fairy tale about him since she makes them up all the time for her books?'

'Don't you know it was the finding of Lachie that started her off writing the stories Lorna? It wasn't long after that, as she carried him about in a sling on her back walking everywhere instead of using the van, she started asking us all, the Coll ones that is, about the old stories.

'And we are very glad she has written them down and made them better and other ones too – from Uist and Skye and the standing stones one from Lewis and we are very pleased for her success on the mainland - tha sin gle mhath, it's very good.

'See, she wouldn't have met her Bill Travers now but for the stories, would she?' she says. 'Him doing the drawing for them. Now that's a proper fairy tale romance so it is.'

When Auntie Ruby tucks me in under the heavy feather eiderdown quilt like a caterpillar in a salmon pink satin chrysalis on the nine foot high bed in the back bedroom that bores into the hill, and the ceramic potty under the bed in case I need it in the night and don't have to fall again on the slippery, rickety back steps like a ladder leading to the outside toilet, it is part of our bed-time routine that I ask her. 'Can I not come and live with you Auntie Ruby?'

And she says what she always says, she says it with her big arms wrapped around me and my tiny head nestled in her bosom and the smell of rose-scented cold cream that still makes me feel safe when I put it on my own skin now, she says, 'you know I would love to have you here a gradh. I would love it. But he needs you. You need to look after him a gradh.'

I thought she meant her brother, my father. Now I wonder was it not Lachie?

- 5 -

I'd like to say I fell asleep that night cooried-in like a
wee grub in my satin eiderdown and dreamt of the
seal folk - of seal maidens and men of such beauty the
sea waves kept them hidden lest they be stolen by
mortals, precious treasures of exquisite shimmering
colours that would brighten the nights inside black
houses, trapped sea fire flies, and make the dour
world of grey and black and urine-soaked tweed a
magical place of rapture and heavenly blessing.

Seal folk who would keen for their kin in the sea.
Who would walk the shores of the whole, tiny island
to find their seal skin and return.

I could have dreamt of a seal maiden on the rocks
at Elleraig that I saw first as a seal which stood up and
became a tall woman with long, dark hair and darker
wise eyes in a face of such perfect loveliness that I
gasped.

My daughter, Freya, who is six years old, dreams
of fairies and demons, of witches and dwarfs, wild
woods and fathomless seas. She has the benefit of a

deep folklore education at her Waldorf school. But not I. No, I did not dream of sea fairies.

I could say to you now that I saw whispers of such transformations on the rocks in the corners of my eye as Lachie and I played in the rock pools and fossicked for what the flood tide had left us.

But I never did.

I never saw Lachie gaze wistfully to the sea with anything other than the need to be immersed in it and swim. I never heard the wind send his name to us, I suppose it would be his selkie name that he would recognise, from the ocean depths to dance around our ears.

We never heard his parents' voices in the spiked shells we clapped to our ears, only echoes of longing. We never thought of dog fish cases as anything but mermaid's purses. But I do remember Lachie telling me that mermaid's purses were the place to hide your secrets and we stole a penknife from his mother's tool bag and for a while would slice open the leathery hard cases and poke our fingers in to make sure they were empty.

We would think with morose gravitas about a particular secret, I cannot remember a single one of them now, and tuck in inside, under the groove next to the slit and then we'd kiss the case and set it free into the sea again.

He wouldn't have been sending messages then would he?

I must not be so daft.

And yet.

There is something.

It is indelicate to mention. I will ponder it later.

The whole thing is wrong. It is just all wrong. That

they're saying he drowned is particularly wrong. That he is dead on Struan beach is wrong.

The only thing right about it is that I am here; a peculiar co-incidence for I have just arrived, just this morning on the boat and with no-one here knowing I was coming.

It was only that I left my medical bag here with all my instruments when we came up at Easter. I left it inside the front door of Rose Tree thinking Johnny would put it in the car. I have been using the spare surgical instruments at the surgery for this past week but I am wanting my own bag, my own tools, with me.

I think of my husband, my little girl and my older boy back on the mainland in our home in Glasgow. I see them at the dining table eating breakfast, blackened toast and scrambled eggs and sunshine streaming through the window I've just washed and my mind goes blank. I've been considering too many disparate notions and now two worlds have battered their heads together and I am locked out on Struan beach.

I only came on my way to see Lachie and say hello like I always do. I always drive down to the beach, there is a fence and gate at the road now but you can drive down very easily.

I always look ahead before I turn to the left, get out of the car engine running, and open the gate and put the heavy hook of the chain on the leaning post on to the rung of the gate. I always look ahead and think of Lachie to let him know I'm on my way but just making a quick call to look at our beach.

I jump back in the car, noticing the fresh tyre marks that have crushed the tiny orchids and wild geraniums further down and after I close the gate behind me I notice the prints of boots in the wet sand near the gatepost and I know right away something isn't right for there to be such traffic here on a Saturday morning and me first off the boat.

I drive slowly the few hundred metres across the flat plain of flowers and grass that the sheep love to graze. The sheep are not here.

Around the hillock I see the backs of vehicles; a Landrover, Jordan's; a strange car I don't recognise, green it is; the doctor's Mercedes and oh mother of God there is John-Mac's truck.

If the doctor, the special constable and Jordan are here someone is dead. There is no question of that. I want to turn back and head over to Lachie's at Elleraig, take my wellies off and toast my thermal-socked feet at the fire while sipping one of his famous coffee-in-a-dram's from an old mug we both remember his mother used to drink from and not be involved at all in whatever drama is happening here on our beach.

When you're younger these things are exciting but now I have seen enough sadness that I am not curious to see more. I don't want to see ugly on my beach. But, of course, I can't suddenly turn around and my tracks there for all to see and say how strange, and maybe even suspicious, it was that I turned away.

For Christ's sake.

It is just infuriating when you're just going about your life and next thing, you're in the middle of some event and involved and your life is hi-jacked and it is always something I have battled with, this need to feel I can get a run at something instead of constant interruptions.

I'll need to go down and see them. It's not so bad, me being a vet, people are always happy to see my professional self because vets, I'm happy to say, seem to have a more amicable status amongst folk than doctors, as if we have something 'other' about us, the mysteries of the healing of animals lending us the kind of reverence doctors enjoyed before the internet, and google especially.

I park my car to the side of the others, a bit away. I light a cigarette from my emergency packet in the glove compartment using the car lighter. I have to replace my emergency packet regularly.

I step out of the car and the wind nearly blows the cigarette from my fingers but manages to blow ash into my eye and it stings so that I keep both eyes closed and wait, gladly, until my tears wash the ash away.

When I reach the edge of the machair I'm relieved to see the group is away down the other end of the beach, a good five or ten minute walk, more if you're the beachcombing kind.

I've left my binoculars in the car in my overnight bag, I remember I put them at the top so they were handy. I'm not going back for them. I would look odd standing here looking at them through binoculars.

So I let the loose white sand, clumped where other boots have been this morning, spill down some more as I follow the trail the boot steps have left despoiling the perfect wind-rippled blue shell patterns on the sand just below the high-tide mark of dry, black seaweed.

The wind is threatening to bring rain and there is a swell of salt already in its breath. I pull my waxed jacket hood up and hold it clasped under my chin. I lick the salt from around my lips and am not sure it is salt from the sea wind when I was on the ferry gazing at Coll coming towards us this morning, a view my soul is awakened by as though from deep slumber, or is it fresh from the private sea that is mine and Lachie's here.

They are intruders this lot at the end of the beach and as I watch them come closer with each of my sluggish steps and my heart sinks with the sand under my feet in big furrows here where the three sets of boot steps come closer and one set is in reverse, someone must have started to go back and then changed their mind and onwards I go on this track.

I see now that it is not a person they have found. It is a small whale. A seal maybe? It is a bulging grey mass that if I didn't know this beach so well I would take to be a rock. But what a funny place for something to beach. I have never seen anything in that spot before.

I make the wrinkles round my eyes deeper as I screw my face up to see better. I can't see much at all because the three of them – the doctor's floral scarf is being tugged at by the wind – are standing with their backs to me and between me and the whale, seal, whatever it is, rounded beached thing. Maybe they will need a vet after all I think except I've left my newly-reunited med bag in the car too.

The tide is well out so it is unlikely whatever it is has survived.

I am spotted. Jordan is running towards me with his arms waving at me furiously as though I am right in front of him and he is pushing me away. I hear his voice like a very quiet foghorn but can't hear the words, the wind is scrambling them into code.

He is running at me. I've never seen Jordan running before in my life. It's quite a sight; his olive green oilskin has fallen down his left shoulder showing the pale tartan grey coloured lining and his waders are flapping and slapping together where he's folded over the tops so he's like a giant walrus coming at me beating his flipper arms and making foghorn noises.

I stop.

Behind him I see the other two, the doctor and John-Mac are looking at me. They are like the standing stones at Totronald transposed there onto Struan beach. Quiet, ancient sentinels to something no-one remembers or knows.

As I stand, not realising I have stopped, I see the flashing light of the beacon on Sul-Ghorm further down the inlets and skerries of lacy-rock coast. I am centered and grounded by its flashing because my heart beats know its rhythm and I can feel my heart beats and hear them behind my ear.

"Go back!" whispers John-Mac in his shouting that's filtered by the wind. I tilt and turn my head with my ear towards him to hear better. My arms raise themselves from my sides, my hands are open, my fingers spread apart as if to say I can't hear him.

"Go back Lorna!"

Who the hell is he to tell me what to do? What is going on here?

When he is close enough for me to see his face I am suddenly aware of my knees being joints after all that might give way and there's a sense of the sand moving downwards beneath my feet.

His face is ghoulish and wet and it's as though his

sagging skin has been dragged down to his throat, his mouth is open, he is panting, stupid man, now he can't speak for all his running.

I just wait. I look over at the standing stones who are still looking at me. I have a better view of the beached bundle – is that denim blue?

John-Mac is in front of me, blocking me with his body. "Lorna! Oh Lorna!" he wails at me and then he says nothing at all. He's shaking his head from side to side and his arm is pointing limply behind him and, is he choking?

I go to move past him, wanting more than anything to end this stupid charade of him and his inability to form a sentence.

He grabs my arm, 'Don't look Lorna. Ma 'se ur toil e, *please*, don't look. No'

'Get out of my way, you fool' I say, shaking off his knobbly red knuckled hand. I sprachle my way onwards until I am close enough to see blond curls tangled in seaweed, that is neither a seal nor a small whale that has beached but Lachie, a bloated Lachie, the sea has filled him up and he has swollen and how long has he lain here alone? Surely not long for the tide has just left him for us, for me.

And then I fall forwards meaning to reach for him but instead there is sand in my hands and I am Lorna-the-vet on her knees howling and I think I did scream, for I felt it come up from my guts and wrench itself out of my mouth that was too small to hold it in and my whole body tingled with the strength of it when I screamed with the seagulls and all of my longing.

'Get your hands off me' I say to John-Mac when I realise the heaviness of my shoulders is the weight of his arm and he is crouched down next to me. I had thought he was Jordan the wife-beater.

'He's been in the water a while Lorna. We're not sure where he went in. It doesn't look to be here, at least.'

I'm grateful for my liking of John-Mac for it is that which makes me become quiet and attempt to get to my feet. I manage to do without his help so that standing I am Lorna-the-vet and not LachieLorna and remain so while I am able to stay standing and stop keening. I am unable to move. And so I stand. A fourth standing stone.

The day me and Lachie went to the standing stones at Totronald was a lost day in the west end. For all it is was only 6 miles from home on a two-track road we always lost our bearings there with all the peat bogs and cairns and it always seemed to be dark there and raining or about to rain.

I had brought sandwiches from Auntie Ruby and cake, of course, and she had gone and bought us small glass bottles of lemonade from the shop and waved us off from her front door as we headed towards the left road at the fork, the road that ran along the low side of the hill and along past the village hall to the west end. This was 1977 and the first summer holiday after our first year at the high school in Oban and it was now we felt able and adventurous to explore the whole island and not just the East End.

I had gone up to visit Mr McMurchie in one of the council houses on the hill of Arinagour near the school and he had made me coffee and wanted to hear all about how I was doing at the high school and what subjects did I like best?

Of course Lachie hadn't come and I don't think he said as much as 'hello' to Mr McMurchie from the last 'good mo---orn--ing Mr McMur-ch-ie' singsong hello of our last morning at the primary school until Mr McMurchie left the island for a new job in Orkney when he did indeed wave him goodbye.

Lachie is scuffing up all the tiny stones on his track of the road, occasionally kicking out at the tall grasses in between our tracks. My heart sinks.

It's not just his brooding or his hanging head or slinking, low shoulders. Nor the lack of natural synchronicity of our footsteps. Nor that when I look down our feet are so different, mine wrapped in brand new training shoes bought by Auntie Peggy in Oban, all white and newness and his in old black sandshoes. No. It is not these superficial things. It is the feeling I have that I need to ask if something is wrong? Is he unhappy about something?

It is so new this need to ask him things. With our first year in high school, me in the warm embrace of my auntie and uncle and empire biscuits, him in the hostel, forsaken and bullied, he has changed and it is not just that he has changed for we both have grown-up too suddenly on the mainland but it is that there is a space between us like there never was. It is change, this thing. Change. I don't like it.

'Did you want to take the old cattle track from the old dairy?' I say trying to catch his eye under his veil of golden hair.

'Maybe' he says and sighs.

'We could always go back a bit and cut through the field?' I venture.

'No Lorna. Don't you know you can never go

back?'

I stop walking. He is full of these forlorn statements now Lachie is. Deep statements that close doors in your face. He continues to walk on, scuffing his feet still.

'Will we just go home then?' I say, annoyed already with his mood and even annoyed at being on the road to the West End which I have never taken to. It has always felt like a different island to me with its bogs instead of rocks and its quick, hidden ditches of peat banks filled with tarry water so that you don't feel safe off the road for fear one leg will go down and the rest of you carry on walking so your ditched leg breaks and you're dragged down by the West End's equivalent of Wights on the Barrow-Downs.

He turns to me. 'This is home Lorna. Come on.'

I hate this new habit he has of calling me my name. It's as if he's bossing me about. And when he started doing it at school on the odd occasion we'd see one another, me loaded with books and plastic tartan pencil case heading into class and him with a duffle bag of who-knows-what but not books that's for sure, heading who-knew-where he'd say, "Hullo Lorna" as if I was a stranger.

It is funny the way I attempt to regress a year in the hope of keeping LachieLorna happy. I remember making a mental effort there on the road past the doctor's surgery and the Lodge and heading for a silver line of sea across miles of brown bog and crannog-crowned lochans.

By the time we get to Totronald and sink our backs against the standing stones we are in better mood and LachieLorna is happy. We unpack our food quickly, we are starving and we eat it all in a rush and take our time with the lemonade and its bubbles which lead us to a burping competition. Lachie wins.

'Why do you not like the school?' I say. It's a question that's been burning my brain for months.

'That's simple' he says.

'It's not simple to me. Why?'

'I don't think you'd understand Lorna.'

I am affronted, 'Me? Not understand?'

'I don't mean to offend you Lorna. That's the thing you see. I am stupid. And you won't understand because you are clever.'

I notice at that moment a green hairstreaked butterfly resting on the stone above Lachie's blonde hair. I know if I ask him Lachie won't know its name and I am proud that I do know it.

I feel that by knowing it I have captured the essence of it. I have its perfect wings in my mind and I know the colour of its chrysalis and the plants it feeds on. It is probably looking for some Birds-foot-Trefoil right now and I can see some just over there - We have just studied butterflies in science class, a class I am thoroughly enjoying.

The butterfly takes wing and lands on Lachie's right hand, flattening its wings on his skin so it looks like a dead leaf.

Most people would want to lift their hand to their face to look more closely at this beautiful creature, maybe lift its wing up to see the emerald underside. Most people would want to invade and interfere. They would disturb its chosen resting place without a thought except to examine its splendour. I notice now that Lachie has never done that. He lets nature rest upon him.

Right now his eyes glance down and his lips move

outwards in a kind of a smile and his eyes close and his hand remains still on his thigh until the butterfly alights and is instantly gone.

I have met so many people in Oban, throngs of tourists near the pier from all over the world. I hear American accents and German, people speak French and Spanish and it excites me and stirs me and makes me feel part of a huge, wide world. I have many friends who seem just like me, from other islands and with a craving for knowledge that lets us compete with one another without jealousy.

Through this multiplication of humans I see all humans differently as though I am already looking down a microscope and as I look at Lachie, me brushing heather bells off my jeans and him not bothering I frown. Part of me is drawn to his wildness and another repelled by it. But he is my Lachie and we are LachieLorna.

Of course he's wanting to swim at Crossapol but it's miles more, only a few really, and I am wanting to get back to Auntie Ruby's, my legs are weary.

But it is too much for me that first summer after high school in Oban to consider letting Lachie go on to Crossapol on his own and me head back to the village and so we do go to Crossapol and when we are closer he runs ahead so that by the time I am on its sand he will have had his swim already and be ready to head back.

I meet my Uncle James who has seen us passing and not coming back yet when he was out on the hill at Friesland and has come over in the Landrover with his sheepdog Cap to ask me are we wanting to come for our tea on the way back?

I tell him my legs are aching and I need to get back

to Auntie Ruby's and that Lachie is swimming at Crossapol.

'We'll go and get him. I'll take you both back to the village. I've to get petrol anyway' says my Uncle James.

I jump in the open back of the Landrover with Cap whose fur is dusted with water and salt and sand and he smells like the sea and the farm and wildflowers and I breathe all that and am happy cuddling up to his warmth as the wind whips my hair into my face and Cap points his nose into it, then turns quickly to lick my lips once with authority before going straight back to the business of sniffing the wind.

I see a swollen grey tick on Cap's face at the side of his mouth and, I have done this a hundred times on various animals including myself, I expertly dig my fingernails in at each side and twist and pull and it's out legs scrabbling for a hold and I chuck it out into the wind behind us. Cap keeps his nose in the wind; he's on-duty.

My Uncle James is lighting his pipe as we stop at the Crossapol gate all stark and lonesome on flat shell sand and rough marram grass and the wind always whipping and I jump in the front of the Landrover next to him after I've shut the gate behind us and Cap comes in too, sitting between us. 'Good boy Cap' says my Uncle James.

We will wait on the beach in the Landrover with the salt smattering the windscreen and the tiny wipers wiping and squealing now through the sand dunes, the Landrover rolling on the curves and sharp slopes and deep, narrow valleys like a boat used to such stormy waters.

And from here at the beginning of the huge expanse that is Crossapol beach, miles and miles of white sand, we can sit watching Lachie in the water through the greasy, narrow windscreen but not well enough it seems because my Uncle James is getting his binoculars from the short shelf near his door and is hooking the latch of the door to stand with the door like a shield against his body and his elbows leaning in between the door and the cab of the Landrover like he has done to look at sheep in the distance a thousand times before and now he is looking at an altogether different sight: Lachie, like a porpoise in the wild sea water bobbing and rushing under and my Uncle James puffs and watches and contemplatively says to no-one in particular, 'aye, it's right enough what they say about his swimming. Look at that now. It's a funny way to be swimming right enough, without your arms.'

I scrabble along the bench seat like a little crab when you lift seaweed off them at low tide, 'I'm going to be a vet Uncle James' I say for I have just decided.

'Well now that is very good' he says. 'I am pleased to hear that right enough'.

Once Lachie is in the back of the Landrover with barely a word exchanged between the three of us I notice that I am wanting to stay in the front with my Uncle James when ordinarily I would always sit in the back with Lachie and love sitting in the back, bouncing on a bruised bottom, the hard metal of chipped paint and sand-scores, bare arms and legs exfoliated by wet sand on Landrover panelling, the possibility of nettle leaves lurking in the corners near the fencing wire with its barbs or maybe the plastic container of chemicals with skull and crossbones

POISON label that seems to be dripping.

"Don't fall out now!" shouts the driver with such a load and me and Lachie priding ourselves on never having fallen out of a Landrover in our lives which is more than can be said for most of the adult population on Coll.

No, Uncle James isn't coming in for tea he says to Auntie Ruby. I can see she is keen for a chat with him but he is wiping the corners of his mouth with a huge blue cotton handkerchief and pushing his black-rim glasses up his nose with his thumb and middle finger and sucking at his dentures so that she knows he is at least keen for a cup of tea if not the talking but has realised he is running behind schedule.

There is broth on the stove when we get into Auntie Ruby's sitting room and the wee white-washed house is the height of heavenly cosiness. Dish cloths and towels are hanging on the bar across the mantelpiece above the stove, the kettle is already whistling its tune, a sound which to this very day makes me feel happy and warm and safe all over. And now we have bowls of heat and carrots and potatoes from Auntie Ruby's garden and red lentils and huge chunks of bread and butter and after all of this slurped and burped we are sleepy and my legs are water-logged. Lachie says he has to go.

'Go where at this time?' says Auntie Ruby

'Home. I have to get home' says Lachie.

'You're not going home at this time' says Auntie Ruby looking out the tiny window to the sea and noting the colour of the sky to judge time and weather forecast instead of at the mantelpiece clock on the heavy, dark wood sideboard carved with deep flowers and foliage and with a sliver of mirror its full length.

'The rain's coming in; it'll be dark soon' says Auntie Ruby.

Darkness is nothing to Lachie. He can find his way anywhere at any time of the day or night on Coll. And we have the darkest nights of the whole of the UK on Coll as I turns out, no light pollution you see. I read in my library book that you can see the Aurora Borealis from Lewis and Uist, also Benbecula, Harris and possibly even Skye on the Cuillens.

'Can you not just stay here? I don't like to think of you on that road in the dark. Have you a light on your bike? If you stay here sure your mammy will know you're with me.'

She taps her fingers, one, two, thinking things through. Making a first attempt at something new, moving with the times, making adjustments.

'I can go the phone box and call Donald at Cornaig and he'll maybe go and tell your mammy on his bike. He's maybe heading out Sorasdal way anyway.'

I am liking this idea of Lachie staying over with us. He's not done that since … a long time.

'Will your legs make it Lachie?' I say thinking of the walking and the swimming and cycling to come to get him home 4 or so miles. It'll make today a triathlon' I say, smiling.

'A what?' says Lachie.

'A triathlon. You know when you run, swim and cycle in a competition. You know, triathlon!'

Lachie shrugs his shoulders. I can see he doesn't know what I'm talking about. He thinks I'm trying to make him feel stupid by using fancy words.

'I'm away' he says, 'Thanks for the food and …

everything' he says to Auntie Ruby. She makes a clucking noise like she always does when she's not sure whether to disapprove of a thing or not.

When he's gone she says, 'At least he'll be safe home with his mother and she'll not worry about him.' she says.

'She never worries about him Auntie Ruby. He always knows what to do no matter what. He's very good like that.'

'Aye, you're right there Lorna. He might not be good at school but he's the one you want to have around in an emergency right enough.'

'Aw' she sighs, taking her apron off and I can see she's wearing her white blouse with the pearl buttons, 'You won't remember, Lorna, how we'd put you and Lachie in my wee garden and you'd be lying next to each other in the pram – you know the big pram that Violet had?' I say nothing because she'll not stop now until she gets to the story about how one day Lachie managed to get out of the pram and how she and his mother found him eating the nasturtiums but just at that moment when she's started about the pram cover that my auntie Kate made there's a crashing roar from the front door and I don't know if it's the fumes of alcohol that alert us first or the complete derangement of my father but either way we jump out of our seats.

'Get your stuff and get in the car Lorna!' he says.

'What's going on? She's not leaving in the middle of the night!'

'It's the boat! I need to get to the boat. Hurry up Lorna! Move! Now!'

As I'm rushing to put my jumper on and my wellies and feeling befuddled and my fingers not working because of all the adrenalin, which is weird because I read it actually helps you when you're frightened and it does look like I am in flight as opposed to fight mode but then I seem to be flighting towards danger as opposed to running away from it, I hear him telling Auntie Ruby in short, abrupt and drunkenly panicked answers to her clever questioning that Donald has phoned Dougal at the Hotel where my father has been drinking to let him know that his boat has come loose.

Dougal, who helps out on Cornaig Farm has seen my father's boat at the head of Bousd Bay nudging the rocks and dancing with the tide.

"What time is it?' I hear my father shouting as if he doesn't know the clock is right there in front of him. Maybe he can't read the face.

'The tide won't turn for another hour or more' says Auntie Ruby who never looks at the Tide Tables like my father makes a study of them and yet know everything there is to know from her view onto the harbour of Arinagour.

'Hurry the hell up Lorna!' he's shouting again.

'Can you not just leave her here?' says Auntie Ruby and it is another of the same conversation I have heard so many times already.

'No. I'll not.'

'You're drunk Malky!' she says in her best firm tone, the one that always makes me jump-to.

'She's left me Ruby! She must have got on the first boat this morning!'

'Malky!' says Auntie Ruby, 'Tt's more than eleven years! Look! Lorna's not a baby now – look at her!'

'I see her well enough.' He's grabbing my by the arm above my elbow, I'll have a bruise there tomorrow, he doesn't know his own strength, and my wellie does not come off like I thought it would and he's got my kagoule and we're out the front door and I am in the car in a rush and wanting to be in the back but somehow I've landed in the front and already I am closing my eyes and it is much later at my first Carnival at the Kelvin Hall in Glasgow a few years later that I wonder why people pay to have fairground rides that scare you when you just be in the car with my father drunk at the wheel negotiating every bend and slipping ditch-sided curve and flying low of the top of the Windy Gap and bouncing like a plane making an emergency landing and only just making it through the black and white painted posts that mark the narrow bridge and wondering will he stop in time or will we hit the Fishing Gate again and all the while him white-knuckled like he's pulling a creel from the depths of hell and silent like the eyes of a hurricane probably is, furiously calm and dangerously still.

If I put my kagoule over my head he will break his stillness to look at me, eyes off the road, and shout at me for being so foolish so I sit up very straight and make it seem like my eyes are open when they are half-shut and I've made them see in a bleary way.

It's no use anyway for I know every bend and straight of this road with my eyes shut, every cattle ramp and bridge, every turning and I have to think about one of my school books and imagine it in my mind.

I can see my Basic Biology book right now with its beautiful photographs and here I am in Chapter Three and there is the picture of the parts of a plant and I am studying them as I read the names, 'stamen', 'petal', 'pistil', 'sepals', 'stigma' and I do this so my mind doesn't automatically follow the route of the two-track road and trying to sense by the speed and the sways to the left or right are we going to go off the road or hit a sheep, a lamb, a cow, a calf, a hedgehog, frog... and I think about how much I love biology and school and I start to count the days then of how many days it is until I am back at school in Oban and I have worked it out very quickly so I choose another book in my mind, "Chemistry for Today" and I am in Chapter One which I did grapple with I have to say.

Lachie! Oh, Lachie's on the road! White coldness slides through my body and the top of my head is tingling. I'm aware of the insides of my thighs being chaffed and burning. I am still as a lochan on one of those days when there is no wind and the earth seems to have sucked all the oxygen from the air.

How far will he have gotten on the road? It's impossible for me to determine how much time has passed since Lachie left Auntie Ruby's. I feel sure in my guts writhing that he is peddling his old black bike on the track in front of us somewhere; somewhere dark.

He'll hear us coming for miles! He's sure to get off the road when he hears the car coming. But a car at such speed? Caught by time on the walled bridge near Toraston? A slipped minute trapping him in a noise-flattened dip like the one near Cloiche?

'What?' shouts my father gripped in his tempest. I must have said 'Lachie' out loud. So I say 'Lachie! Lachie's on the road.'

'Well hell mend him if he doesn't get off it' says my father and the car rushes forward finding speed I never knew it had and we are in an airplane right enough that just touches its wheels down now and again to tap lightly the tiny stones and pummel hard the bigger potholes of the two track road.

It's only at the turn-off to Bousd harbour that the car does skid and a wheel is caught where later there will be a gate post driven.

My father curses and throws open the door and goes running down past the white house that is the old schoolhouse and I run after him not knowing what else to do. I see the figure of Donald at the edge of the rocks away out at the narrow-lipped mouth of the harbour; a space of only about 10 metres until sudden open sea. There is no boat there now.

The wind, if it had been a North-Westerly, would have kept the boat inside, the boat being only about five metres long and happy to bounce its nose against the teeth of the rocky inlet. But it is not a Nor'Westerly and the boat has been blown like a lover's kiss on an open palm out and away.

It's not just the embarrassment of not having secured your boat; the main investment of the work you do to feed your family. It is also the possibility of the boat being smashed and sunk like molten glass being pummelled between anvil and hammer. It is also the chance of a fine for having creating a hazard in the shipping channel. So it is all these things that are the reasons for my father's fury.

And yet, I see as I look at him, for the first time with a certain pity, that there may be other reasons too, reasons I would never fathom at twelve years old, not even a teenager yet for all I am feeling quite the young adult.

Donald is raising his arms as my father stumbles and collides and ramshackles his way over stinking sea wrack and bits of broken creels and stagnant, lime green algae covered peaty rock pools and I can see from my stance at the head of the harbour inlet where there is a little concrete pier of sorts set amid the ancient giant metal rings attached to rocks by my ancestors for a gentler kind of fishing, that Donald is showing his resignation with his arms out for the loss of the boat; that he cannot see it anymore.

I think to myself that if I was my father I would've hoped Donald would've thought to come meet us rather than have me go all the way to the headland to be told my boat is lost.

But perhaps it has only just gone down, is right now floating silent to the bottom of the sea. My father could easily be in Hughie's boat right now, heading out to catch his own instead of sprachling on dry land.

Hughie's boat looks proud and honest resting on her side in the dirty brown peat shell sand; lain down by the withdrawal of the sea. Her fresh-painted oars with their white lines so clear are tidily stashed. Her rollicks have fine new ropes through their eyelets to prevent their loss. Her flat wooden planks for seats would never give you skelfs on your buttocks and thighs.

Her sides are curved wide and full in such a pleasing way you want to run your hand down along them to feel that splendid sweep of old, varnished wood. Her name, "Aila", which I learned years ago means 'from a strong place' is painted in a steady hand with a fine paintbrush and has Celtic knots on either side and everything about the Aila is beautiful. She is an old boat that has been loved for three generations and she seems to sing with the waves and

fly with the seagulls and terns and dive with the great
northern divers, easy and gentle on the ocean.

- 6 -

'It was you, you weirdo!' My father is raging. 'I know it was you, you Devil-stained heathen! You stole it and I'll have you for it!'

'No, no, rest yersel Malcolm' says Donald a moment too late with his easy voice and gentle manner that calms men as good as it calms lambs.

My father has gone for Lachie and it is years of loathing that make his arms so powerful as he rushes at my friend who looks suddenly taller.

There's an almighty scuffle of arms and tucked-in heads and my father has Lachie's neck in a lock and punches Lachie's fair curls with his fist. Once, and now the arm is raised high again and Donald has grabbed the hitting arm and has a a hold on my father from behind and they are like two bears dancing on their back legs to the music of huffing and puffing.

Lachie falls to the ground as my father is forced to release him by Donald's massive bulk. 'It wasn't him Malky now, he's only a boy. It wasn't him. Leave it now.'

He's taking my father away and I am wishing he'd walk him to the end of the old pier and push him in whether the tide's in or out doesn't matter; he can't swim and maybe he'd smash his own head against the exposed hard sand.

I have to wait a minute or two to go to Lachie otherwise I'll be getting a beating myself later on. I wait until they are over the cattle grid heading for the hotel – whether it's the bar or Donald's car they're heading for I don't know.

'Why would he think you stole his boat Lachie?'

'Because it was me took it back, that's why.' His eyes are closed and the skin is crinkled at the side of them.

'What do you mean took it back?'

'From the sea. I swum out and got it and towed it back in.'

I look past Lachie lying on the muddy grass flats of pot-holed peat near the shore and see the hunched, oil-skinned figures of my father and Donald at the car park.

'Shall we get some chips?' I say, 'I've got enough money for a portion.'

'Alright.' Lachie gets up and pushes the hair off his face, 'but no tomato sauce, remember'.

I glance at his head looking for blood as we walk side-by-side but see none. Everything is fine.

In the café it is warm and the windows are steamed up and there is no funny atmosphere so it seems nobody saw a thing.

'Portion of chips please Maggie.'

'Are you having them here or do you want them in a bag?'

'We'll have them here thanks' I say and we sit on

the two-seater floral sofa to wait for our chips not saying a word and watching the yachties, the people who've sailed into Arinagour harbour in yachts, holding cups of coffee in red fingers and sniffing up snot in their red noses.

They are like another species entirely on Coll and I rarely notice them at all as they fill their water containers at the tap at the middle pier – or, if they're holding an empty container, they will come up and ask me do I know if there's a water tap and where it is?

They make their way to the hotel for a meal and a hot shower, maybe even a sauna in the Finnish-style hut at the back in their waterproofs of many colours and huge labels to let everyone know where they bought them from – that they are not only expensive but made especially for people who own yachts.

Their sleek yachts dance in the bay for a night and are gone in the morning. Little petrels with folded wings floating, taking sanctuary from storms both sudden and forecasted in this safe harbour.

It is Lachie the yachties are always drawn to, no matter be they old men of the sea or young sailors. And, strangely, he to them.

I have never heard Lachie use so many words with anyone but the yachties and always of the sea and the wildlife and the birds and tides and waves and channels of rocks. Always it's to do with the water, the sea.

It makes me wonder now why did he not take advantage of the offers he got later to crew a boat, to join them on a sail up to Lewis and they'd drop him back on the return, or take off with them for the rest of the summer, or crew for them next year when they were headed for faraway waters, for he had many such offers as he grew older.

It was yachties that took me and Lachie over to the bonfire on the island at the head of the bay a few years later. Lachie had swum to that island many times before, a dangerous swim not least because Orcas and sharks swam around the island and the rip could pull you out towards Fingal's Cave and your death, but it was like a foreign country to me.

How desolately beautiful it was with piles of pale grey rippled driftwood and rusty bits of metal and bones of seabirds and whales even which had lain against heather and shell for years and years.

The bonfire of driftwood was lit and roared and someone had a guitar and played country music songs and we all sang. All of us sang and I heard Lachie laugh and his laugh was sweet and sacred and not like a normal laugh at all so that the singing stopped suddenly and everyone looked at Lachie as though he was singing a song so pure no guitar could ever match it and there was a pause, an elegant, appreciative pause and then joyous laughter from the yachties, a whoop-whoop or two and Lachie chortling and blushing in the firelight.

- 7 -

MALCOLM

'You're looking a bit ...' the cuntstable paused and made a big point of looking at my fingers. The fingers of my right hand, which are always the worst for the shaking '... nervous, is it, Mr McLaren?'

He stretches his long black-trousered legs out in front of him like the eel he is and lifts his arms high, stretching them and even his own fingers splayed. Showing me just how relaxed he is about my guilt. I always take the line of 'say nothing'. Let the bastards hang themselves with their own words.

Of course I am shaking. It's the drink. It's just the way it is. I'd thought I could manage this trip to the Police in Oban no bother without a drink.

I knew, in fact, it would be smarter to remain sober for a few days before.

I don't mean for their benefit.

I don't mean so I'd appear to be an upstanding member of society, no, no.

I just wanted to be able to remember the details of things.

The damn details have all just merged into a big mess in my head. My brain is like a useless thing, a torn fishing net tangled up and half-buried on the shore. That's it. My thoughts are buried with the sand, dead fish rotting and seagulls picking at the guts of them. Flies.

Louisa. Lorna. Ruby. All these damn-it-to-hell women messing everything up for me.

No-one's going to tell me what to do, least of all this one sitting here asking me questions like I'm some kind of rat, a sheep in the fank, a lobster in one of my creels.

Watch it now Malky boy you're getting worked-up. Just relax. I'm getting worked-over is what it is.

'I'm saying, and I'll repeat it nice and slow for you Malky my man, did you kill him or did you not?'

'Not.' There we are, one simple word. All that's needed.

'We think you did. We know you've been threatening Mr Dundas since …' he picks up a bit of paper from his plank-high stash on the chipped formica table and looks at it earnestly, '… forever'.

The top of my head is itching but I will not give him the satisfaction of scratching it.

I see that big white-faced clock on the wall with its black hands, time ruling like a godly idol on the wall for us all to worship, and notice there's no second hand on it. The big hand clicks to the next minute as I look at it. It's all just passing the time. There's no point to any of it at all. I just need to sit here and keep my head together as much as possible and then at some point they'll either jail me or let me go.

I feel a tinge of sweat popping at my forehead, around the sides of my face. I'm glad I've had a shave before I came. That freshened me up a bit. I'm also glad I sat in the bar on the boat over and that I've come to them on my own terms rather than be dragged off by the boys in blue, not that I care what anyone thinks mind you, but on my own terms I can have a dram or two on the boat and am able to get a half bottle at the Co-Op near Peggy and Charlie's. When are they ever going to die for Christ's sake? Jesus, it's like the walking dead up there. There's no point telling them why I'm in Oban. I wonder how much they've got in the bank now?

I'm just not liking this at all. It's not as easy as I'd thought to myself. I'd thought I'd just sit and say nothing. They don't frighten me, these tossers in Oban. They don't know a thing.

But I have to say it; I've under-estimated how bad it is in this tiny wee room with that clock ticking. The clock is really annoying me now I've noticed it. Its ticking is distracting me and I'm losing my concentration.

I do not know why I did not have another mouthful before I came in. I've got a packet of Fisherman's Friend lozenges in my pocket and they take away the taste and smell of everything. I'm thinking, will I have one now? I could offer him one. How would that go down I wonder?

Ah, Jesus H Christ. Now I've missed what he was saying. He's looking at me the same way Alec did when he got the 'best catch' at the fishing competition last year. As if I cared. Some of us need to make a living. Not you bastards with your bloody fancy Tesco lures that aren't worth shite.

I know now why I'm looking at the clock. The pubs are open. I don't need to stay here. I've come 'voluntarily' as they say. Doesn't matter what he's just said.

'If there's nothing else cuntstable' I push my seat away from the desk and he says, 'Aye, but there is Mr McLaren, there is.'

I wait, Stand over him. Waver a bit, unfortunately. Feel myself sway a little.

'Sit yourself down now Malky. I know it's not easy. Let's start again eh?'

Start again? Holyjesusmotherofgod. 'I don't need to be here. In fact, I need to go. I've come here of my own accord. I can go of my own accord too.'

'That's right Malky. You're right enough there my friend. Just so's you know, I'm Detective Inspector, not cuntstable. But not to worry.'

It's an Edinburgh accent he's got. What's he doing in Oban? Why can't people just stay where they belong? What the hell was it he said a minute ago? I can taste whisky at the back of my throat if I do a backwards gulp.

'Here's the thing Malky. You've got an opportunity here. A very good opportunity. I can see you're feeling a bit uncomfortable and I understand that very well. The small space. You used to the open sea. Aye, I get that no bother.'

He looks at my fingers shaking again and wipes his face with a big white hanky from his trousers pocket as if he's sweating and I can see fine what he means with his theatrics.

I think this was where I started to lose it.

'I feel for you Malky I really do. You're just starting out on a new life with a beautiful woman,' he pauses to check another piece of paper as if I can't see he knows her name already and if he says her name I am going to smash his face in, ' … aye, Louisa.'

He tuts and sighs, 'Lou-isa. Beautiful name too. And so there yeese are; two young people in love, a wean on the way, living the high life of freedom from care on Coll, your whole future ahead of you and …' he snaps his fingers, ' … gone. Gone, just like that' he snaps them again. 'Damn shame Malky. It's not easy.'

I've got that milky feeling in my head where everything is swimming about as if the sea is in my brain, a flood tide about to make my skull explode. I'm fighting to turn the boat back over. It's a strain. Christ. It's a strain.

I cannot hear a word he says over the swell running between my ears. Just be calm Malky. Quiet now. Keep your mouth shut.

Arms by your sides.

I just need a moment and she'll be here.

There.

Louisa.

Thank God.

' … Not only losing your beautiful, young wife Malky. But all that future possibility.' he shakes his head from side-to-side, 'And in such an unusual way too.

'It's very hard when things aren't explained isn't it now? And you raising a wee girl on your own? Och, you've done very well Malky. Very well indeed.' He puts his hands together as if he's about to applaud me

– applaud me! – throws his palms apart and says, 'do you want a coffee Malky? Do you good.'

I've lost. But she's here now. She's here now. She's whispering my name while I am inside her and everything is alright.

- 8 -

She was beautiful too. At the bar she was, leaning against it with her elbow, her breasts pushing against its side. She would ask me what it was about it that drew me to her and I never said it but it was that. Her full right breast pressing against the wooden curve of the bar, pushing against it like it was a wave pressing the side of a boat.

Her hair was blonde. Natural blonde it was. Wavy. She had a big smile. She was a bit pissed when I met her. I met her when she looked at me through a swirl of smoke coming from the cigarette of the fella who was chatting her up. She looked at me and I swear to God it was as if we had been going out for months and I was just a bit late to meet her.

So I went up and stood in front of her, my back to the fella with the cigarette. I could feel him moving away. I stood there in front of her feeling confident. Confident. It was an unusual feeling. I was a hard man. And ready.

It was just before Christmas, 1963. She had on an

orange blouse. That same orange blouse. I was down in Glasgow to see to my mother's brother who was getting put in a home, dementia. I was far too young for the job but my ignorance seemed to help things and anyway, Ruby was busy with her training at the hospital. She was thinking about going to America. Louisa I mean, not Ruby. Definitely not Ruby.

'I could take you part-way' I said to her, 'You could come and live with me on my island in the Atlantic Ocean. At some point when we wanted to we could take my wee boat, put a sail on it and cross the Atlantic together. We'd ride a whale for a while. We'd maybe see a walrus. Or an iceberg. But on my island you could see the seals.' Something poetic like that I said to her.

I loved her.

The next day she told me when we met at Central Station to go for a drink somewhere that wasn't the Park Bar where we'd first met, that she'd handed in her notice at the cinema where she worked.

She was coming with me to my island. 'Your family?' I said to her and she said nothing. I took it to mean she had no family. Maybe she did. I never knew.

Was any of it real at all? I look at Lorna and it surely was real for here is our baby. But this stuff? Where did she live? Where was she from? I don't know.

She had green tobacco and we smoked it in the Necropolis after drinking in some pub in the Trongate, walking up the hill and her giggling all the way past the Cathedral. Everything was possible. My Louisa. Was that even your name? Who were you?

You had a white blouse on that night for it shone

in the moonlight and you had another dress thing on top of it with flouncy bits at the shoulder and was it spotted? You took off your shoes and I felt I was enchanted by the fairies. Were these the fairies I was told were bad? The ones who swapped your baby for one of their own? Were you a real person Louisa?

Christ but if you're not more real to me now dead and a ghost than you ever were as a creature I could hold in my arms.

But that's only because you are not dead. I know you'll come back to me. It's only a matter of time before you come back to me and I am a patient man.

On the boat you had just a wee suitcase. A tatty old cardboard thing that looked like somebody's uncle's. You sang 'She Loves You' to me and we'd both go, 'yeah, yeah, yeah!' and I'd sing, '… and you know that can't be b-a-d' into the wind on the starboard side where it was gusty and visitors might occasionally slam open the wooden door and spew on the deck not making it to the side so we had to stand upwind of them. You with your rosy cheeks and sparkling blue eyes and not a patch of green seasickness tint on your face like you'd been on a boat your whole life. You wanting me to have sex with you in the lifeboat, pulling me over to it by my good tweed jacket lapels and me being horrified at never having had such an idea myself.

You opened me up Louisa. And then you left me.

Nobody was surprised when we stepped off the boat together. You in your short coat, the very height of fashion apparently, and the wellies I'd bought you. Ruby loved you the minute she laid eyes on you.

Everyone loved you Louisa.

You had that way with you. Old Pat the Irish with

the second sight brought you fish and me a fisherman but it was what he had to give.

'Are you still with us there Malky?' he says and as I look down from the ceiling I've been staring at, I see there's another, older one with him. 'This is Detective Inspector Johnson. He's brought something with him as you can see.

'Here's the thing Malky. I'll get right down to it now. As I said, you've an opportunity here. Confess now, get it over with, this is your chance. Much better for you.' He glances over at the plastic zip-lock bag the other one is grasping with knobbly knuckles like a wee fat boy holding his cock.

'Otherwise, with what Detective Inspector Johnson has here, well Malky, I'm afraid we're going to have to arrest you.'

'Arrest me?'

'Aye, Malky, I'm afraid so. Arrest you.' he sighs in a obvious way. 'But you're better to just confess just now. You know you are. Best thing so it is.'

'Confess to what exactly?'

'Aye, we've all committed our sins Malky, sure enough' he turns to the other one and they both guffaw at each other like a pair of billy goats.

He pulls himself up and puts his face in a serious position, 'No, sorry Malky. Confess to the murder of Lachlan Dundas is what I'm saying.

'Confess now and it'll be all the better for you. And Lorna, of course. Much better to come clean. Make her proud of you. Eh? Your honesty I mean.'

The other one clears his throat. He stares at me all of a sudden, it's like a pair of floodlights coming on.

'We'll give you a minute or two to think Mr McLaren.'

He pats and fondles the plastic bag. What is in that thing? Anything at all? A bit of scrunched up paper? His butt plug? Is it bulky that bag? Something else in there? Is it a bullet? I can't see. As he gets up, he puts it under his arm, tucked and hidden and protected by his strong arm of the law.

The slimmer, younger one with the friendlier face, did he tell me his name? He rises too and they're away through the door and I'm on my own, desperate for a drink and damn it to all Hell this drinking. How can a man have such a strong liver? Just die would you? Just die.

They've left the first bit of paper that's been filled-in on the table alone too and I turn it around to face me and read: Malcolm McLaren of Struan, Isle of Coll, Argyll, PA8 6TE Marital Status: Widower Occupation: Fisherman DOB: 12.04.1943 Age: 62 years.

So that's me. I don't need to read any more. Dependants bullshit. All neat and tidy and on paper there I am. They're always wanting this postcode for everything. Everything needs a postcode. Can't buy a bottle without needing to give your postcode.

What is the postcode for Rose Tree? Would everything have been different if I had lived there? If it was me that'd looked after my mother and father and not Ruby? If I had gotten the house and Ruby stayed in Glasgow? Maybe she would've married a John or a Jimmy or even a Benjamin.

No, I can't see it. Everyone seeing all my business in the village. Competing with Alec for the fishing. No. No. The caravan was ideal. Better fishing over there. Better to be away.

'What's it to be Mr McLaren? The money or the

bag?' They're both laughing as they settle themselves down in front of me, adjusting their black suit jackets neatly as though ready for story-time.

'No, seriously Malky, we've brought the form for you to sign. Makes it easier. OK?'

I honest to God can't remember where we're at now. What form? Do they mean the form I was just reading there? 'Yes, that's all correct' I say, meaning, of course, the form I was just reading. That's the only form I know about.

'Good man Malky. 'Cos we've got Lorna here. She's a vet I hear, very good that. Good for her. And has her own practise with her vet husband in Glasgow she was telling us? Very good so it is. You must be very proud of her, doing so well.

'But she's very upset Malky. Very upset indeed. She saw him, you know? On the shore, all bloated up and putrid. Aye, she's very upset, isn't she Detective Inspector Johnson?'

'A lawyer'

'What's that Malky? You want to see Lorna is it?'

'No! A lawyer! I want a lawyer.'

'Och well that's a shame, I thought you said Lorna. In fact, maybe you did say Lorna right enough. Because if you had of said you wanted to see Lorna, that would be quite normal, wouldn't it Detective Inspector Johnson?' DI Johnson nods his chin slowly into his flabby neck.

'And then we wouldn't have a whole lot of fuss and bother. You could just sign this form here, your confession, then we'll take a quick statement and that'll be us. All done and dusted.

'DI Johnson here can put his wee baggie away. Now, what do you say Malky? You're an old man after all. You want to do the right thing. You know, after so many wrong things. For Lorna. Eh?'

- 9 -

LORNA

Even as I sit here looking at curled-up leaflets, mainly about domestic violence and knives, pinned to a notice board at the police station in Oban I have no sense of shock at all.

It is as if I have at last reached my destiny. I am at last at the destination I was always going to arrive at for the exact reason I always knew. But it's only now I'm here that I know it.

I have my medical bag with me. Why, I do not know. I find myself now attached to it like some women are to particular handbags so that I take it to some places like I am a soldier taking his weapons on a peace mission, because you never know do you? And best to have what you need to hand.

This was one of the things I noticed when I first took over Rose Tree after Auntie Ruby died and left it to me. She had had a place for everything and sure enough, everything was in its place.

It struck me after living in various rental apartments and shared houses before me and Johnny married that I had never known before the joy and security that could come from knowing the butter knife is next to the bread board, the front door key is hanging from a hook next to it in the hallway, the dish cloths are under the sink, the plates fit neatly in their individual slots so you know if one's missing.

I have the house kept in exactly the same way. The same way as Auntie Ruby. The same way as my grandmother. The continuity of womenfolk, a thread of steel through our homes wrapped in the bright, new thread of each generation.

I think Auntie Ruby knew too. She probably thought it would be she and not me at the police station in Oban and her brother in the cells. She would have died worried that the task had skipped her and was left to me.

But she would never have guessed how glad I am that it is me. It could only be me. I deserve this sweet revenge.

The friendly policewoman on the front desk said I should go and have a wander about the town, it would be at least tomorrow before I might be needed. But I have no mind to. I know every crevice of Oban like the creases of my med bag. Here I became a woman. Here I explored and adventured in city streets. Here I learned how different life could be.

It doesn't feel like any kind of home now, Oban. Peggy and Charlie died long ago, though my father thinks they still live here, the house sold to a young family. The money used to update my father's caravans: new creosote roof, a plastic porch, a wood burning stove, a new toilet.

I like the feeling I'm having in this police station hallway. He is here. Caught. Soon to be punished. The wooden panels must be from the 1950's. It is all more modern as you go through those swing-doors. Like an office building, which I suppose it is now. Not really a gaol. Shame. It makes me think of Glasgow University. The School of Veterinary Medicine was all wood panels and sharp implements, heavy-handed healing and rote learning. I loved it.

A cave of academia from which to creep, hoping sick calves and cats might not hear me. Not like that now. I have loved my job, my life, my husband and children. I love that they and I can say "she's a vet" when anyone asks what it is I do and I am there defined and labelled. So neatly. Possibly also in a book or journal somewhere.

My graduation and me trembling to think he might come and embarrass me. Wishing he would come, sober. Hoping he had died at last.

He never spoke of my mother. Not one word. If I cast my mind back, flick my thoughts away far out across the water of my memory, I have a sense that I asked him questions about my mother until the silence drowned my words. Little child questions of what was she like and was she beautiful? Did I ask why did she die daddy? Was that the first time I was hit maybe? Could be.

There's a copy of The Oban Times newspaper on the coffee table next to the water cooler. It is from last Thursday and this is now Tuesday so a visitor must have left it. How long will it live here?

My cell phone vibrates against my hip through my jacket pocket. I cannot stand the noise of a ring tone. Seeing "home" on the screen always makes me feel good. 'Hullo' I say. 'Sweetheart, just phoning to see everything's OK?' says my husband Johnny, the father of my children, my own sweetheart Johnny. 'Better than I ever thought' I say.

'It's really very good here at the police station. I'm just staying here.'

'Are they making you wait?'

'No. I'm happy to spend the time, you know, thinking. It's good to have the time to think about things. You know. How are they?'

'Perfect. They're great. We're all fine here. Finn's finished the ship-building. Freya's nearly fallen on it three times so far. Finn's not liking going out in the rain, poor dog. Pearl watches him from the window purring and cleaning herself.' He laughs and I laugh and we are all one and he and I connect and there several heartbeats of moments of silence in which we are simply together without the need for words.

When I shut my phone, this is my family phone, I have another work one which I only turn on when I'm working, I feel I've received a transfusion of normality.

The hallway here looks different. Unearthly. A police officer comes through the swing door holding a polystyrene cup of something that steams. I feel like an intruder. I decide to sit outside the front door a while, it's sunny in the cold.

I can see part of the wide bay. Lachie would have swum here at night, sneaking out of the hostel and slipping into the dark water swimming with the ice cream cartons and oil slicks from the ferries, guts and severed crab claws from the fishing boats, ropes stretching taut from sea floor to yacht side like bars of a cage, tampons with strings bobbing with the current like jellyfish. He was as suffocated by the sea here as he was at the school. It's a wonder he lasted a full year before he left to be, as his mother wrote in her letter to the Education Board of Scotland, 'home schooled'.

Aye, home schooled in the sea.

As I am tucking the back of my jacket under my bottom to sit on the low wall I happen to see a ferry coming in.

It has just passed the Isle of Kerrera which acts as a breakwater for Oban alongside the hook of the mainland.

That'll be his ship coming in then. All his sins visiting upon him like wretched, blood-dripping viruses of darkness, eating away at him now like wee ulcerated malignant cancerous tumours, turning him inside-out before he gets to die.

'Be kind to him now Lorna, a gradh. Be kind.' I hear her in my mind, her words often blow through me like an unexpected cool breeze on a hot, thick, thundery day.

'He's going to die anyway, a gradh. Whether in jail or at home, what does it matter? Remember the snowflakes Lorna. We all disappear.' And yet today, here at Oban police station with my father being interrogated by the police for the murder of Lachie I tell her no. No. I will not be kind. Not now.

- 10 -

I notice some horsetails growing among the hebe shrubs in the concrete beds that separate the police station from the pavement. They are like the ones I have in my garden in Glasgow, our little patch of private nature behind our tenement flat. A space I have filled with plants from Coll, collected by me and Finn and Freya roots and soil and water and all in plastic bread bags knotted at the top to be relocated like myself into strange, urban soils.

I never realised that until now. The wild poppies haven't taken. The soil too rich perhaps. But the horsetails and plantain and bracken are happy. The tougher, more flexible species.

I did not wait to see them load Lachie's body into Jordan's Landrover. I have put enough cats and dogs and calves and even a bearded dragon or two into black plastic bags at my surgery to know I don't need to see them do it. I am thinking of the eel suddenly in the back of the Cortina.

I am walking back across the sand looking at my

car in the dip of a grassy sand dune and the wind is in my face so I don't hear her come up behind me until she is panting at me and pushing her face into the wind so the strands of hair that have come out of her clip are not in her eyes.

'Lorna. Do you know you're down as his next-of-kin?' says the doctor.

I look at her.

'You'll need to go over to Oban to formally identify him. With Kirsty being in Australia. Is that OK? John-Mac's just told me.'

'That's fine.' I say and she stops walking as I continue, I haven't broken my stride at all. So I am his next-of-kin am I? And that I think was the very first secret disclosed when Lachie died.

Solving the mysteries of an animal's ill health clue by clue over the last fifteen or more years has given me the skill of joining-the-dots-together. It is automatic that my brain be programmed to at this very moment show me a scene that has long perplexed me. The time when Lachie proposed to me.

Right before I was to start Vet School at Glasgow Uni.

'Lorna' he said with his eyes staring into mine, me aware of the strength of his fingers as he held both my hands in his, aware that he was a man and me a woman.

'Will you marry me Lorna?' he said and there was no doubt in my mind at all that he meant it most sincerely and everything his proposal entailed. That if I should 'yes' we would be married at the church in Arinagour. That I would still be free to pursue anything I wanted to do on the mainland or anywhere. I could still go off and become a vet. But that LachieLorna would be formally trysted.

Lachie, so strong and fragile you were in that moment. I see you now like you're encased in glass in a filigreed locket, a seagull flying high over your head as you looked at me and held my hands.

You gave me a power over you I never wanted. There was a blankness to me then which you took to be surprise of a different kind, you took it to be an insult that I would be surprised that you asked me to marry you, me going-places, clever, and when we had barely seen one another that last summer, me working as a waitress and chambermaid at the Coll Hotel and you over at Elleraig.

And now I was leaving Coll for Glasgow you're asking me to marry you and me I'm wondering was it a big rope you were wanting to throw over me like the thick ropes that hold the ferry tight against the pier to keep me close?

Why did you ask me Lachie Dundas? Was it just a simple way to make me your next-of-kin alongside your mother, able to stand between you and the world?

My fingers are under the door handle of my car when I'm gripped by a sense of needing to run back to Lachie's body. I have to put my other hand on the car's roof to attach myself to its metal to prevent getting pulled back to it by some magnetic force. I'll see him in Oban I hear myself saying aloud. I am speaking aloud. To myself. Get in the car. Drive to the gate. Open gate. Panic.

I was about to head off to see Lachie at his house at Elleraig. This was my original mission and I have been side-tracked by some event on the beach.

Oh yes, I had just wanted to have a quick look at it

myself. So rare to be by myself these days what with Freya and Finn and Johnny, of course.

I've been to the beach and now I'll carry on to Lachie's because that's where I was heading. But I'm realising in some insulated part of me that Lachie won't be there because, because. I need to pull the car over. Think Lorna. They'll be coming up over the machair soon enough and you do not want to sitting here in your car watching the preview to his funeral procession driving past you sitting here in your car.

will I go over to Lachie's? Should I not just continue with my plan? Keep things consistent. But what will they think of me going to Lachie's now he's dead? Would that be wrong? Should I head back down to the village? But that would be too soon. And worse to go back to Lachie's later?

I decide to phone Johnny. Yes, I must phone Johnny. I take my phone out of my tweed bag but once it is in my hand I hear myself having to tell Johnny about Lachie. I would have to say the words aloud. About Lachie on the beach, Lachie on the beach, but dead.

This seems like a sensible idea; to talk with my husband about what has just happened. But would I not be in some will o' the wisp way be letting Lachie down? The police might want to know what I did directly after seeing Lachie and what is the most appropriate response I should give? What is the appropriate thing to do right now?

I need to get away from the gate and I do not want to be anywhere near the road when Jordan's Landrover and the doctor's Mercedes and John-Mac's truck go past. Whose was the green car I didn't recognise? Where is the driver?

I pull into the lay-by at Elleraig which is almost never used. I look at the sea through the cleft in the heather-covered hills. It is dark green and welcoming me with little waves.

My throat is constricting itself involuntarily. It is acting like a little floodgate. There's a rush building from my belly. I hold tight to the steering wheel. I have the sense to turn off the engine. The quietness is like a muting blanket. I hear a bird trilling. I open the car window and I cannot hear the sea because my ears are playing the pulse of my blood through my veins. I just need to get to the ditch halfway so I'm not in sight of anyone that might pass.

I am a fugitive walking briskly from grassy clump to grassy clump through the bog, glad to be away from the road because it's occurred to me that someone might come from Sorasdal and want to pass the time of day with me, 'hullo! what's news Lorna?'

When I am there I cave into it. I fold up in the middle of its coolness, the tiny trickle of water at its fold turns the leather of my shoes a darker shade of brown and grasp the top of my head with both hands and squat parallel to its bank and I rock myself in sobbing heaves in the scoop of peat, cradled and hidden here, nestled and rocking with the earth either side of me nursing me and saying, 'it's alright a gradh, sure it's all right'.

I pull another emergency cigarette out of the packet which is now more handy in my tweed bag and not the glove compartment of my car. I even have a lighter in there. I suck at the cigarette when I am done with my crying.

I am officially allowed at Lachie's. I am his next-of-kin after all am I not? I am officially permitted. But this realisation makes me feel awkward, pushes me into a professional mode which I do not want to feel right now. I want to feel Lachie.

I take another cigarette out of the packet. When I light it, I cannot get a hit of smoke from it, I look at its stark white paper and the tear near the filter and tiny curls of brown tobacco poking out. I am not sure what to do with this useless cigarette; too smelly to put back in the packet, too long to hide in the heather. I cannot stand cigarette butts in wild places. I wrap it in a tissue from my pocket and hold it in my hand thinking that I can put it in Lachie's bin. But would that indicate I had been there sooner? Maybe before Lachie died?

I need to talk myself down. I am very well aware of how paranoia makes the innocent seem guilty. I feel I have done something wrong. Even wishing I hadn't come, on a whim for my med bag of all things, how unlike me. I am glad that I have. If I have been guided in some way to come then I must not attempt to be in the driver's seat at all. I must learn to move instinctively and see where I am taken next.

I am drawn to Lachie's house and so I will go and confidently so. Now. The other cigarettes in my packet, how many? Twelve of them. Four are a bit creased, the rest are pristine. I pull out a creased one and straighten it out through my finger and thumb tips which reminds me of when me and Lachie stole one of his mother's cigarettes. Poor Kirsty. What will she say to it all?

Did he have the kettle on the stove? Has the house burned down? Was he even living here recently? I can't imagine anyone will have been here to check since they've only just found Lachie's body. They won't have had time. Does that not make it a crime scene? Stop it Lorna.

When did I last speak to Lachie? At Easter when we were in? How was he then? I am trying to remember him as I walk through the petalworts and sea pinks, harebells and yellow Birds-foot-trefoils and here, as always, purple self heal in abundance.

In the little garden Kirsty created years ago a flourish of eyebright and thyme, primroses and orchids are blooming and only me to see them. It is not a garden that has tried to control nature but one that has given the wildflowers a close, appreciative audience.

I see the horsetails poking through the cracks in the cement and hear Lachie telling me he wished I hadn't told him about how I had read they were ancient plants, horsetails, that they had been around at the time of dinosaurs. 'I don't want to know Lorna! Don't you understand that?

I didn't understand. I had thought he didn't want to know because my telling him made him feel inferior to me. I was wrong about that. I had felt him sulky for years whenever I shared, excitedly, my knowledge of our world with him. One day he managed to say it aloud to me: he did not want to know.

All looks as normal. The giant rope laid to rest against the short stone wall that runs alongside the house-end facing north is still resting in place. The huge pile of empty oyster shells is as big as its ever been. The glass fishing float balls are still piled in their torn wicket basket that turns more grey each year. Kirsty found that basket not long after Lachie was washed ashore.

The rusty horseshoe makes a 'U' shape above the door. If they are hung the other way around all the luck drains out of them. The half-barrel at the side of the door holds the old, wild honeysuckle still which is not yet in flower and I see that Lachie has trained its searching stems up the wires to the side.

I take off my shoes out of habit. And my socks. My sweaty feet pick up the loose sand on the rough concrete strip at the front door. I brush my bare soles against the bristles of the doormat. I notice the grey-painted door of planks is open a little, but that is not unusual.

I hear a yowl inside and my body goes rigid. I hear it again but this time I identify it as Sula the cat. She rushes me as I walk inside and I say, 'are you hungry Sula?' Yeow! She yells at me, indignant and desperate. Sula has always been a great hunter so I know she cannot be starving as I open a tin of cat food on the kitchen bench. I know where it is and the tin opener too. It is the same tin opener his mother brought over from the mainland when the house was finished. It feels good in my hand. I give Sula half a can in her enamel dish. We have done this before, many a time, she and I.

I fill the kettle from the spluttering tap. I put it on the stove. I light the fire. It is already set with twists of newspaper, looks like The Oban Times, and dried driftwood in tinder pieces, some lumps of dried peat on top. I long for the smell of its sweet burning. I don't need to use my lighter because there are matches here in the pewter Charles Rennie Macintosh matchbox holder that belonged to his mother on the mantelpiece. And if I need more, I can get them from the store out back, the old toilet it was and now taigh

110

beac, the little house, is the store.

I look at the stack of old books on the table next to my chair and flick my fingers over the titles on the spines. I take the faded paperback copy of "Ring of Bright Water" and hold it like a bible. Auntie Ruby gave this to Lachie one Christmas before he learned to read and I would read it to him while we sat on the pebbles of the shore in front of his house and we would wonder if the sea otters would come and listen and sure enough, the mother of the pair at Elleraig would often swim towards us and race up the peat turf at the side of the beach.

It was from this book that Lachie learned to read, reluctantly, eventually. Lachie had a waterproof resistance to Mr McMurchie's teaching. He was stubborn in his refusals to read a word on the blackboard or write his name in our jotters. All through primary school he was this way; a rock of granite blocking the glacier of education coming his way. It made me feel I needed to learn enough for the both of us. I needed to understand the big, wide world across the water. But I needed Lachie to know how to read, and to write. I needed him to.

And so I would carry this very paperback, its corners coffee brown, its cover with white creases on both corners. A tear on the back repaired with sellotape, look at it now, a work of art it is. And here it is in the back crease between the back cover and a list of other books to buy, a fragile harebell, faded from pretty purple to the palest of lilac, dry and precious.

Lachie had picked that flower and handed it to me as we lay on the heather just here at Elleraig. He pushed it at me like a magical weapon threatening the telling of the story. I had calmly tucked it inside the back cover and calmly, as I had seen Mr McMurchie react to a distracted child, continued to read. We were only on chapter two or three I think. I knew he was listening. I knew he was beginning to like it; the listening to the story.

Only after I had read Ring of Bright Water to him in its entirety could I see that he was captured by the pleasure of escaping to a different world and so I moved from the cannabis of sweet summer days with Lillian Beckwith through to the heroine of George MacKay Brown's poetry so that he has a stash here of books about fairies and warriors, foolhardy adventurers and Celtic princesses, sailors drowned by mermaids and birds that talked.

What was it he said to me at first? 'I do not like printed words Lorna.' I'd thought him ignorant, which he was. 'I do not like things to be captured that way.'

'How can you not like words Lachie?' It was a mystery to me, as if he were saying he didn't like food or water.

'But if you only learn to read Lachie, the stories will give you solace. And it means people won't have something over you. They will laugh at you and feel sorry for you if you don't know how to read and write.'

'How can they give me solace Lorna when learning the words and their meaning takes me out of myself? I cannot describe it to you. You don't understand at all. You like all this learning you do but I do not. It makes me unhappy to reach for things that way.'

The fire catches, clicking at me and little flames dance but I leave the stove door open until the fire has enough air to get going. Sula is making a racket eating, slurping and chomping, so it has been a while right enough. If Lachie had a diary it might be helpful in seeing what page it's left open at. But he's never been one for dates of days and names of months nor time either for that matter.

I am unsure whether to return the book to the pile or put it in my bag. It has become treasure. A memory I can touch. Something I want to think about. Should I maybe not have read it to him? Would things have been different for him had I not interfered? It is clear to me now, sitting here alone, that interfering was what it was. A determination to make him what I thought he, all of us, should be; clever, quick, knowledgeable.

But he let me read to him anyway. He indulged my determination. He allowed me to boss him. He let me show-off how smart I was. He loved me. We were friends.

I have been here alone before, fetching something while Lachie is out, usually a jar of his preserves, or visiting when he is not at home, or to feed Sula or the hens. I should go check the hens in a minute. I am surprised not to have heard them cluck at my arrival.

This house is peaceful. It is the home I always wanted. Kirsty has made it a home with her knitted patchwork quilts all tweedy browns and greys made from small hand-wound round balls of sock wool remnants that Auntie Ruby gave her. The rock walls left unpainted, much to the amusement of the boys that laid them one top of the other, driftwood and wooden fish boxes collected from all over the island and used to make the step ladder to the upstairs sleeping place.

Almost everything in here is natural; stone, pebbles, rocks, wood, bone, wool, antlers above the stove for hanging damp clothes. Everything was once alive. Wood from a tree. Wool from a sheep. Bone from a fish. Horns from a cow. Teeth from a seal. From the outside the house looks as though it is an extension of the pebble beach and cliff, like it has been washed up by the tide, flowing pebbles and rocks piled in walls of a storm during a flood tide.

I feel the need to see if Lachie's bed's been slept in, for why I do not know. Perhaps it is really that I am wanting to feel the ladder rungs under my bare feet again, the sides against my palms. Kirsty was wise to swim against the tide of the influx of plastic and formica when it came; to house the old things, the long sideboard of solid wood Mrs Cuddy was going to send to the dump. I know without opening it that the narrow top drawer will contain long tined bright silver forks and slivers of thin, worn, bone-handled knives stamped, "MCPHERSON BROTHERS BUTLERS AND SILVERSMITHS GLASGOW" laid against green felt and separated in wooden compartments.

I decide I will just stay here and not go back to my own house. I will just have a quick look-in there before the boat. I am booked on Monday. I will spend the weekend here, with Lachie instead. It is good here with the smell of Lachie and all his history as if he is out somewhere and me visiting when he is away swimming or checking his Hebridean sheep.

The kettle is beginning to sing and I take the thick linen mitt from the rail above the stove and carry the kettle to my mug near the sink. I see someone coming through the gap in the hill towards the road.

I lean in.

It is my father.

I am sure of it.

I can't see the figure or even their gait to identify them by but inexplicable though it is that he is heading down here to Lachie's house, a place he has never been, and today of all days, I know it is my father.

Hide.

I am 5 years old.

I am putting the kettle on the hotplate and tucking the mitt under the rail.

No. Make your coffee. Take it with you. Don't leave the mug there. I am relieved to notice the door is open. I slide up to it and close it slowly with my fingertips from the hinge side. It clicks shut loudly.

Not locked but that is normal. I head through the back door, closing it behind me, and along the back of the house wall where Sula sees me and raises her tail, jumping down towards me off the low dry stone wall. He won't notice her doing that; giving away my presence. He never notices the animals.

I sneak one eye over the corner edge of the house and yes, it is him right enough. Would he have seen the smoke from the chimney? He's looking down.

What does he know? I am well-trained in reading his body language, fear and its prevention is a very good incentive for the reading body language. It has helped me in my practise. Helped me understand the animals that come to me. I watch them carefully when their owner is talking, more aware of what their body is telling me, far more accurately than their owner's words.

Does he know about Lachie?

Damn, but he's walking very surely.

Is it his experience of walking across bog and rushes and rock that's making him take the shortest route to Lachie's or is it as it looks to me, that he is no stranger to this house?

I go into the wee storehouse with its fishing boxes nailed to the wall and filled with jars of preserves and cans and bottles of vinegar, a bag of basmati rice, opened and re-tied on the floor, not a mouse hole on it, well done Sula.

I am like a NASA satellite dish receiver in here, tuned at high frequency to every nuance of sound and vibration in the house.

There is no wind.

The house feels like a person.

She is glad I have shut the door.

And yet, there it is, the sound of the door being opened and not tentatively either. Footsteps unhesitating, one, two, three, four, five, six, heading into the sitting area, another sound, something sliding, pause. He's standing. Footsteps: one, two, three, four, five, six, no hesitation whatsoever, no looking towards the fire, the kitchen, nothing. I put my mug on the shelf behind me because I am clutching it so hard the side is burning my finger.

Creak and the front door is shut.

Is he coming round the outside of the house to the store?

No. I feel him receding. I feel it. And I feel something else too in this state of hyper-vigilance. A shiveryness running this way and that on my back, up the back of my neck, shivery nerves on my scalp. Lachie. I can feel Lachie. I put out my hand, palm up but no ghostly hand is put in mine. Not a breath of coldness there or on my face.

I am wanting to tell him all the things I have realised already, how wrong I was but it is all just nonsense to him and for the first time I do not resist him.

'You didn't drown did you Lachie? I know you didn't!'

I have more confidence creeping out of the storehouse and peeking from the corner of the house. He's nearly at the top of the gap already. What has he taken with him?

I wait until he has disappeared before I go to the front door. I am him. I know his stride. For years I had to run to keep up with him as he strode on ahead. I open the door. I am him on a mission. I know what I've come here to get and I know exactly where it is. I walk his strides one, two, three, four, five, six and facing me is the bookcase. I don't think he leant down. I don't think he stretched up. He couldn't have gotten to the top without standing on something and he didn't do that so it is something from this shelf or this one. What is different here? It all looks the same to me. It must have been a book, there are never any ornaments on the bookcase.

What was it Lachie?

I am thinking too much, I've activated the investigative part of my brain. And it is useless. I have no idea what he has taken. Maybe a book.

I've left my mug in the storehouse and on my way to get it I see them. Lachie's trousers hanging over the back of the chair at the kitchen table, the front crotch facing me. A new kind of coldness rushes up my body from my legs to my head. My heart heads off the other way. They'll see!

117

When they take off his jeans they will see it! And what will they make of it on the cold stainless steel slab? Whatever will they say? Their report; it'll be in their post-mortem report!

- 11 -

'Lorna, honey, I am glad you were next to your phone.'

I hold it against my ear and say nothing. I've answered it automatically. And now here's his voice. I slouch down the throw-covered, feather down filled cushions of Lachie's sofa. How long have I been sitting here?

'You don't need to say a word now, Lorna.' He pauses, listening. 'Are you there Lorna?'

'Yes' I say, vacant. 'I'm here. I'm at Lachie's. His house, I mean.'

'That's good Lorna. Now, you don't need to say a word just now Lorna. I wish I was there with you. I can't imagine how upset you must be. If you want to talk about it, you just go ahead. Or call me back. Whatever suits you, Lorna. OK?

'OK.' I sound like Freya. 'Is everyone OK?' I say.

'Yes, they're all fine. I haven't told them anything yet. John-Mac's only just off the phone to tell me. They're playing in the living room and in the kitchen.'

I feel better thinking of Johnny in the kitchen in Glasgow. I envy Freya and Finn not-knowing, playing.

'We'll tell them together. I didn't want them to be upset and you away. You never know. How they might react. I'm not wanting to give them bad news and you not here. It's their first time. Anyway … ' he pauses and I'm not sure what he's said but am struck my how glad he is my husband, this man who has a calm voice, who can be trusted to know the right thing to do in an emergency, who thinks of his children and considers his wife and makes decisions based upon their wellbeing.

'Aye, well, you know how much they loved him' he says 'they' in a way that means himself too and I think I will just stay on this phone, with his voice in my ear and his breathing, steady, honest. My little family cell phone becomes my ventilator.

'Me too.' I say.

'I know, honey.'

'It was good of John-Mac to phone you.'

'Aye. I told him so. Very good of him.'

'They said I'm the one who's to identify him in Oban.'

'Aye, he said that right enough.'

And my husband lets there be silence between us and I love him fiercely.

'I can see why people are always wanting you to put their pets to sleep' I laugh, 'you're very good at this Johnny.'

'Och, I'm very good at a lot of things you've yet to discover Lorna.' I hear his smile.

'He came. To the house, here.'

'Who?'

120

'Malky.'

'Malky? Eh? What was he up to? Are you OK?'

'I don't know. It was very odd. I hid in tigh beac!'

'Good for you. Don't give him the satisfaction.'

'He came into the house. As though he'd done it plenty of times.'

'No.'

'Aye.'

'What did he do?'

'Went over to the bookcase I think. Think he took something.'

'Let's stop thinking about him just now. Prick. What are you going to do now?'

'I'm going to stay here at Lachie's. It feels like the right thing to do.'

'Aye, I can see that. Everything OK at the house? How's Sula?'

'She's fine. I fed her. I'm just going to check the hens. I haven't heard them at all.'

'Do you feel a bit better?'

'I do.' I pause. 'Thank you Johhny. Give them a kiss from me.'

'I'll try my best. They always wipe mine off. I'll call you in a wee while if I don't hear from you. You'll call me if there's anything?'

'Of course. But don't panic if I don't. I'll put the phone on the charger just now.'

'OK. Lorna my love?'

'Uh-huh?'

'I'm very sorry. I'm deeply sorry for your loss. He was a very special man and it's an absolute tragedy.'

'He didn't drown Johnny. I know he didn't.'

'Aye, John-Mac told me you'd said that. I can talk to you about all that later. On Monday, when you're home. I'll call Adrian and let him know you won't be at the surgery on Tuesday. So don't you worry about a thing.'

But as I am walking towards the hen house, a beautiful wee hut made of fish boxes and driftwood, I am already worried. Limpet, cockle and mussel shells and an occasional cowrie or mother-of-pearl razor shell are glued around the arch where the ladies go in at the top of the ramp but the shutter is open and before I even look I know the hens are not there. I look around the hills for them. Nothing. Not so much as a feather on the ground. Not an otter then. And yet the hen house does not seem disused.

My heart thumps loudly as I see something washed up on the pebbly shore of Elleraig below the house. I'm fast developing a beachcombing phobia. I can't not go and see what it is. It would be worse to sit wondering what it is and imagining than to just go and see. Dread.

No hens. Something on the shore. Every step I take closer to it, on my own, no-one else around, no sense of Lachie even, has me flashing back to walking towards Lachie and I start to laugh at the ridiculousness of it all. But my laugh is spluttery and sounds wicked and strangled as it echoes off the small cliffs of Elleraig bay near the house. I've always hated that echoing thing that happens here.

Aside from the house itself and the run down to the sea, I do not like Elleraig bay, I never have. It is a place of no logic that seems to defy science as though it is haunted by the souls of seals and whales and their hunters. In this small, lagoon-like bay whales and seals were dragged, roped to small boats and tied off on huge metal rings staked into the rocks and their bodies would be cut and their blood would muddy the pale green water and the wading birds would fly away to another less familiar bay lest their feathers be stained with blood.

When I told Lachie years ago, we were maybe 13 years of age, that I sometimes felt if I squinted my eyes I would see our ragged-clothed ancestors walking up the shore from the water he said he often squinted his eyes looking to the sea.

Now as I come closer I see it is a seal on the beach. I think of Lachie, a baby, being found on this beach. Tears spring to my eyes from some silent place inside me. I don't know why I am sad. It is a seal. What is the big deal about that? I have seen hundreds of dead animals. I have euthanised animals. I have carved my scalpel through the flesh of animals and suctioned out their fluids and run a sewing needle through their skin and hacked out tumors and yet here I am, Lorna McEwan, nee McLaren MRCVS, crying over a seal on the shore.

It is rotten, I smell that right away. I've never seen a dead seal on this or any other beach on Coll. Lachie would never leave a seal, or any other animal, this way.

It is dry and bloated, the light grey fur is mottled I see and feels much softer than a sealskin sporran, I stroke it without thinking. I do this with the patients at my surgery too, without thinking.

I can see it has been sliced the way I was taught by Malky to gut a fish; from the throat below the chin to the anus and all the organs have been removed.

As I am examining the seal's carcass I automatically reach for my med bag to get a small clamp to hold the skin aside to see better this something that is not as it should be inside, deep in that empty cavity. My bag is not there. I am going to have to go and get it from my car. Or use something from the house. I am loath to leave the gutted seal carcass here though it is clear no seagull or otter has nibbled at it, there are no beak or claw or any other marks on it. Strange.

What is that thing in there? It is not natural, I can tell that. I am going to use my bare hands to get it.

- 12 -

There was only one book I hated as a child. No. To be precise there were two. Alice in Wonderland and, even more repellent, Through the Looking Glass.

Mrs Cuddy was surprised by my vehement dislike, they were her oldest, Helen's, favourites after all - and by my furious, resentful determination to finish it. She expected I would fall in love with Alice, would revel in adventuring with her. But from the minute Alice faced her first ridiculous choice I wanted to close the book and never see the world through her stupid eyes again.

But I couldn't. I was stuck down the rabbit-hole with her. I had to know: what stupid choices did she make? What more ridiculous possibilities would she have to choose between next to get home?

Oh why was she so foolish as to forget to take the bottle off the table before she made herself small? How much more stupid could she possibly be? How can someone ride on a griffin through water if there are no griffins?

What sort of parallel world was she in? How would she ever get home? Was she just delirious? She had no control over anything at all that happened. Creatures interacted with her and yet she had no effect on them whatsoever. It didn't matter what she said or did, things just went along whatever nonsensical way regardless. Any intellect she had was useless in the face of ludicrous creatures such as bong-sucking caterpillars.

I had nightmares about the anxious White Rabbit for years. I tormented myself with thoughts of the Mad Hatter and his unpredictable nature.

Now I can feel exactly why I hated that book. Here I am – Alice.

Standing in Wonderland. Coming across all kinds of weirdness and needing to make strange choices.

Unfortunately, I am 40 years old and the 'it was all a dream' just isn't doing it for me. Maybe my 8-year old self had a prescience of all of this wildness coming up around me. That would be less weird an explanation than Lewis Carroll's imagination, would it not?

Later, much later, when we were grown-up, Lachie told me the poem he loved best of all was "The Walrus and The Carpenter" from Through the Looking Glass. He especially liked the illustration of the Walrus and the Carpenter speaking to the Oysters. 'I love oysters! I can't help it!' he said which was funny because he really did eat a phenomenal amount of oysters.

Thereafter whenever we were about to make dinner, go to the beach for driftwood, go to bed, head off to the village on our bikes and later my car, or anything along those lines, Lachie would announce,

"The time has come, the Walrus said, to speak of many things!" and I would say 'Argh! It's not "speak" it's "talk" - TALK of many things!'

And this was one of our things. And the way we were. Me hating/fearing the freakshow world of Lewis Carroll and the lack of effect reason and intellect had upon it. Lachie loving/welcoming it for those self-same reasons. And yet we made our little bridge.

I am glad Freya and Finn picked up 'the time has come the walrus said' from Lachie, calling him 'the walrus' at bedtime. We will make a point of continuing that. We shall make it a new McEwan tradition.

- 13 -

MALKY

I am the secret-keeper. I am the secret-keeper. I cannot say a word. She told me not to say anything to anyone. She told me I was the secret-keeper. A mermaid's purse I was she said to me.

But now, what was the secret?

What is it I am supposed to keep?

I know I have it somewhere.

I wouldn't lose an important thing like that now.

No, no, no. Where would I keep it now? In a wee box? Oh, I must not think of boxes. They put my Louisa in a box, they did. Or was it me put her in a box? A box in my mind? Whose was the box? No-one was ever in a box. When was that? Louisa? Has she not come home?

'Has she not come home?' I ask the police officer.

'Who Malky? Lorna?' says the police officer with the kind face. I'm not sure who the other one is. He looks very dour. I don't know him at all.

'Louisa. Did you say she'd not come home?'

'What are you talking about Louisa for Malky?' says the one who spoke before. 'Are you trying to confuse me now? Sure it's my job to confuse you.' He laughs.

'What happened to her?'

'Louisa?' The police officer is sitting directly opposite me across a table. The table should be replaced. Look at it, all chiselled away at on my side. I can see the cheap plywood chips and they even have a sooty dirt on them. I can feel it against my fingertips. The dirt of strangers rubbed off here. Who else has sat here? And this doesn't seem to be a very nice place to tell someone the love of their life is missing.

He clicks his head to one side and looks at me like a cockerel.

'I think we maybe need another wee break, eh Malky?'

'But where is my Louisa?' I ask him as he and the other officer push their plastic chairs back screeching the legs against the linoleum on the floor. I can see lots of black scrapes where the linoleum has been rubbed away at before.

What are these fools playing at?

I am deeply worried now about my Louisa. I have every right to be upset. They said she was missing, she hasn't come home, what has happened to her? 'What has happened to her officer? You can't go without telling me!'

I get up quickly to grab him, stop him leaving me but my legs, like sticks breaking, go out from under me and I'm holding the desk leg and looking at – is that my hand? Christ but it's old-looking. Where am I? I am not at home.

'Where I am? What has happened to Louisa?' I manage to get it out but I can hear it sounding like vomit and the officer is stepping away from me, fear in his eyes and he backs up to the shiny pale blue door that the other one who looks wrapped in a cloud to me from here is holding open and he slips out through it.

Where the hell am I? I nearly miss the chair when I go to sit on it. My arse seems smaller than usual. I can feel the hard plastic through on the bones of my arse. I look at the backs of these hands of mine again and sway my head in wonder. My palms are etched with deep lines and I lean over and rest my face in them. There is a wetness between my fingers and for a moment I think I am in my boat, my beautiful boat, but the salt water running between my fingers and dripping on to my jeans is my tears.

'Malky!'

'Who's that now? Talking in the fog of my ear. Someone walking through the hairs there, hairs like marram grass I feel when I stick my finger in and poke about.

'Malky! You hear me?'

A woman's voice. It's not Louisa. 'Aye Ruby. I hear you. how could I not? I would've heard you at the end of the village.'

'Did you bring the tools?'

'Yes.'

'Well go and sort it out then. The babbies are in there enjoying a wee bit of the sunshine.'

'Sunshine?' I look up at a sky that's slate-white like a coating of ice on a puddle. I see the two babbies, two blobs of knitted whiteness lying like grubs on a cream blanket. I recognise it as the one from our parents bed, the wool one with the four dark grey lines at each end.

'I need to see Agnes for a minute. Watch the babbies Malky.'

Why would I want to watch them? I'm here to fix the latch on the gatepost. It has dropped so the gate is not shutting properly. The metal bar of the small gate of planks is not slipping into the metal catch of the gatepost. I decide I will move the bar down a bit and take off the loop of rope Ruby has put over the gatepost to hold the gate closed and stop the sheep pushing in.

'She's got you busy has she Malky?' It's Wullie from next door, walking slowly towards me with his pipe unlit in his hand. He leans against the thick, round trunk of a corner post at the road on his side. 'It's a grand day is it not?'

I wish these people would just keep what they think to themselves. Leave a man alone.

'Aye, the shipping forecast said a force 8 later, nor' wester.' He looks out towards the sea across the calm waters of Arinagour bay, 'I can't see it myself.'

He pulls a cream sachet of tobacco from his pocket. I've seen him do this a hundred times, a thousand times. I know the smell of that tobacco. He rolls a wad of it between his fingers. He pushes it into the pipe. He takes another wad. Pushes it in.

'Och, aye' he says and sighs the sigh of a man contented.

Another wad is grasped in his fingers. The slow deliberateness is already annoying me. It's as if he's marking time by whole minutes with wads of tobacco.

'Why do you not use one of those proper metal tools to make up the pipe Wullie?' I say as I push the gate I'm to mend so hard the whole square of fenceline around the garden at Rose Tree shoogles.

'Sure God gave me a pipe-making finger Malky. It would be wrong of me not to use it.'

Every day for five days now he's stood against that green corner post, watching and waiting at me. 'Maybe you could use that finger to better purpose Wullie?' I say as I get the screwdriver out of the khaki canvas bag that was my father's tool bag and is now mine and point it at him.

'Aye. You're probably right about that Malky, you're probably right.'

He looks inside the bowl of his pipe. There will not be a single thread of tobacco hanging over the side. I've never seen a man smoke a pipe the way Wullie does. Not for him the huffing and puffing and flick-flick-flick of a lighter. He puts the pipe shaft in his mouth so that now his face looks complete. A brass petrol lighter appears, a flame, purple and golden, a raw redness from the bowl and at last, at long last, the release of a wisp of smoke. His lips tightening and relaxing which always reminds me of the old steamer boats that used to come, he has the same rhythm as them, those old smokies. Everyone knows not to speak to him while Wullie takes his first puff.

I unscrew the old bar off, my father would have put these two screws in. I can tell he did because they are perfectly set flush to the grain of the wood, nested just deep enough to hold tight and not catch on your clothes when you walk past.

There's a moan from the blanket. We both look over. I look away, back to my task, while Wullie says, 'Aye, hush now wee babbies. Hush now wee babbies or the sea dragon'll come git yeese.'

'Could you not do some of these things for her Wullie?' I've been wanting to ask him for days.

'Aye. I could.'

He's not looking at me.

'They're bonny wee babbies, are they not?' he says. He's still looking at them.

'The furred one is not.'

'Maybe. But he'll be wise enough, so he will.'

'It has a mother. At least that's something.'

Me and Wullie are smothered in thick air. Denseness in my throat. I clear it, the sound of hawking comes at the same time a sheep calls for its big lamb. Nearly a year down the track and she's still calling for it.

I take the hammer out and use the claw end to yank the metal bar off the gate. I haven't the patience now to footer about with these damn screws. I've bent the plate and the screw holes are empty. Screws lost in the sandy shells under my feet. I'm just going to nail it back on. What the fuck do I care? It's nails I've put in my pocket anyway and not the screws I meant to.

'Why am I having to come every day, traipsing to the village, to be her handyman?'

'You know the answer to that Malky. It's your sister's way. She's like her mother. And praise the Lord Jesus for that.'

'I've got plenty to be getting on with in the East End. I've the fishing for a start. And the wee caravan needs tied down.'

'A man can get lonely on his own Malky. Away over there in the East End. No use. No, no use at all.' He taps the pipe bowl in the palm of his left hand.

'Have you thought any more about staying down here?'

'No. I won't.'

'Sure it would save you the daily trip. What is there for you out there Malky?'

He reminds me of my father when he says this and it's no surprise at all since the two of them were so close and not only because they were next-door neighbours.

I maintain my silence. I think about how I've known Wullie my whole life. Wullie, who retired from being at sea not long after I was born, around the same time my father was working for the Laird over at Breachacha in the West End on a good wage and glad of it. Wullie, who walked all the way to Breachacha and back to get him when my father broke his leg.

'Have you finished that yet? I'm needing you to put a new plank on the steps out the back.' Rose is talking to me the moment she strides out of Agnes' the five steps it takes to cross the road. There's a ram heading down towards us I see, the evil one with the massive horns that goes for the dogs.

'Do you want me to build you a new taigh beac at the same time? Order you a new porcelain toilet while I'm at it with wee stickers of pansies on it?'

'Och Malky, come in and have something to eat. You'll have had no breakfast as usual.'

I can smell whisky. Whisky. Yes, it's definitely whisky. Where it is coming from? Oh, here in front of me is a white polystyrene cup with smoke, no not smoke, what is it called? Don't know. Smoke off it. And black. Oh, it is coffee but smells of whisky.

I pick it up and sure enough, it is whisky I'm

smelling. Strong whisky in weak coffee. Hot.

'You get that coffee down you, Sir. You'll feel the better for it' says a very young man in a police uniform. He's all shiny silver buttons and I wonder does he shave yet? I think I had a son once. Is that right?

I cup both my sets of wrinkled fingers around this chalice of heaven. God looks after his own right enough so he does. I am like Jesus drinking from a cup a beggar has given me. I remember a picture from our bible books at the Sunday School in the Minister's house. Jesus had lanky hair and a pointed nose. He looked a bit like my auld auntie Dolly. He was grasping a cup and water was spilling down the side of his lips and I had thought, how can you be Jesus if you can't take a drink without spilling it? So I make sure not a drop of this medicinal coffee toddy escapes from my mouth. I am parched like a desert wanderer myself. I open my throat and let the whisky slide so easy in a few mouthfuls that I can see now why people say a man drinks like a fish.

Where are all the fish now? My creels are empty. It is hopelessness I feel when I drop a creel into the water. I have tried every skerry now with my darrows, except a couple that I've long avoided.

When there is that wriggle between my fingers of a fish, caught and flicking, I do not have the youthful joy of winning I used to have. Now I check the fish for tumors. Jesus H Christ. How did it come to this? The worst of it is when I think of the old days. I can see in my mind all my fishing boxes, good plastic ones from Oban given to me by the captain of the Eriskay Flow. I say given to me but I recall there was a bit of drinking involved and a bottle of The Famous

Grouse.

I can see those boxes now, in the bottom of my boat. Full of silver, running with the oily purple and black stripes of hard, thin mackerel and pale gold leafs of saith and treasure it was did I but know it. You can't know.

I am a fool for still going out in the boat. The empty sea torments me. If there were mermaids here I would gladly throw myself into their arms. But even the mermaids see no use in a fisherman without fish.

I am feeling warm. I better get back to the caravan. There's a gale coming and I need to tie down the wee caravan. I should re-tar the big caravan. Where am I now?

My guts writhe. It's all come back to me now but the damn of it all is that as soon as I have it all, every detail, absolute knowledge and king of my kingdom, total control, the wave turns and most of it flows away again on me and makes me think I am in my boat because it is so like the waves receding.

I just need to take it one thing at a time.

I am at the police station in Oban.

I have come voluntarily.

I got the boat on Tuesday.

I got the boat on Tuesday because John-Mac said to me I should. He's a good man John-Mac. He's always been good to me. We went to school together in Oban after his parents came from the mainland to Coll when he was 14 and I was … Goddammit. Stop getting caught in these details. I'm busy picking up fish eyes and all the time Moby Dick is breaching behind me.

I am brand-new after the young policeman shows me where the toilet is and I splash water over my face. The tap keeps running and I wonder will it ever stop on its own or do I have to press the top of it again. What's wrong with a tap you twist to get it flowing and twist again to stop it for Christ's sake? Am I not even in control of how my face gets washed?

Calm down Malky. Aye. It's all fine now. Get in there. Sort it out. Get to the pub. Come on. Let's go.

'Detective McWilliams' I say to him and I know I have only a short time here before it all goes to hell on me again. Details. 'I'm sorry. I am here to help in any way I can. What can I do for you?'

'Aye. Very good Malky. You're back with us. We'll just take it easy this time. It wouldn't suit us at all if we had to get the psych in. Doctors. Let's just you and me and Detective Johnson here sort it out.

'We're thinking you killed Lachie. We think we know why. What we want is for you to tell us all about Lachie. Start at the beginning and see how far you get.'

I rub my hands over my face. I can feel my skin sagging and dry over my cheeks.

'Or, if that's just too much, I realise you want to get away as quick as you can, we can just get a quick confession and we're all done for now. What's it to be Malky? Your choice.'

'Did you say Lorna was here? I wonder. I wonder if I...' I've lost it. It was a great idea but it's gone. Too big to manage.

'Lachie.' I say, 'Aye, Lachie. He was my son.'

'No. No Malky. Stop right there. He wasn't your son. There is no way in God's heaven he was your son. We've taken his DNA and we already have yours' he says staring at me, 'As you know.'

'Oh aye. The assault thing.'

'Aye. The assault thing Malky. We know how much you disliked him Malky. Beating him when he was just a wee boy. How much did you hate him Malky?'

'I did hate him. Spawn of the devil's work. I did hate him. But not now. I like him now.'

'What? Now he's dead? You like him better dead Malky?'

'No. Yes. Yes. I like him since I found out about ..' What the fuck did I find out about? A letter? Why am I here?'

'But Lachie is my son. Isn't he? Where's Louisa?'

The big, old, quiet mountain of a Detective pats his pile of papers on the table. Looks at the other one. Shakes his head.

'Back in a minute or two Malky' says the McWilliams one.

- 14 -

LORNA

I get up quickly off my wee wall. I notice my backside feels damp. I hope I haven't got a stain there. I am conscious of the cigarette in my fingers. I hate the way it makes me feel like a tramp as Detective McWilliams comes towards me.

'How's it going Detective? Has he confessed?'

Detective McWilliams gestures me to come inside the station. 'Would you mind Lorna, coming inside for a minute?'

'Has something happened?'

'Yes and no. I need to have a wee word with you.'

I'm watching every door we pass, alert for the sudden appearance of Malky as we walk down the blue-painted corridor. I notice a fluorescent light flickering at the end. I wonder does it take the same expensive bulbs that ours do at the surgery.

This is quite a good atmosphere for our surgery to have I'm thinking as I follow the detective's black back. He looks like a cockroach walking because I can't see his head, just his black jacket. His plain clothes are all black just as if he was in uniform.

We are in tryst he and I. We have shared the identification of the body, he and I, the day before. 'Is that the man known as Lachlan Dunbar?' he said. 'The man?' said I. 'It's Lachie'. It is odd that Lachie looked more himself there on the stainless steel than he had at Struan. I leaned over his face. I expected his eyelids to open, maybe just one eyelid if two were too difficult for him to manage. I had waited for a sign that he knew I was there.

I had lifted his hand, such a very big hand. He'd always had hands too big for him. People would say, 'Can you give me a hand Lachie since yours is such a big hand?' He didn't mind that.

I can only slide my hand under his. We often held hands me and Lachie.

His face was waxy. I touched his cheek and it was a candle; hard and cold and too-smooth. I took the mermaid's purse I had brought with me from his house, with my secret in it, and tucked it inside the slight claw of his fingers. There was nowhere else to put it.

'You might want to wait and put that with him when he's in the coffin' said the detective, a kind soul.

'I want him to have it now.'

'What is it anyway?'

'It's a secret-keeper.'

Now, today, Tuesday, as it all is beginning to feel so much like routine already, he opens the door for me, what a gentleman, holding it open and waving his right hand inside.

There is a long window of glass with a grid of fine

wire in the door. Two small blue sofas sit in a welcoming L-shape but the room is cold and barren with nothing but the two sofas and a small coffee table where their sides meet. I take the one that is parallel to the door with the arm of it on my left side. I put my tweed bag on the sofa next to me. The detective sits on the other sofa with the arm on his right. We are both perched on the edge. I move back a bit so there's no danger of his knee touching mine.

He has an air about him that reminds me of Johnny. Compassion in his professional manner. But I am irked by his opening the door for me and this condescending carefulness; treating me as a victim, making sure not to further upset the bereaved. Being privy to all the facts, sharing only those he deems necessary. I do not like being on the other side like this. I am usually the one in that position.

I am the one who knows all the facts, the prognosis, the progression of the disease, the consequences of the accident. I am the one who is in charge of what happens next to an animal. Who gets to know what. I have to choose which facts I share and all of this is only partly to do with the owner of the pet and whether I can tell they want all the medical details, discuss the information they've found on google, how tied up their love is in their pet. How easily they will let go. It is a powerful position. It is me who chooses whether the animal will live or die and most importantly of all, in what way.

There is no point in me suggesting intensive home care when it is obvious this mother of three, much as she wants to, will not be able to do it. She would feel guilty if I did. And yet I know that if this cat were with different people it would probably live.

At the same time to suggest to an obsessive, repeat-visit client that intensive care is an option I know I am putting the animal through a special kind of medical hell; the hell of the search for a cure, the time before death spent in the cells of my surgery where the lights are put out at night and no-one is there to hear you meow and you don't know where you are or why your people left you because no matter what owners think to make themselves feel better, animals have no idea why we put them through the medical procedures we do. The idea of experiencing this pain to postpone death later is a human one after all. And so we see the selfish nature of people. We cannot help our humanness.

I am thinking all this through while the detective looks through a wee notebook he's brought. I'm thinking about the science of whether I share the finding of a secondary tumour or the research I read last week on an experimental treatment, the results of which show it will not work but may lead to a cure in five or ten years. And all of this is in my hands as I stroke the fur of my patients.

The detective is stroking the arm of the sofa. I am glad I kept my knee out of the way. I feel at last a professional connection and it calms me. We are both quiet for a while in this space for waiting and hearing and being told things.

'Lorna' he says and shuffles his backside forward so he's only just balanced on the wee blue sofa, a funny blue, not quite electric. His fingers are knotting and un-knotting themselves away out in front of his knees, elbows resting on his thighs. 'You never heard me say this. OK?'

'Fair enough.'

'It would have been better for everyone involved if John-Mac and the rest of you had quietly buried this one.'

'Buried?'

'Aye. Buried Lachie. Reported him missing maybe. But this…' he claps his hands together. 'I can tell this is going to be bad for all concerned.

He laces his fingers together. He has big thumbs. 'If it wasn't for all this new procedure crap we could have stopped it all right here in Oban all the same. We can't do that sort of thing now. More's the pity.'

'I'm not sure I follow Detective McWilliams' I've always been good at retaining client's names.

'I've seen a lot of broken men in here Lorna. And then there's the criminals' he splutters an empty laugh. 'Your Da Lorna. He's a broken man.'

'Oh aye, I've seen that act. He's very good at it. Poor Malky, he's a broken man.' I make a huffing noise. 'Nothing wrong with him.'

'I know what I'm talking about Lorna. The man is totally broken. It's not just the crying. And the shaking. And the confusion. The man's a total wreck so he is. We can't do anything for him. We can't get anything out of him.'

'He's playing you.'

'No Lorna. He really isn't. I've had to call the doctor to him. We had a good shot at him confessing. He seemed to be pretty compus mentis when he came in, he had a wee drink in him, but it's been downhill from there. Now he's just gibbering rubbish. Doesn't know where he is. No clue what year. In and out of reality.

'He's obviously got a lot to be guilty about, Lorna. And I'm not saying he didn't hurt Lachie in some way. But not only is ... how will I put this, not only is he ordering a drink at the last pub before the desert of raving lunatics but ...' and here is the pause that I recognise so well, I do it myself every day with clients, 'I'm no doctor Lorna but I'm seeing all the symptoms of dementia. My own mother had it. Same thing.'

'Dementia? The bastard. That's just very convenient isn't it?' I straighten my spine. I'm aware of my jaw clenching. 'Did you ask him about the seals?'

'The seals?' he shakes his head. 'That's the last thing on my mind. I know you're a vet and you care about the seals but my job is to go for the biggest crime first and all the rest is incidental. People are forever shooting at seals you know that Lorna. It's a crime right enough and we're serious about ... Anyway, let's stick to the main issue.

'The thing is, with the dementia, he can't be interrogated. Anyway, it would be a totally pointless exercise. Nothing he says would stand up in ...'

A vibration from my bag. I see "home" on my phone. 'Would you mind? It's my husband. He'll be worried.'

'No problem' says the detective and gets up and starts walking about the room, hovering in my space.

'Johnny? Listen. I can't talk just now. I'm talking with Detective McWilliams. I'll call you back when we've finished.'

'Hold on Lorna. You remember that day you had the Labrador with gunshot, the RA cat and the poisoned horse all in the same half an hour?'

'Uh-huh.'

'We're having a bit of that now, but at home. Now look, we're all fine-ish. But I'm about to take Freya to

146

Yorkhill A&E; looks like a fractured tibia is all but need an X-ray, so that's OK. You can have a word with her after you've finished with the detective.'

'Right. What else?'

'Just call me back after you've finished. I'm heading up to the hospital now.'

'More bad news?' says the detective.

'My daughter has fractured her tibia. My husband's taking her to Yorkhill.'

'That would be right. Never rains but it pours.'

'Have you gotten hold of Kirsty yet?'

'We have. She's flying back from Sydney today. Or was is yesterday?' He shakes his head. 'I think she'll be here tomorrow. Time difference: gets me totally confused. But aye, she's on her way. She'll be here soon enough.

'Oh, wait, here's her itinerary she emailed us.' He pulls it out, a folded piece of paper slipped in the back of his notebook and puts his glasses on.

'Let's see, here we are: she's BA7313 Sydney to Bangkok arriving Monday 11 June, BA10 arriving Tuesday 12 at Heathrow 06.25, arriving Glasgow Airport on flight BA2960 Tuesday 12.45. That's right they are a day ahead of us. Tomorrow with them.'

'Well that's one thing.' I rub my fingers along the furrows on my forehead. I've forgotten to put moisturiser on again and I'm wondering if I might even still have some salt spray from the boat on my hairline like dandruff.

'OK.' I say. 'So. Are you saying to me that he's going to get off Scot-free? He's managed to get away with everything?' The last word is a screech.

'Lorna.' He's sat down next to me on my sofa now, facing me sideways. 'Listen to me now' he claps his hands like a wee baby seal, maybe he should have been a teacher, 'Life's a bitch and then you die. You're a vet. Sure you know that.

'The doctor's taking a look at him now. It's a blessing in disguise. At least he'll get a diagnosis and everyone'll know what's what.'

'You mean he'll be forgiven for all the bastard things he's done because he can't remember? Because he's got dementia? It's all OK because he's got Alzeimer's poor soul?' I curl my hands into fists and tilt my head to heaven. I notice my fingernails are digging into my skin because I haven't trimmed them for nearly a week.

'Excuse me detective. I just need a wee moment' I get up and walk towards the wall and am staring at the burst bubbles of old paint as I say, 'You fucking fucking bastard. You fucking motherfucking bastard!'

'Aye, that's better Lorna. I'd be thinking the same thing myself in your position.

'People say this dementia is a terrible thing but it works out well for many of the less savoury kind.' He stands up. 'Not only do they not get punished but their conscience is totally clear. God love them.

'I wouldn't mind spending my twilight years in some nice, cosy hospital away with the fairies myself' he says. 'For folk like Malky it's an avoid-the-jail-all-tha-gether card.'

'So what happens to him now?'

'Do you want to see him?

'No.'

'We'll see what the doctor says. We might be allowed a couple of sessions with him once he's diagnosed and in the hospital at Avonlea so they gauge how bad he is. Looks to me like there's no way he can live on his own anymore. A couple more sessions with him once he's levelled out a bit might be helpful for information, satisfy our own curiosity, but I'm not sure we'd even get that.'

'So you're saying even if he was to confess just now to what he did to Lachie it wouldn't hold?'

'Aye. I am.'

'But surely you don't need a confession?'

'No. If it wasn't for his distress. And I have to say it is distress Lorna. A confession would just have made the whole bad mess of it go away. Let you and your family heal faster. And him get what he rightly deserves. But the fact is Lorna, it makes no difference whether he goes on trial or not. He's a sick man and he'll end up in the Avonlea regardless. And paid for out of our taxes too. A guilty verdict would send him there anyway. And without the stress of a trial, which would likely send him right over the deep end if he's not already dipping a toe in the water there, you might get some of the answers you're needing.'

'The cunning bastard. You know, he's always been a cunning bastard. I would much prefer him to set alight to the caravan and burn himself to hell.'

The detective purses his lips. I put my bag on my lap. I am needing a cigarette. I suppose that's me back on them, officially.

'So, let me just re-cap detective. You're telling me that the sweetest man that ever walked the earth is dead and the one that … the one that tormented him his whole life and killed him goes free?'

'He's far from free Lorna. But yes. That's the truth of it. Listen, I'm just going to get us a coffee. There's something else I need to talk to you about.'

'I can guess what that is. The post-mortem?'

149

'Lachie. Aye.'

'Will you be wanting my professional opinion detective?' I say with a smile.

He raises an eyebrow at me, 'So you know then?'

- 15 -

Saturday

Once I take the foreign object out of the seal's carcass I put it in the inside flannel pocket of my waxed jacket. It's important to always wear something with pockets or take a bag with you when you go down to the beach. You always want to be able to take necessary things home.

If there is one of these things, there are bound to be more. I am sure of it. I leave the seal; a cavern of furred skin, and head off towards the short heather-clothed basalt cliffs on the northern end of the small beach.

It's a steep climb, me tucked inside the narrow ravine of where the overflow of rainwater runs down the cliff in a stained brown line. You have to use the woody heather stems to steady yourself and pull yourself up. It's always felt like walking an endless fresh grave.

The last time Lachie and I climbed up here was

only two summers ago. We felt old. Nearly four decades to account for. But we put gritty sandshoes on in the front garden, bleached by the sun and parched by the wind, sandshoes of different sizes for anyone to wear, and did it anyway. I said the sand was good for exfoliating the dry skin on the soles of my feet. Lachie said dry skin was a terrible condition and that seawater was the only remedy for that and shouldn't I know it?

When we get to the top we watch Johnny with my children on the beach at Elleraig. We see Kirsty come out of the house with a tray and she's made lemonade and we see her and Johnny laughing and it is good to see them down there. The bright colours of Freya and Finn's clothes, the blue denims of Johnny, the fudge-coloured jersey of Kirsty and the wagging tail of Finn our Malamute frightening all the whaler hunter ghosts of Elleraig away.

Johnny is adding more wood to the bonfire pyre we're going to set alight tonight once it's nearly dark. Flames to beat back the spectre beasts.

'I'm pleased for her she's going' he says.

'To Sydney?'

'Aye. Australia. It'll do her the world of good. And Alfie too. They'll have a grand time of it in the sun.'

He smiles as he watches the figures moving around, Kirsty pouring lemonade into un-matching glasses. 'She's always had to look after me.'

'When have you ever needed looking after Lachie?'

'It's ones like you and her that's done the looking after. And your Auntie Ruby. Women seem to understand these things well.'

'What things?'

'Och, you know.' his long whiskers are rolled into

a musketeer handlebar and goatee affair, he twists one end with his right hand in a way that is pleasing to watch; the same way I saw John Byrne the artist fondle his on television. 'The moon. The tide. The beasts' he laughs. 'Are you happy Lorna?'

'I am Lachie.'

'You've done well.'

'So have you.'

'You mean because I've not had the jail or the loony-bin?'

Now I laugh, 'wild spirits like you can't be jailed Lachie. It's against the Wildlife Act of Scotland so it is. I know about these things.'

'Aye. Mammy would agree with you. You know how she gives me an allowance to live on?'

I nod my head and chew at the grass stem. 'She says she'd rather support me than World Wide Fund for Nature. Better to take the direct route she says. Cut out the middle man.'

He nudges me on my arm with his elbow and we fall over backwards laughing, looking at the sky, blue and with drifts of white tendril smears.

'You know what I miss?' I say.

'What?'

'I miss tickling the tentacles of sea anemones. I miss them sucking my fingertips into their mouths. My fingers are too big now to fit. I love it when the tentacles grab hold of your pinky and sort of suck at it all sticky. I was showing Freya the other day down at Struan; you know the big rockpool? I envied her her wee fingers.'

'Was there much in the way of wildlife in the pool?'

'I think maybe more. Plenty of whelks. Nobody's

gathering them so that's good.'

He takes the stem of a bobbly purple self-heal flower and snips it between his fingers. He hands it to me. It's funny that the flower looks tiny when it always used to look so big in our hands when we were young. Lachie was always picking wild flowers for me. 'Would we have been happy if we'd married do you think?'

'Maybe' I put the flower in the breast pocket of my flowery blouse, tucking it in deep so I don't lose it. I think about how I used to tuck them in my jeans pocket and make a wee collection of them drying next to my bunk bed in the caravan. I would press them in my palm and breathe in their machair scent in the darkness of my father's snoring.

'You would have learned all my secrets' says Lachie not looking at me but facing the sea.

'Sure I've got all your secrets collected in mermaid's purses'

'Remember when you called them devil's purses?'

'Aye. I'd read that they were also called that.'

'They bring everything they don't understand back to the devil. I think they invented God just so there'd be a Devil to blame for everything. Or explain everything.'

'Look,' he says sitting up and pointing out over the water. Porpoises are playing just past the island at the mouth of Elleraig. 'Tha iad bòidheach?' he says, aren't they beautiful? 'They've seen us and they've come to say hello.'

I sit up next to him and tug my jacket off my shoulders. 'Are you still swimming with them at night?'

'Oh aye. I'll never stop doing that. They're more

fun than the seals.'

'What about the Orca?'

'He went away a while ago. There's been no word of him for a while. But I think a female may be on her way with her calf. I'm looking forward to it. I'm a strange one, am I not?' he laughs. His laugh so like the spill of a wave on a smooth sandy shore. 'I'm awful glad the whales can't get stranded at Elleraig. Especially the wee minkes. It's a good horseshoe bay with the two channels and deep.'

He's turned to look at our family on the beach. They've moved past the big grey and white and black and marbled stones near the grassy peat, past the smaller pebbles that glint metallic with minerals in the light and their backs are bent over drawing heart shapes in the wet sand with their fingers. Johnny has Freya on his hip as he leans over the sand. Kirsty is sitting on her side and Finn jumps on her back.

'Do you still want me to teach them to swim?'

'Oh, yes.'

'The tide'll be in before dinner. We can take them in then. You can show me if you're any better yourself.'

I laugh. 'No. I'm definitely still not swimming out to the island. I think a whaler might catch me on the way.'

'You and whalers' he snorts. 'You know fine it's the seal hunters you've got to watch out for.'

I slap him on the back of his shoulder. I pull him towards me. He falls in on my side and I hold him the same way I have always held him since we grew up. Not just in my heart but against it, tight. The way I hold Finn and Freya and Finn. The way Pearl comes and curls her furry body into me in bed at night, soft

155

paws resting on my arm.

'I love you Lachie.'

'I know that. Tha gaol agam ort-fhèin.' he says, I love you too, in the same flowing way a wave climbs up a rock without breaking.

When I get to the top of the cliffs and sit in our spot near the flat lichen green rock I see nothing out at sea. It is grey and flat and does not even seem to mirror the sky.

I notice the bones of a seagull's rib cage, a cluster of yellow-tinged feathers held by white stringy membrane. Perhaps the golden eagles of Mull have come this far. More likely the hen harriers.

I am looking down the other side of the cliff now, certain I will see another seal carcass. There it is. No. There are two. Small curved rocks lifting out of the sand always look like seals. The colours are the same.

I can't see the next beach inlet from here. It's possible there are carcasses in the rock pools from here to Sorasdal. I am too weary-hearted to check the whole coastline. I will look down here and as far as Traigh Lekavic, the most beautiful beach in the world, and then I will walk back along the road.

I find five seal carcasses on my trip. All have been gutted. All have the bullets inside them.

When I'm on the road and nearly home to Lachie's I call John-Mac on my cell phone. The family one. He answers in his official special constable's voice even though he knows it is me calling. The finding of Lachie's body has already changed the ways of the wild folk.

'Someone's been shooting the seals out the East End John-Mac.'

'Eh?' he says.

'I said, someone's been shooting seals from Elleraig to maybe Sorasdal, maybe more. I've found five carcasses on the beaches with bullets in them. They've been gutted but there are still bullets in them. You better come and have a look.'

'No Lorna. That can wait. It's not a crime to shoot seals. I'm busy sorting out the paperwork for Lachie. He's to go on the boat on Monday. The doctor's on her way over to help me with the report. What do I want to go looking at seals for Lorna?'

I take a deep breath. 'Just a minute' I say. 'I put my hand over the cell phone and scream. And as I scream I see someone moving on the hill past Elleraig, near Struan. On the hill, watching me. 'I said John-Mac, someone's been shooting seals and you need to get over here and check it out or else I am phoning the police in Oban. I'll meet you at Lachie's …' I say. I press the end call button on the phone and say, '… you cock' and feel better.

I get back to Lachie's and my feet are soaking. I pull my socks off, my pale skin has a curved high tide mark of brown peaty scrapes of bits. I hang my socks over the rail in front of the stove. The fire has gone out but there's still a big piece of log in there so I add more kindling and set it alight again, blowing my angry breath in short puffs so I start to feel light-headed.

Sula comes and meows at me, on her tippy-toes flicking her tail against my folded legs and back. 'Just a wee minute Sula' I say. 'I'll get you something in a wee minute.' My feet are cold against the big rock in front of the stove. I am suddenly freezing cold. I need to eat something too.

I get Sula a fish out of the fridge, it looks like one

Lachie has caught and it is smelly. I put it in Sula's dish and she is growling with fierce pleasure. There's no milk in here as usual but I have brought my box of groceries from the car on my way back and I've plenty of milk and bread from the supermarket in Oban. I've even got an Esky with frozen pumpkin soup I made in Glasgow in it. I put the freezer bag of orange soup in a white bowl from the shelf and put the bowl on the stove so the soup begins to melt. I put the kettle on and take a jar of instant coffee from my cardboard box pantry and the carton of milk, I put the other cartons in the fridge. I'll put the rest of the stuff away later.

I touch Lachie's trousers on the back of the kitchen chair, the canvas is dry and has salt on it, I can feel it between my fingers and I can smell the sea off them, the smell of the sea off Lachie, and for a moment he is not dead for here are his trousers, regular as you like, nicely dried on the back of the chair.

I know he won't come. Poor John-Mac. The biggest crime, a dead man, and him needing to make sure it is all done exactly by the book. He must be terrified. Completely out of his depth. He'll be down there in the village with the doctor and him looking up his special constable folder of what to do in such and such an event.

It wouldn't do for me to hunt him down myself. I could just walk out of here, and hunt him. Check his caravan lair first. Have a look at Bousd for his boat. I could take one of his guns from the wee caravan, the key will be in the same place if that is, he has happened to lock the rifle away in the strong case. And I could just put a bullet in his head and that would be the end of it.

If I find him near Bousd, I could take one of his old faded turquoise fishing nets from the wee caravan, wrap him up in it and drag him to his boat, bumping him over the small dry brown cliffs and green lichen rocks, tie him off to the bow, start up his new Yamaha outboard and reverse out of the safety of the sea channel, watching him all the while, his body rolling and turning and me feeling a bit like a crocodile death-rolling my prey and how long would it take I wonder until he drowned?

This is a good plan.

I wouldn't have to listen to him crying. Or swearing. Or calling me names. Names like 'Louisa'. He would just be in the wake of me at the bow end until I cut loose the rope that binds him and let him drop, float, float away. A new kind of bait to bring all the fishes back.

A sense of righteous dharma floods me as stoke up the fire in the hearth with the long blackened poker. It is as straight as a fine arrow with not a single dent in its line. It is a thing of beauty. The wee sparks fly and after a while of this poking, harder and harder, the red embers livid, I put another log on to last the night through. I check the wood for nails and such – beetles and bugs - as we always do, me and Lachie, and notice it is a round fence corner post.

My coffee has gone cold but the frozen soup has succumbed to the heat and I put it in a pan, the smallest one in the row of five hanging on hooks from the beam above the kitchen. No, I think, as I pour the hot soup into the pan and stir it with the wooden spoon that's dark brown at its edges and worn not just thin at the bow end of it but at the handle too.

No, it wouldn't be the done thing, this kind of restorative justice. I take the dull, grey bullet from my inside pocket and examine it closely. It's not a crime in Scotland to shoot seals. You can shoot nursing seals in the water, fire at them from the shore to the island where they're lolling about. You can shoot the baby ones, the big males, whatever you fancy. And of course you've every reason to as a fisherman, they are stealing your livelihood after all are they not?

And that must be very annoying for you when your nets are so impotent, your boat so slow, your diesel so expensive. How justified you must feel maiming the seals that eat 'your' fish.

I've pulled gunshot from ducks and gun dogs alike. BB pellets from cats who lived too close to small boys. Even once a red deer, a stag, accidentally clipped. But this delving with my naked hands into the carcass of a seal, its innards removed, a bullet wedged in blubber, no latex shielding my sense of touch. It is this seemingly inconsequential task that turns me.

If I look back far enough I can see my young self so full of dreams and trust and vigour. All I had to do was fill my mind with knowledge, every fact available, know the words, know the anatomy, know the reason and I would know it all. I was queen of all things because I knew. My Certificates and Degree were my pennants of splendid education. My servitude to text books devoted. My lectures on 'Advances in the Treatment of Feline Cancers' were attended by my peers and professors in Glasgow and London. The transcript distributed around the world.

And here I am with all the knowledge in the world

I could ever hope to retain and I am lost, defeated and like that bloody irritating Alice, I am bewildered. Filled with anger and sorrow. I would be clueless yet the clues keep coming to me through this grief-stricken looking glass.

I pour my soup into the white ceramic bowl, take a silver spoon with a deep, round bowl from the sideboard drawer and sit at the table. Sula jumps up on it next to me. 'You're not supposed to be up here Sula' I say but who am I to push her off the table in her own home. 'If you come and live with us, if Kirsty goes back to Australia that is, you'll not be allowed on the table you know'. Sula looks at me and shuts her eyes and opens them in one single movement.

My legs ache. My feet are cold again. I long for the wool loft as we call it, the sleeping platform up the driftwood stairs. I take my hot water bottle from my overnight bag and fill it from the kettle, I go to the bookcase thinking to choose something to read, maybe some Scottish poetry, and I remember Malky taking something from here. What could it have been?

I shake my head. I am too full of things and too empty. I climb the ladder and climb on all fours across the piles of sheepskins scattered like clouds fallen from the sky on the floor, I slop myself onto the first low palette bed. I can smell the salt linen and seawater. I am asleep before Sula can get to me with her kneading paws and purring.

162

- 16 -

Sunday

Again I do not dream of mammals in the seawater. Nor dead men on beaches. Nor the gutted carcasses of seals. Instead I awake knowing exactly where I am and looking for Freya because I have just told her to be careful on the top rung of the ladder on the slide because I know it is a little shoogly up there because Johnny has still to plant it deeper in the ground and she doesn't need to tell me she has hurt her leg because I can see the bone between her right knee and her foot is now two instead of one like a railway track in switch.

It is Sunday. It is definitely Sunday. Here is Sula sleeping next to me, her paw twitching. My perfume smells stale. I should probably have a wash. Swim with me! No. I will not go in that water today or anytime soon sun or no sun.

Its rays are splashing through the small inset windows of both the kitchen and sitting areas. It has

163

always fascinated me how this house caught the light through such humble windows. I open the front door and breathe the sea air. A movement, rapid in the bracken, and a tail like a big rat's disappearing and it'll be one of the otters looking to see has Lachie left them a wee something. Not today. Not tomorrow.

Perhaps they already know. Perhaps they saw it all. There are waders on the shore, I can see worms casts in conical spiralling bumps on the sand and I remember trying to get Lachie to dig up the worms with me one day for bait, huge giant sand worms, and the idea was so disgusting to him it surprised me. And me feeling it was not a good idea after all to go digging on Elleraig bay when the tide was out. 'Leave them for the birds' he said to me.

And here were the oystercatchers and redshanks, lapwings and snipes, all of them as you'd never see on one beach on Coll, gathered here for the plenty.

Should John-Mac not be coming here to check it all out? The thought curls up to the surface of my mind, looking for something to attach itself to, a fact of some kind, something important.

I suppose not if he thinks him a suicide. My knees disappear on me until I feel them hit the heather in front of me. I was on my way to the shore and now I am on my hands and knees and I raise my head up and from my womb comes a sound and it bursts out between my lips and clamped jaw and I think it is 'Lachieeeeeeee eeeeeeeeeeeeee eeeeeeeeeeeeee' that comes out. The wading birds burst off the sand like shot from worm cast cannons, straight up and away without circling.

All this primal yelling. It's exhausting me. I have no control over it all. Is it years of suppression rising up now there's a wee, bitty chink in my floodgate? It's like water bursting out of me. A rogue wave spewing through my lips.

Sort yourself out Lorna for God's sake. I brush the sand off my flannelette pyjamas, an indulgence to be so childlike as a proper grown-up. Wrapped in flannelette I sleep soundly. No satin negligees for Lorna the vet. I see a sprig of heather twig has attached itself to my knee. I leave it there.

I am glad I am alone today. I can spend time absorbing the loss of Lachie. Be pragmatic about it. Get through the grief quickly, deeply, with myself here so that I can get back to work and home and Johnny and Freya and Finn. I should call Johnny right away.

I head back into the cottage and unplug my cell phone. I fill the kettle, add a thick, short sliver of driftwood, a meagre piece of peat and the heather sprig from my knee to the fire and leave the door open for it to draw and smoke. I do all of this before I can bear to turn the cell phone on and look at the messages. The act of the kettle doing something purposeful helps, its gathering simmering bubbles building in the background.

I hate the way this phone beeps at me about everything. I hate how it feels in my hand, all plastic and pinkness. I cannot read the letters and numbers on the keypad without putting on my reading glasses because some idiot designer has made them prettily pale coloured against the pale gold keys and therefore perfectly impractical. I remember when I did not have reading glasses. I do not send text messages. I am quite happy to receive them. I send symbolic acknowledgements of xxxx and 'yes' or 'no' in return.

I could use the house phone to call Johnny. But it is an old rotary phone without a long cord. Since it was installed by Kirsty at the insistence of her agent in Edinburgh years ago, 'for emergencies Kirsty!' it has long been referred to as the 'emergency phone' and therefore never used. But here we are with an emergency. And yet it is not. The emergency must have been prior. The patient is now dead.

I don't bother to check the messages though I can see the little envelope symbol on the screen of my cell phone. I hear a kerfuffle as Johnny answers, '… put her down now Finn …' I hear him say as his lips move towards his cell phone. He must have been carrying it about with him to answer so quickly.

'Is that Pearl he's got?'

'Aye. For some reason he won't leave her alone this morning. He's going to get a scratch in a minute!' his says the last part to Finn and sure enough I hear an "OW! She hurt me!' from a wailing Finn so I know Johnny will be having a quick look at the scratch so I just enjoy feeling like I am there and with the added luxury of being an observer instead of an active, cotton-wad-bearing participant.

'Do you think I should put the telly on? Isn't this the sort of time we said it was OK to use it?' he says to me.

'Why not?' I laugh. 'You sort that out and call me back.'

'Everything OK? You sleep well?'

'I can safely say I am sure much better than you. Were they both in the bed with you?'

'Aye. That's how it ended up. At about half past ten as I faintly recall.'

'OK. Call me back then.' I flip the stupid phone

shut.

It's odd how we now shut up the phone instead of putting it down.

I've fed Sula and made my coffee and begun an attempt at porridge, filling the pan with oats and milk and leaving it on the ancient oak kitchen table that came from the Manse, I've even managed a fly cigarette out the front blowing smoke downwind and away and crushing out the stub in a clay saucer in the front garden before my phone shrills its pretend rotary phone ring.

'All quiet on the western front then?' I say.

'A ceasefire for the meantime. Peace talks silently in progress during Balamory. How are you honey?'

'I'm fine. I had a dream Freya broke her leg.'

'Well, as long as I don't we'll be fine. How are you?'

'In denial. I feel like it's still yesterday and I'm caught in a never-ending loop. Did I tell you about the seals?'

'The seals? No. You told me about the hens being quiet.'

'Oh, yes, that's right. The hens are gone. And I told you about Malky coming round?'

'Yes. Has he been back?'

'No. I don't think he'll be back. Listen, I phoned John-Mac last night to tell him about the seals. I meant to phone you too but well, I fell asleep instead.'

'Aye. You'll be exhausted.'

'Listen Johnny. A whole lot of seals have been shot from Elleraig as far as Sorasdal. I found five carcasses on the shore all the way down.'

'You walked all that distance yesterday?'

'Aye. Hence the tiredness. Listen. I phoned John-

167

Mac and he is not remotely interested. He's gone into super-officious mode.'

'I don't blame him.'

'No. But still. People can't go around shooting seals. And on Coll! At Elleraig!'

'But you know they do it elsewhere. The fishermen. On the quiet.'

'Don't get me off-course Johnny. The thing is I know who shot them.'

'Let me guess.'

'Yes. The bullets are from his gun. I've got the first one in my pocket. As evidence.'

'It won't be evidence in your pocket Lorna. The police collect the evidence.'

'Damn. You're right.'

'It's probably just a one-off. He's lost the heid and gone off with his rifle. That thing should have been taken off him years ago. It's only the one he's got isn't it?'

'No. He's got at least two. And some kind of pistol, hand-gun thing he plays with.'

'Christ Lorna. You don't think he's walking about just now with a gun on him do you? Did you see him with anything yesterday? He definitely didn't see you? Christ. How old were the carcasses you found?'

'A few days. Maybe a week. They were quite dry and decomposed. Also, they had been gutted.'

'Gutted? That's weird.'

'I know fine John-Mac won't even bother coming to have a look at them. He could easily take one of the bullets are evidence. The carcass near Sorasdal is quite easy to get to from the road.'

'There's no way Lorna. He'll know it's not illegal to shoot seals. Damn shame. He's far too much on his plate already just surviving. Dotting his i's and crossing his t's.'

'Aye. You're right. I feel bad about them just lying there as if nobody cared.'

'What about Lachie?'

'They've taken the body to the doctor's surgery.'

'Aye. John-Mac told me.'

'What? Has he phoned you?'

'Yes. He phoned last night.'

'Last night? Did he mention me calling about the seals?'

'Not a word.'

'That's odd, is it not?'

'I suppose not. He's very worried about doing the right thing. He sounded like a different man. I hardly recognised him when he phoned. He said the doctor had just left.'

'Aye. She's helping him. Keeping him right. She's good like that.'

'After he called me I started to wonder…'

'But hold on. Why was he calling you?'

'I don't know really. I think it was just a courtesy call. Like, officially letting us know what was happening. Maybe he didn't get a chance when you called him and he wanted to put in his report that he had called us. He did ask why you had gone back up to Coll and what we all did when we were there at Easter.'

'Did he now? Very conscientious. So what did you wonder?'

'I'm confused about why they're taking Lachie to Oban. Why are they not just keeping him on Coll?'

'They said I had to identify his body in Oban.'

'I know. But why? Why in Oban?'

'Oh yes, because surely I could just officially identify him here and John-Mac sign off on it and the doctor give the cause of death.'

'But what is the COD Lorna? We're all assuming he drowned. But you said right away he hadn't drowned. Why did you think that?'

'I don't know. Why did I? I still don't think he drowned. I mean Lachie? Drown? No way. I just can't see it. No.'

'If John-Mac and the doctor think he didn't drown either then that'll be why Lachie's going to Oban. It must be a suspicious death Lorna.'

'Oh for God's sake, you're right Johnny. Oh my God.'

*

I look around the house of wood and stone and wool and horn and it is a like an empty womb. It has never looked like this before. It's become overcast outside and I need to put a few table lights on. The fire in the stove catches some salt and spits loudly and I jump and feel foolish.

A suspicious death. That is an unnatural death. That means they don't think it is suicide. Or could it maybe still be suicide? I am ashamed to realise some part of me had supposed Lachie had killed himself, like some poor lost romantic throwing himself into the sea. But now I think about it, he would never have died that way. There's no way he could have drowned.

There is something here to explain it all to me. I can sense it. There's no feeling of Lachie around me like I had yesterday but all the same I'm being driven to look around me, slowly and with great care. To look at everything with new eyes. To put my vet's eyes in and cast about, poke and touch and stroke and listen with what I like to call my dog senses.

I know it sounds daft, me flaring my nostrils and lifting my nose, being aware of the undercurrent of living things but being my 'dog-self' is the way I deal with using my senses of instinct and intuition in my work. These you have to learn yourself as a vet, or maybe expose them from deep inside, there's no class on it at Vet School. Doing this I feel I am cheating. I should maybe teach a class in it myself, volunteer for it. Would they all laugh at me? Intuition over science? Oh yes, there would be laughter indeed.

This house is a living being. I can feel it opening up to me. I can almost see different areas flaring in different colours of green and red and blue like that game me and Finn and now Freya play; looking for a hidden object – you're getting warm, hot, hot, hot, hotter, very hot, boiling, cold, ice cold, so freezing cold, until that which is hidden is found.

'Can you show me where it is Sula you clever girl?' I say as she stretches her front legs and bows to me. No, she's wanting out. I open the front door just enough for her to see it's not sunny. She hesitates on the threshold. 'Don't dither Sula, do you want in or out?' I say, knowing it is pointless and I'll have to stand here for a few minutes. I leave the door partly ajar. I don't want to lose my mood. I am sure there is something here for me. Something especially for me.

What would it be and where? I walk around trying to imagine my body feeling hotter or colder as I go. I am sure I am hotter near the bookcase I think as I walk past it on my third circuit of the large room, around the kitchen table, past the front door, through the sitting area.

There are no internal walls of course so the job is much easier. What about up the stairs? Something hidden under the wool mattress? No, that doesn't feel right. It is in the bookcase. Or is that just my own belief that all can be found in knowledge drawing me there?

I can't help that. But I am definitely drawn to the bookcase and after all, was this not where Malky took whatever it was he took from? I decide I will go through each and every book. There must be a hundred of them, mostly vintage books with linen covers and pale brown edges to the pages. No small amount of Penguin paperbacks from the 1960's and '70's. On the top shelf are first edition sets of Kirsty's own books; Fairytales for Small Folk, Mysteries of Moonlight, Tales from the Dawn of Today, Forgotten Stories.

Not a single text book among them. It is still a mystery to me. Now where would Lachie put something for me? He would put it in the most scientific of these books. Something I might be likely to pick up. Or more likely, something that reminded him of me. Little Women, of course.

And it falls out as soon as I put my finger to the top of the spine and pull, an envelope. Cream, A5 size, and on the front in childish cursive writing, "Lorna".

I let out the breath that's been sitting on my chest. Tears spring annoyingly in my eyes so that I have to move the envelope in front of me so as not to spill my stupid tears on it. It looks old. I don't know why. The brown ink – I remember his mother's fountain pen and her sucking brown ink up from the ink bottle by drawing up a silver clip on a special cartridge and how me and Lachie coveted that pen with its scrolling curliques on a golden nib, its mottled green and black plump body, the elegant way it wrote our names.

And while children nowadays, my own too, might search for sweets and gaming controls when their parents are out in the garden for a minute, it was this pen that Lachie and I would look for and find when Kirsty nipped out. We would hold it so long, feeling its weight and pretending to write with it, not daring yet to pull off the lid. We would hear Kirsty coming and always she caught us before we had time to write with it and no doubt bend its nib with our fumbling, over-excited, virgin fingers.

And yet, Kirsty has at some point shown Lachie how to use the fountain pen because here is its ink and the writing is his. It is curling cursive, it is the cursive that Kirsty taught him quiet and slow for years after I thought I had taught him the letters in lower case and capitals.

Lorna the handwriting is tentative, unsure of itself. I turn the envelope over and can see the flap is perfectly aligned and seems to have been sealed years ago. I hold it up toward the kitchen area where it is lighter and I cannot see if there is anything inside. The vellum is thick.

Is this his suicide note?

What will it say? I am afraid to look. For 'to read is to know' as Auntie Ruby used to say and I don't think I am quite ready to know that Lachie is dead. To know it in his own handwriting. But it may explain to me why he killed himself. And it would be him telling me, just me and him in private, the two of us.

Bloody envelopes with results in them. Laboratory results with words I've never heard of, I'm sure the lab technicians make them up to test us. Exam results from school, university and me with an ache in my stomach, a fierce life-threatening desire to have passed with honours, flying colours. To be the smartest, the cleverest, the most intelligent and with an official piece of paper, a Degree no less, letters after my name, to prove it to the world. I exist and I am smart! Look Mother, I am Lorna McEwan, nee McLaren, your daughter and I exist!

Holding this envelope I feel dread inside. I have no foreknowledge whatsoever. I have sat no exam that I knew of. And yet I am holding the results in my hand.

Rip the thing open and get on with it Lorna. Stop tormenting yourself, a gradh.

I'm not even going to look for the horn-handled letter-opener. But here it is in an old biscuit tin that's open in front of me on the bookshelf. Did Malky open that? I rake open the top folded edge of the letter, corner to corner, clean. There is a wad of folded paper inside, the fold facing me, the same vellum as the envelope but with no writing on the back.

I unfold the paper. On it is a scrawl of brown ink cursive writing. No mistakes. He has taken time with this letter, a lot of time and care. And yet he has not given it to me. There has been plenty of time for him to give it to me because right at the top, so very unlike him, Lachie has written the date, or at least, the season and the year.

Autumn 1976
So not a suicide note then?

- 17 -

MALKY

Tuesday

The stupid girl at reception takes an eternity to understand what I am saying.

'Are you an actual police officer or just a wee dolly bird?' I say

'I am a Constable, yes Sir.'

'Well, get a move on, there's people waiting here!' I wave my arm at the chairs behind me but there's nobody there. 'I said, Chief Superintendent em, you know, the Chief? Ahm here to see him.'

'What's your name Sir?'

'I already said, Malky! Look, you better hurry up. He's expecting to see me.'

'Do you mean Detective Inspector McWilliams by any chance Sir?'

'Aye! McWilliams! That rings a bell' I say, my elbow sliding unnecessarily along the counter. 'I'll just take a seat here. OK? I said OK?'

'That fine Sir. I'll just call the Detective Inspector.'

I can see her on the phone, glaring at me as if I'm taking her job or something. She's whispering away into the phone.

'Detective Inspector McWilliams will be with you shortly Sir.'

'Aye. Very good. At bloody last.'

'I pay taxes you know. Expect a better service.'

She's not listening. Stupid cow. Ah! Here's the man himself. I get up as he comes in. He's frowning. What's he got to frown about?

'Malky? Oh for God's sake. How did you …? You're supposed to be with the doctor. Has she seen you yet?'

He helps me up, very kind of him. 'The doctor? Oh aye. Very nice. Very cold hands though.'

'Come through here Malky. What a state to be in. Were you at McCaig's Return for a wee snifter?'

'Aye. I got fed up waiting for you in that wee room. Thought I'd just go for a wee half in the meantime. You know, save me … Wait! Listen to me now Chief Inspector! I've something very important.'

Damn it to hell if I can't find the thing in my inside jacket pocket. I've not left it in the pub have I?

We're in the corridor and he's pushing me if you don't mind in the back and the next thing I'm shoved in a plastic seat with such force I very nearly miss it completely. As it is, it just tilts over a bit and I right myself.

'What's going on Malky? You're in a terrible state so you are. You weren't supposed to leave the station.'

'I can do whatever I damn well like! But listen …'

I lean over the table and gesture him to come in close to me, wiggling my fingers. He doesn't lean in far enough so I have to shout.

'I found it! I've remembered why I came here in the first place. I found what I brought you. In my pocket.'

I wrestle with my good raincoat, getting it off and I'm looking for that deep pocket, putting my hand down the sleeve first of all and I may be a bit four-sheets-to-the-wind but I can tell he's losing interest. Where is that fucking letter?

I present it to him with a flourish 'Have a look at that now why don't you?'

'What is it Malky?'

'It's the letter from Kirsty! It's proof!'

I am waving it in his face. He steps back.

'I am not his father at all!'

Now, why has his face fallen like that? I've just solved a mystery for him here. 'I'm telling you Chief Inspector, Lachie is not my son!'

'Yes. I know that Malky.'

'But how do you know? How do you know and ah don't? You think because I've had a few drams ahm stupit?'

'Sit yourself down Malky. It's all A-OK. I'm very glad you brought the letter. Very good of you so it is. Can I have a look at it?'

'That's why I'm here you stupid fuck! I've got my arm stretched out and he's still not taking it from me.

'I've come all the way from Coll to show you this fucking letter. Give it to you. It's indisputable truth so it is. He has nothing to do with me at all.'

'Very good, Malky. How long have you had this letter do you think? A few years?'

'What are you talking about? I just got it out of Kirsty's house the other day.'

'Why were you at the house Malky?'

'To get the letter!'

'But how did you know the letter was there? I see it's got your name on it.'

'B-e-c-a-u-s-e' I have to say this really slowly because I'm talking to an idiot and also I'm trying to remember who it was exactly told me about the letter and had the message from Kirsty.

'It was Dougal! That's right! Dougal at the hotel told me. He said, what was it, let me just think a minute …'

'Dougal MacKenzie? The owner of the Coll Hotel? OK. Don't worry about it all just now Malky. I can speak to Dougal myself. Listen …' he takes the letter off me at long last, 'I'll just go and photocopy your letter. From Kirsty is it you say? Very good. I'll just go and photocopy it and you just sit tight here for a minute or two.'

He's away. I've done my duty. I've brought the letter. Saved the day. Now I better be off. I've the roof to tar and the wee caravan to tie down.

*

LORNA

Monday

There is only a straggle of cars driving from the pier onto the boat, bumping on the ramp that sometimes moves nearly a foot without warning in the sea swell so the cars are like ladybirds and shield bugs trying to stay close to each other and jerking about when one stops, dithering.

Oh damn it. Here he is. Pissed, of course, and with that wee suitcase he's had since before I was born. A tatty old cardboard thing that looks like somebody's dead uncle's. Look at him; what an utter disgrace. John-Mac is intercepting him and has his arm up barring the way. I've seen John-Mac and Fergus do the same with the beasts on the pier when they're heading towards the end of it instead of up the vehicle ramp.

Every time I think of the cows on the pier, being sent to the market for slaughter, pretty brown and white Ayrshire cattle, strong of hoof and wide of pink nostrils, yellow-tagged ears flicking at flies my guts clench. Eyes full of terror at the noise, the metal under their hooves, the sea and its waves and the boat that dips and lifts, dips and lifts.

And Ruarhi with his bamboo cane that's split into four or five razor-sharp slivers at the end using it to direct the cows on which way to go whacking the pale skinned noses of the once dairy now meat cows, whacking at them until there is blood and even when there is wind on the water the backs of the cows steam and there is cow shit everywhere, runny, slippy green mucousy cow shit so that the last cows to go on the boat have to slither their way on this shitty ice slide, skittery and sometimes falling on their sides and all the men shouting at them and Ruarhi with his split bamboo cane whacking and whacking.

hat a shame it is that John-Mac doesn't wield that truncheon of his.

179

I know he can't see me, he only ever sees what's dead in his sight but I creep behind the metal curve that joins the promenade deck with the one above. Tucked in here, I light a cigarette and blow the smoke in a plume that for some reason makes me want to make smoke rings. I must be old. I can't remember the last time I blew a smoke ring. I would look like an old monkfish doing it now.

I lean around for a peek and thank God of all creation, John-Mac has his hand in the small of Malky's back and is guiding him back the way he came up the pier.

'You're not getting on the boat' he'll be saying. He knows how to keep Malky from losing his temper. 'You're drunk and the Captain won't let you on. Don't cause trouble Malky, I've got Lachie on the boat and I have a lot to do. Help me out here.' I don't know, is it the authority he has as Special Constable or their having been to school together on Coll, I don't know.

John-Mac never says a bad word about anyone, never has. Maybe that's his magic weapon since he has no truncheon ever on him though apparently the one he was issued with hangs in his shed, the leather thong as pristine on the nail it hangs from as the day he hung it up there … I'm guessing thirty-odd years ago? Look at that now, their progress towards the pier office, both pairs of legs in perfect unison, reminds me of Agnes and Jack dancing their Highland Scottische at the summer ceilidh dances at the village hall and everyone would clear space for them, so good were they at the Highland Scottische.

They are at the pier office now and I wonder is John-Mac timing the whole thing so he'll be last on the boat before the pedestrian gangplank goes up and maybe he's even told one of the boys on the boat. Sure enough, I step back to see the Captain's wee booth at the top of the grand old ferry and he is looking straight ahead and not at the rocks of the shore next to the new pier but at the pier office. Poor John-Mac. I hope he's got all his paperwork on the boat safe. Maybe it is with Lachie. I saw the container with him in it go on.

Silver paint on rusty metal. The container that is a strange size unless you know what it is for, not big enough to take a load of groceries for the island shop or building materials and animal feed for the crofters nor small enough to be a visitor's load. Just the right size for the biggest, and smallest, of bodies. It is usually tucked away at the back of the pier office storeroom but we all see it when we look and know that if we are lucky we won't go in that container to the mainland but be buried here on Coll.

'Sure I would die if I was ever put in that' Lachie said to me when we were snooping about the store when the pier master's back was turned and the village had become an exciting place for adventuring, just before we both went to school in Oban.

I sigh and walk towards the stern of the boat. There are several passengers, not locals, probably day-trippers, with bright coloured waterproof jackets, shop-bought woollen hats and binoculars and fat lensed cameras for necklaces. I turn back and see John-Mac walking briskly onto the pier and shutting the pale grey metal gate that is usually only used when the cattle come on board behind him. The Pier Master, Niall, comes up behind him and stands at the gate. Malky is still at the Pier Office, looking down at his feet, holding the wee suitcase in his arms against his chest.

Why the hell was he wanting on the boat anyway? He never leaves the island. I can count on one hand the times he's left and none of those times are in the last five years.

I hear the tannoy announce the breakfast service is closing in the cafeteria. It just sounds like a grumbling from the engine out here but because I have heard it umpteen times before while inside the boat I know it and all the messages. Johnny and I play a game guessing where the announcer's accent is from. It's always disappointing to hear a Glaswegian accent and best of all is the North Uist or Lewis accent, all melodious and precise with its English.

The giant ropes are thrown off the bollards on the pier, they fall into the water and are winched up. The dark green water swirls into murky pale green against the reverse thrust of the propellers and the water is white foamed and furious as we back away from the pier. We are away and the tiny houses of Arinagour village will soon disappear into the rocks of the island and the island will flatten as we head towards Mull and then it will be a dark line on the horizon and then taken by the waves.

Why was he wanting to get on the boat? What did he take from Lachie's? I had forgotten about that. I see the weakness in him grow stronger. As we pass the buoy at the head of the harbour, just past the island where me and Lachie had our first bonfire ceilidh with the English yachties amid the whale bones and driftwood, I look as I often do to the spot near the jagged edge of the coastline where we saw the fin.

It was not the first time that I had seen my father afraid. But it was the first time I saw two grown men, strong and sure of themselves, panic and gibber and make me afraid with their whimpering.

We had gone out fishing from Arinagour. I don't know why this was decided. Ruarhi did not like boats nor the sea. He did not fish. He was a reluctant farmer. He was a better, though untrained, mechanic. But my father was taking Ruarhi out in his boat and not from Bousd but from the village which is on the opposite side of the island.

Alec was on the pier checking the netting on his creels, only a few were there and my father said to him, 'we'll be sure to bring you back some lobsters Alec!'

The lifting of other people's creels, either for profit or plain wickedness, was an assault that was easily done. To lift another man's creel was far worse than lifting the skirt of his wife. Much easier than confronting him in the pub. You could take what was in there, you could move the creel somewhere else, scupper it, cut the rope, tear the netting, let loose the lobsters, leave something troubling in there for him to find.

I was excited. I felt favoured. Out fishing for pleasure with my father and Ruarhi. Out with the men folk.

It was not long before the fin came. It came up the side of my father's tiny boat like a black sail and I swear it was so close to me as I sat on the middle plank of boat, that if I had managed to unclench my fingers gripping the plank on either side of my scrawny bottom I could have touched that blackness, that wet dark skin of danger. The boat did not rise though the body of the basking shark must have been directly beneath us and did the shark know we were even there? Did she come to play with us, her mouth wide as a skerry cave, her body slow and mountainous. The fin sailed past and turned across the bow as if to come back and the burst of activity from Ruarhi had me thinking he was going to jump out of the boat so desperate was he to be on land.

Yanking and yanking at the rope starter cord of the seagull engine, flooding the engine completely so it would not start. Yet he kept on rewinding with trembling, clumsy fat fingers and yanking that cord as my father stood like Captain Ahab, perhaps he thought he was the Captain, he stood still and watchful for a moment then he too panicked, 'Get us the fuck out of here Ruarhi!'

'The fucking engine!' said Ruarhi no doubt disbelieving his stupidity over something mechanical when his life depended upon it.

When you are a child the things you notice in such a sharp-magnified situation as this are: basking sharks are beautiful. Nature always trumps man. Buoys make an echoing –ting-ting, ting-ting metallic noise in the waves when everything is quiet. That men don't care about little girls. Men care about their own skins.

Is that basking shark dead now I wonder. I would love to see her again, her fin, her stately manner. So close to shore. Now it is porpoises I see all the time playing near the buoy. Maybe the ones that Finn and Freya see are the sons and daughters of the ones I saw at their age from Rose Tree.

This past week since our ferry trip last weekend, Freya has entered the dolphin and whale phase and we have no less than five picture books about marine life from Partick Library. She refused the encyclopaedia I offered.

I'll go read my book in the cafeteria and get a coffee. I have brought Lachie's copy of Alice in Wonderland to read to Finn. It may help explain to him the change in mammy. And if I sit reading this the locals will certainly understand why.

After I rip open three paper sachets of brown sugar at once and spill the shiny grains into my black coffee I see John-Mac at a table near the window.

'Hello' I say.

'Hello Lorna. How you are today?'

'Not bad' I say. 'How's yourself?'

'I'm fine.'

I start to sit down opposite him but he says, 'No, Lorna. I'd rather you wouldn't sit down with me.'

'Why not?'

He looks around at the other passengers, there are only about ten or twelve in pairs and families, none are from Coll.

'It wouldn't be right.'

'Oh.' I say, forgetting for a moment, how incredible of me, why he is here.

'Yes. Of course.'

I put my tweed bag strap over my shoulder and unwind my scarf in the heat of the cafeteria amid the smell of cold bacon and the scraps of fried eggs and shrivelled tomato.

'Can you not talk to me at all John-Mac?'

'No, Lorna. Not just now. It would be unprofessional of me. You know how it is.' He looks at his coffee mug and lifts it to his mouth, taking a too-slow swig of it and holding it against his lips like a barrier to stop any words pouring out. He is not

185

looking at me but straight ahead into the gift shop with its red and yellow Caledonian MacBrayne Hebridean & Clyde Ferries tea towels and car stickers, blocks of sweet tablet and Cowan's Highland Toffee, cans of Irn Bru and guide books on Barra and Coll and Tiree, cassette tapes of Gaelic song crooners wearing kilts and seal skin sporrans, postcards of long, earth-tied clouds of golden sand beaches. They are clean and free from flotsam and jetsam.

I know I should not stand here like this hovering over him. I can see his cheeks are blushing. 'I wanted to ask – whose was the green car at the beach? Was it the person who found him?'

He takes a deep breath. 'Lorna, I am so very sorry to say it but I cannot talk to you at all. I am here on official business as you know. It's critical I do it by the book. You will have to speak to someone else. Someone in Oban.'

'I'm sorry John-Mac. You're doing a very good job. I know how it is right enough. I'm sorry to have said anything. I'll leave you to it.'

He glances up, relieved. I see the white rim near his hairline. It's like an accidental outdoors-men tribal tattoo this white line of skin the men folk have when they take off the Greek fishermen hats and farmers tweed flat caps that cling to their scalps.

*

'They've been saying he was all washed up years ago' says Mrs Effie MacPhail, proprietor of the Toraston Bed & Breakfast in Oban.

'Ocht, it was only a matter of time. Wasn't it Lorna? Him and his wild ways. And swimming. That's why only the tourists go swimming on Coll. I'm sure when I was there none of us ever went swimming. I still wouldn't know to swim.'

She's poured me a cup of tea from the bone china floral patterned teapot. I collect up my matching saucer holding it in my left hand while my right handles the delicate gold painted handle of the cup. I'm having to sit on the edge of the tapestry seat so I don't spill it all over myself.

'Were you at the police station yet? What time is it now?' she looks at the dull gold face of the brown wooden clock on the mantelpiece. 'Did I wind that this morning? Oh they'll be closed now, it's after 5. How was the journey over?'

She's a clucker and a fusser like all the lost women of her generation. Women like Mrs MacPhail and Auntie Ruby could have led the United Nations to world peace with their rolling pins and heaving bosoms. Instead they boss the rest of us about, confident of full disclosure of essential facts from all parties and no nonsense about it.

'Is Johnny coming up then? What about the wee ones?'

'I don't know yet Effie' I still feel recalcitrant calling her Effie after twenty years of Mrs MacPhail.

'Well I'll get the other room ready for them, just in case. I do like having the young ones about. How are they?'

I'm remembering Auntie Ruby telling me about Effie's sixteen miscarriages. Sixteen. Not a single baby to full term. And she never says a word about it.

'They're great Effie. Sure they loving coming here.

Nothing to do with the shortbread.'

'Aye. I better do some tomorrow morning.'

'Are you going to the police station tomorrow then? What time do you need to be up?'

'They said to be there around 10. They should have the results of the post-mortem then.' I put the saucer and its cup on the curved leg occasional table. I have to be careful to set it down so it is on the lace table runner and doesn't mark the table's veneer.

'They're doing the post-mortem tonight.' I wipe the skin under my eye. I can feel the wetness of a tear.

'Och, Lorna. There, there, a gradh. It's a terrible thing altogether so it is. And you so close to him. What would he have done without you all these years? And his mother away in Aust-ra-l-ia!'

'That reminds me; I need to phone and see if Johnny's spoken to her at all. See if she's coming over.'

'I'll be surprised if she does. She left him on his own there on Coll. Away gallivanting on the other side of the world.'

'But Effie, Lachie is able to take care of himself. And you know Kirsty makes sure he has everything he needs. Sure he's got a roof over his head and lives in paradise. It's a lot more than a lot of people have.'

'Aye.' She gives me one of her kind looks and pats the back of my hand, 'Will you take more jam tarts? They're only bought-ones but they're quite nice.'

I ignore the tarts arranged neatly on a pink and gold plate. 'I think it's great that Kirsty went to Sydney. Her books are sold all over the world, Effie. It was a big chance for her to see a bit of it.'

'Books. Hmmph. The stories she writes just make fools of us all.'

188

'No Effie. People love them. Especially the children. Finn and Freya just love them.'

'Aye, well. For the children. Fair enough. Aye.'

I hear the minute hand on the clock thickly tocking. I've looked at that clock's face many times, usually it's letting me know I'm close to missing the boat to Coll. It's strange to be here coming off the boat, seeing 6 o'clock and having to remember it's not 6 o'clock in the morning. The darkness is descending outside instead of disappearing.

'What I don't understand Lorna is why you were there. You were only just here. Why did you go back on Saturday? Could you not have stayed here Friday night?'

I am wanting to say it was work that took me there. Maybe I wouldn't sound such a fool. But Effie knows fine it's the vet in Tiree who covers the livestock and small animals on Coll.

'I had to go back for my med bag. I'd left it in Rose Tree. Behind the door. I thought Johnny had it. I don't know for-why because I always have it with me. Like a handbag you know, I always feel a bit naked without it.'

'Your med bag? What did you have your vet bag on holiday for anyway?'

'Well, you know, I like to have it just in case.'

'When I think of that poor boy lying on a post-mortem table in Oban it just makes me angry so it does. Why could they not have left him on Coll?' She's as indignant as me.

'I wish I hadn't gone back for my bag. I could have just kept on using Martin's instruments until next time we were up – it's only a month or so 'til then.'

'I tell you what I think Lorna, vet bag or no vet bag, it was Lachie wanted you there. Not a doubt in my mind. It was Lachie who wanted you there.'

'I felt that myself Effie.'

And we are quiet. Two women who know far too much and have nothing to do with ourselves and our knowledge. 'I'll make us a bit of steak and kidney pie and potatoes Lorna. Will I turn the TV up for you?'

- 18 -

LORNA

Tuesday

'Lorna, this is Detective Inspector Johnson.'

'Hello, pleased to meet you' I say. They've very nice here, the police in Oban. I shake his hand. It's an old hand; dry and loose skin over the muscle. Veins are raised. But it's a very fine handshake he's got. Firm, true.

'I was one of the investigating officers on your mother's case, Lorna' he says.

'My mother's case?'

'Aye.'

'What do you mean 'my mother's case'?'

'Your mother, you knew her as Louisa Fleming?'

'I'm sorry. I don't follow.'

I sit down on the blue sofa. He looks like the Mad Hatter to me and the other one must be the White Rabbit. Oh aye, and soon the Queen of Hearts'll be coming.

'The disappearance of your mother? I was on the team investigating it. It was a long time ago. You were … well you were just a wee babbie.'

'What do you mean 'disappearance'? I think there must be some mistake. My mother died from TB. It came on after her being debilitated from having me.'

'TB? Is that what they told you Lorna?'

'Yes … what is your name?'

'Detective Inspector Johnson, Alan Johnson. Just call me Alan.'

'Alan.'

'They told you she died of TB Lorna?'

'She did. She died of TB.'

'No. She didn't Lorna.'

'Yes, Alan. She did.' I am sounding like one of my clients arguing with me about a diagnosis I'm giving their pet. 'No, he can't have cancer Lorna because he's a healthy, happy cat and eating well …' and all the justifications attempting to head off the truth.

I am about to say that Auntie Ruby told me so it must be the truth but it is dawning on me like a wispy veil parting that Auntie Ruby's first priority was protecting me. Protecting me from the truth then?

'I'm sorry … Alan, Detective Inspector, just give me minute would you?'

'I was in two minds whether to say something or not Lorna. Long time ago, some things better left unsaid. No need to go raking up the past. Only, you see with your father here, it's all come back to me and I've dug out the file and had another look.'

'Have you found something? Wait a minute! Is my mother actually buried in the cemetery?'

'The cemetery on Coll you mean? No. Nor any

other one either. We've no body Lorna.'

'But I've been visiting her grave there my whole life.'

'Was it Ruby McLaren told you she was there?'

'Yes, my Auntie Ruby.'

'No gravestone? I think she was just being kind, Lorna. It'll be someone else's grave you visited.

'I don't mean to be rude but what the hell are you people talking about? First you drag Lachie off Coll, put him in a metal container and start cutting him open – gutting him! – on your bloody table and not saying a word to anyone about anything about it at all and I have to identify the sweetest man that ever …'

I push down that plug in my throat because I am going for it this time. I am totally going for it and I don't care if they can hear me shouting all through the corridors, ' … swam the sea, walked the earth, and he has got a line of blood going from this chin to his, his, his …"

I smell perfume and here I'm in the arms of a female police officer and God love us but is she not laying me down on the blue sofa and someone's saying, 'see if the doctor's about and call her husband'.

God give me strength but Alice I am suddenly in admiration of you.

*

MALKY

Tuesday

'Away in there and sleep it off Malky. Where's your wee case? Aye, there it is. Right - lights out!' and he shuts the door. McWilliams.

'You can't lock me up you bastard! I've done nothing wrong. Get me a lawyer immediately!'

'It's for own sake Malky. Just you be quiet and sober up in there. You're not under arrest; you're just to have a rest. Now - sleepytime!'

The metal plate goes across the cell door and I turn around to see where I am and I must admit I quite like it in here. It's quiet for a start. Nobody is hassling me. There's a wee sink to wash my face. Paper towels. A nice wee toilet and a bench to lie down on. Now this is just perfecto. Thank you very much inspector.

A wee space opens up at the bottom of the door and lo and behold there's even room service; a big mug of black coffee, just what the doctor ordered. I go straight to it but it curves away to the left and damn it to hell the door is moving. Ah. There. I've caught ye. Oh! Bit hot in the hands.

'Just you get that down you Malky.'

'Thanks very much cunstable.'

'You're a liability, Malky. A liability.'

'Aye. I'll 'liability' you ya bampot. Just you carry on with whatever you're doing. I'm fine here. Totally compos-mentis, thanks very much.'

I take my mug over to the nice bench seat. I only spill a tiny bit. This is just grand so it is. I have my coffee and I think I'll maybe have a wash and shave. Nice wee sink. Where's my case?

Here it is. Click. Click. Oh, is that blood on there? It's not my blood is it? Christ there's quite a spillage there so there is. S'OK, it's very old. Right, what do we have in here?

Sticking plaster. Don't need that.

Where is my half bottle? I'm trying to get into my inside coat pocket. Or is it in my inside jacket pocket? Too many pockets. I have to get up and whack both sides of my coat and jacket against me to feel for the heavy glass. I pat my hands down my sides. Where is the bloody thing? Did I have it with me? I haven't finished it have I? Oh for Christ's sakes and damn it to hell.

Right. See what's in my case. Have a wash and a shave.

Sticking plaster? Nope. I flick it under the bench.

Comb. Aye. Need that.

Deodorant spray. Handy.

Old Spice Shaving Stick. Very good.

Where's my brush? Oh there. Perfect.

Toothbrush.

Talcum. Imperial Leather. Perfect.

Listerine mouthwash. I've have a go at that after my coffee. Total Care so it is. That's the way boys.

Colgate toothpaste. Excellent.

And there you are. Old Spice Original After Shave.

I've just managed to fill the sink, very clean so it is, with water, lovely and hot, I'm wiping my face and wouldn't you know it there she is nagging at me.

'Stop it Ruby.'

'She's not staying.'

'No.'

'No. I've told you. I'm not having it.'

'That's it. No.'

'It's nothing to do with you Ruby. She's my daughter. She's *mine*.'

'She's mine I'm telling you. She's *mine*.'

'That's all there is to do. Shut up. Shut up Ruby.'

'You're not my mother.'

'You're not her mother either. She's Louisa's daughter and I'm having her. Get away from me. I swear I'll hit you Ruby. I'll hit you and that'll be the end of it. You hear? Do you *hear me* Ruby?'

That's her. Good. Interfering bitch. Bloody bitches the lot of them.

*

LORNA

Tuesday

'No I'm not wanting anything. Thanks' I say to the doctor. I know what he'll give me and I'm not wanting any of it.

'It's only a bit of shock. There's nothing wrong with me. It's totally natural. I've seen cats and dogs cope with less. I'm not wanting any medication.'

'Do you want me to continue Lorna? Here's a wee cup of tea, plenty of sugar.'

'Tea? I don't drink tea.'

'The tea'll do you good' he says and he's quite right, of course. I sip away at it from its polystyrene side, dribbles of it refuse to go into my mouth because of the wide lip on the rim.

'So you were saying my mother didn't die of TB? How do you know that Detective Johnson?'

'I won't go into too much detail just now Lorna'

he thinks I don't notice him looking at his watch.

'The upshot is we're going to section him. Detective McWilliams has already spoken with the Procurator Fiscal. He's a grave risk to himself and others. No question. The psych's already signed him over, just now. I wondered did you want to sign the sectioning order too? It won't do any harm and might be a good idea for you to have your signature on it in case of any future bother.'

'Sign him for sectioning? You mean at Avonlea? The nuthouse?'

His mouth twitches to one side, 'Well we tend to just refer to it as 'Avonlea' here and we all know what we mean.'

'I'm not wanting anything to do with him. I've had nothing to do with him for more than twenty years. I'm not going to start now. What he does is absolutely nothing to do with me.'

'I understand how you feel, Lorna. I would be the same if it was my father. As I said to Malky myself, my own mother succumbed to the dementia, it's very hard so it is. But Malky has the drink with the dementia. He's violent and unpredictable.'

'I know that. He's always been that way even without dementia.'

'Aye.'

'No. I'm not signing anything. I don't want anything to do with him.'

'Would it help to have a look-see? We've got him in the cell just down the corridor. He's havering to himself, talking to people who aren't there, ranting and raving, usual. If you see him it might put your mind at rest. I'd hate for you to regret not signing it later, you know, if something were to happen.'

'OK, I'll take a look at him. He's definitely locked in?'

I rub the shaving stick over my wet cheeks. I rub the foam up with my brush. Aye, that's it. Good lather. Where's my razor? Damn it to hell, the blade's not looking so good. Not to worry. I have a razor and I will use it.

I'm showing it to her in the mirror, blades facing her, 'I have a razor Ruby and I will use it. So don't you be interfering in my business, you hear me?'

I can tell she's gone.

Nobody tells me what to do.

Sliding that razor, nice and easy down my cheeks. Hand as steady as a rock. Aye. A rock at Eilean Mhor.

Least of all what to do with my own daughter. She's my daughter. Mine. Sliding down the other cheek, watch it now Malky near the mouth. And Louisa's. Where did you go to my lovely? That's a good song so it is.

'Jesus Christ!' I drop the razor into the water. She's right behind me in the mirror! She's looking through that wee window in the door. 'Louisa!' I shout, I turn round to see her properly but she's gone, 'Louisa! I knew you weren't dead! Come back! Come back Louisa!'

I scrabble my fingers where the window was, it's all metal again. Where the hell am I? My face is cut to ribbons. I've blood on my hands.

'You can see he's fit for nothing Lorna.' says Detective Johnson sliding back the window shutter.

I enjoyed seeing him in there, bits of foam on his face, a monster caged at last, talking to himself and shouting at his demons.

'Come back! Louisa!'

See, he thinks you're your mother. He's lost the plot entirely.

'Yes. My mother. OK. I'll sign it.'

*

It's just remarkable so it is how they all love her. It's starting to annoy me. There she is, hugging Ruby with one arm round the babbie and you'd think they'd know each other their whole lives. 'Thanks Ruby, I'll leave her in your good hands' she's saying and Ruby all chuffed like a mother hen coo-ing and cluckin at that babbie.

That babbie, always crying for attention, her always there with her tit hanging out feeding it. I've told her not to do it in front of the boys. They way they look at her, like hoody crows so they are. I don't like them seeing what's mine and mine alone.

Aye, well we're off to the dance. Oh yes, now this is the bit I like best, they're all looking at her. My Louisa in her orange blouse and blonde hair flying in the smoky air and whisky fumes and the accordian player is hitting the whirling dervishes and oh it is a grand show so it is, her laughter is like the last rays of sunlight reflecting off ebbing waves and I am so filled with love for her I feel like I am flying.

Certainly my feet don't seem to touch the ground when I flounder my way across the dance floor from the bar tent and grab her wrist and pull her away from Alec and I hear the accordianist falter in his playing as I am pulling her out of the village hall, I am wanting to have a word with her, just ourselves, you know, and a bit of a kiss out the back.

But she's livid and all mouth and that red lipstick is moving at me like a giant jellyfish and I have not a clue what she is saying to me.

'Get in the car!'

'I said get in the fucking car Louisa. We're going home.'

'No you can't. It's nearly the last dance anyway.'

'Because I said so.'

'I don't mind you with Fergus. But no dancing with Alec. I told you that. No way.'

'Because I said so!'

I've got her in the back of the car now and I jump in the front and push both the buttons down on the back doors so she won't get out. I watch her with the buttons so she doesn't pull them up. Maybe I should've put her in the front. She lolling over.

I've got her now. I start the engine and skirl the tyres out of the mud near the ditch at the side of the road and I can see a few people have come out to watch.

She's wailing in the back.

'I *am* your husband. Or ah will be.'

I know this road like the back of my hand. The night is that black tar colour and I can't see the North Star that usually guides me in the right direction. The car knows where it's going. It's a great wee car.

I hear her bump about on the back seat. I hear her head crunch against the roof. She'll be fine. Knock some sense into her. Why does she have to be so airy-fairy?

It's only minutes 'til we're home. I cannot wait to get her in the caravan, or maybe I don't need to wait. Why should I have to? I could just take her on the way. I can do whatever I like.

'Malky!' she wails at me. I like it when she does this keening wailing. It makes me all the harder.

When I push myself inside her, not quite making it to the caravan, it's as if I am in the source of all the world, standing and not kneeling in front of God, right next to him in fact, I am king of all of nature. Nothing can best me. And even though she is a bit looser down there what with that babbie I can smell the metal blood from the stitches coming loose and onward we go boys, and all together, heave we ho boys and oh yes my man, let her go boys, the whole load, ah, there we are now boys.

I'll just lie down here on this bench seat for a minute. I better pull the plug out of the sink. I'll do that in a minute. Oh Louisa you are my true love. Where did you go to?

I open my eyes just like wee slits because I hear her moving about and not behind me as usual. I can see through the kitchenette window that it's still quite dark outside but there is a pale sliver of silverness lifting the black and turning it sea grey.

'What you doin' Louisa?'

'What do you mean 'nothing' You're obviously doing something.'

Is she lying to me? What's she got there. Click. Click.

'Is that your case?'

I'm sitting up in bed like a shot. I'm sitting up on this bench seat. '*Hey*!'

'What you doin'?'

'What you doin' Louisa?'

'That's ma gun!'

'Are you mad Louisa? Put my gun back. What are you doin'? Come back to bed now.'

She's pointing my own gun at me! My own gun! She's not even holding it right. And there are no cartridges in it. I'm sure of that.

'What? Have you gone mad? What's wrong with you girl?'

'I think that baby's sent you over the deep end. Now just sit down here Louisa and we'll talk sensibly. Aye.'

'Aye. Listen, you know how sorry I am about that. I didn't mean it.'

I can see the faded yellow of the black eye that she's covered up with make-up the past week.

'It's the drink Louisa. And I love you that much. You know, sometimes it just overwhelms me. My love for you. It's deep as the ocean oot there. I'd do anything for you Louisa so I would. You know that Louisa. I couldn't love you any more. Sure we're going to go to America soon, are we not? We'll go to America and it'll all be fine so it will.'

'On your own?'

'I don't think so.'

'You're not going anywhere. You come here. Come here you wee whore.'

I get the gun off her, pointless really, but it's annoying me her having it. A man doesn't like looking at the wrong end of his own gun. It's not right.

By the hair Malky! By the hair. All that hair tangled up in my fingers.

'Put yer case down!'

Jesus but the case is heavy. She's packed it already. Packed her fucking case!

'You canny leave me Louisa. I canny take it. No.'

She's away through the door, it slams against the side of the caravan. She'll have put a dent in it. 'No!' I shout and the sound of my own shouting propels me forward like the first blast in the water after I start the outboard motor, whoosh I'm away after her, she slips on the sandy wooden step but she's righted herself but I am so close behind and there's no way I'm letting her leave me. No way. She'll be running to Ruby and that bloody babbie.

'*No!*' I shout and my arm lifts up to stop her and I forget I've still got her case it in and smack the crunch of bone as the corner of it, the corner of her tatty wee case, hits my true love's skull and 'Oh for Fuck's sake. Louisa! Louisa my love! *No!*'

Wah! Wah! Wah! And is that me sounding like a babbie? I lift her beautiful body and Christ is there not blood down her legs as well as running through her beautiful wavy hair

'Ah Louisa you've blood in your hair, let me get that out'.

And there's something else in your hair, bits of something, is it.

'Is that your brains Louisa?'

I am holding my Louisa and I am rocking her, rock a bye baby I sing to her, my wee little birdie, my poor wee henny, and I sing, 'I wanna hold your hand' but I sound crackly, my voice like the scratched 45 record and playing too slow.

'You wait there Louisa and don't move.'

I slip into my wee bed and I pull the blanket over me. There's a concrete wall ahead. Aye. What shall I do? I sleep.

I wake up and where is Louisa? She's not behind me in the bed. Where did she go? Where did you go Louisa?

I get up and make a coffee. Maybe she's gone down the shore. She likes going down the shore first thing, collecting bits of rope and driftwood and a single salt leather boot to plant something in by the door. She's still not come home when I realise I'll need to go lift the creels and then we'll need to go and pick up that babbie. I'll get a wee half bottle when I'm down the village to help my heid.

On my way out I see she's left her orange blouse on the path just past the step. She'll be away naked again. She's like a wild nymph so she is. Wait a minute. Jesus. Lorna's inside her blouse and her head is all smashed in on one side and her arms flopped out ahead of her, reaching for the gate.

'Louisa! Are you dead Louisa?'

I remember now.

Aye. I remember.

I wrapped her up in the tarpaulin Ruarhi gave me to put over the wee caravan until the roof was tarred. I carry her easy over my shoulder. She's easier to carry than a bag of whelks. I caress her thighs with my left hand through the tarpaulin as we walk. I put her in the back of the car. I've parked it badly and away from the caravan, halfway to the gate for some reason. I put her in the back, tuck her up nice and neat. How's the tide? I can see it's nearly full in. Perfect.

I remember I have a broken creel on the old pier at Bousd. I pull the curved willow off it so it just has the wooden bottom, the sinker stone, I think it's one

I took from Glaich, and the bait loop. I put it in the boat with my tarpaulin package.

I go right out to my furthest creel at Eilean Mhor. I lift it. There is nothing there. I have never liked Eilean Mhor, all the seals watching me with their big eyes, I don't like it at all. I wrap my good nylon rope, the stuff John-Mac gave me that was originally stolen, good strong orange stuff it is, and I wind it around the bundle of tarpaulin. I fasten it off to the remains of my creel that has no float to show where it might be lifted.

I drop the creel with its bundle over the side.

The bundle floats a while, nestling in to the side of the boat, filling up with salt water. The seals are watching me, the big dark grey one at the front is a male I can see that and the way he looks at me, I hate him. He is like a person so he is, they all are, the seals, like the people in the village staring at me.

'Bugger off!' I shout at them and a couple of them scratch their sides and their heads with their thalidomide flippers. 'Bugger off you freaks!' I say, 'It's not for you. Don't you dare touch it! Do you hear me?'

I look down to see the tarpaulin begin to sink, it is like a seal itself floating down, rolling, and I watch until I see it no more and the waves lap at the sides of my boat and I begin to hum.

∗

I wanted to make sure you'd already signed the form Lorna before I told you the rest of it. I'm glad I did now because something else has come up too.' says Detective Inspector Johnson.

'I am getting very tired Inspector. Alan. I have been here all day without anything to eat Mr Johnson. I really just want to help with Lachie and be away.'

'It can easily wait until tomorrow. Come back and see me tomorrow if you feel up to it.'

LORNA

Tuesday

The sea wind smacks my cheeks with the smell of old, decaying fish blowing up from the pier where the fishing boats are tied up.

My hands are actually shaking when I press "HOME" on my cell phone. I have not seen my hands shake like this since my first RTA as a vet student, the vet throwing me in the deep end at the last minute before surgery and telling me to take the lead.

I can usually walk and talk but not today. I trip over my feet near the kerb and even stub my toe.

'Jesus!'

'Lorna?'

'Johnny?'

'Of course it's me. Are you OK Lorna? The police called to let me know you were having a difficult time of it. No wonder.'

'No. I just stubbed my toe. I've just left. Am on my way back to Effie's. I couldn't stand it a minute longer. I didn't know what the hell they were saying to me.'

I'm not even aware of any background noise. 'Johnny, I need you to just hold the bus down there. Just hold the bus on everything. School, the surgery, the whole lot. You need to get up here with Finn and Freya.'

'What's happened?'

'It's a total nightmare. But everything's fine. The police have it all under control. I'm fine. But I'm really out of my depth here.'

'Listen Lorna, I was thinking of coming up anyway. No problem. In fact, Kirsty is here and ..."

'Kirsty? Is she here already?'

'Aye, I just picked up from the airport. The flight got in at quarter to one. She's out the back with Finn and Freya. They're playing with the new slide.'

'Kirsty's there?'

'Yes, she's here. I meant to tell you earlier she was arriving but what with everything ... anyway, she's here now and that's the main thing.'

'Great.'

'They're playing on the slide? There's something ... a dream ...'

'She suggested we all just come up to Oban together. She was obviously right. We'll pack up tonight and drive up first thing in the morning.'

I can hear another voice, 'let me speak to her' it's saying. The phone line ruffles.

'Lorna?' her voice is old and firm. 'Everything is going to be alright now Lorna. Just you sit tight and we'll all be with you shortly.' I can feel my throat constricting.

'OK?' Her voice has that authority of wisdom. 'Don't say a word of anything to the police until I get there.'

'But I've already been speaking …"

'No. Don't speak to them. There's things you don't know Lorna. Just you get back to Effie's and sit tight. OK?'

'Uh-huh.'

'Sit tight now and get plenty of Effie's scones inside you. It's going to be alright Lorna. Don't you worry my love. I'll be there as soon as I can.'

'OK'

There are seats on the promenade. I'll go and sit down there for a few minutes before I go back to Effie's. It's only the afternoon. Feels like a week. Feels like a fortnight since I saw my babies and Johnny. It's funny how high emotion makes time expand. I wonder did Einstein get a chance to study that?

The wind coming over the stone wall between me and the sea is sharp and like a cold flannel draped over my face. Perfect. I feel like calling Johnny back and having a more sensible, ordinary conversation. One like we used to have last week, or rather the week before last. Like when we were on Coll.

I remember the envelope in my tweed bag. I take it out and look again at the word, Lorna on the front. It even looks like it is written to 13-year old Lorna. I want to read it again. I will want to read this brown ink letter a lot of times.

Tigh An Roin
Isle of Coll

Autumn, 1976

Dear Lorna,

It's taken me nigh on a year to make good this letter to you. That's all good. It will be the only letter I write. I am sure of that. It is fitting. You learned me my letters. So I write a letter for you.

The waves Lorna. It's the waves and the seals that ride them I want to be with. On land I am always wanting to be in the water.

I am becoming a man, I am more whiskery that even before. But I am becoming less of a man. The roin, my seal kin, pull at my heart. I would have released it to them by now but for you and the way we were. Wild we were when we were children and the rain in our eyes. Now you are gone in Oban. It is over. We grow up. I am glad for you. We are different.

What I want to say is this. You knew what I was and you loved me. That is what this letter is about. I want to say it to you so you know. Finding the words is in love. I know you do too. We are still

210

here are we not?

My seal heart feels heavy on the sand and the rock. Heavier with each day. With you on Coll it floated. With you I was me. I was a boy and a seal and you loved me.

I lost something of myself at the school in Oban. I know I didn't speak to you much. The oysters were bad there. They made me ill. I didn't want to hold you back from your learning. You always liked the knowledge. Your shield so it is.

I lost all desire to be a man in Oban. For me there was never really a choice. I am both and neither. I do not see any men that I want to be. The bull seal has taught me more.

The orca want me for the mankind in me. They smell revenge there for the taking in my leathery skin and they would tear it apart with the tenderness of the wicked. I understand. They want the chance of tormenting me worse than they do my full-blooded seal kin. In truth I would prefer that death to living as a man on the machair.

You will be a very good vet. See here you have already saved a beast like me. You helped me be strong in who I am.

In the sea I am free Lorna. I would not sweep you into the sea with me. You are of the earth. The moon shines for you.

There are things of blood and bone that I cannot say. Secrets in mermaid's purses. The dogfish laugh. My boy skin shrivels at what the seals say when they know I think of you.

Maybe one day you will find out. I might not give you this letter. I don't know. I feel better for having it written down.

On land I put my arms around you. You don't swim with me. That's as well. It is all good so it is.

We both of us cry tears of salt water. With you I felt the best of the landward ways. You saved me. In the stillness before thunder I hold you in my soul. You are safe there. I will bring you the wildflowers.

My love always,
Lachie

I stare out to sea. How stupid I have been. And thank God for the mercy of my stupidity.

All this time, the whole of my life, I thought it was a joke.

I truly thought it was a joke.

That his mother had blessed him with a fairytale. And Auntie Ruby thinking it was a lovely tale to tell on dark nights next to the stove, hoping there would be no heavy wader-clad footfall on the doorstep. But he must have thought I believed it, that I was laughing at how wondrous it all was; him being different.

Did he?

I flash a fast rewind in my brain through every single time we've had a laugh about swimming, about seals, about the way he crossed his bare ankles and rubbed his feet together like the tail flippers of a seal, about him being a selkie, about the Orca, about the fishing at the new pier, conversations with yachties and the trawler men with their clam boats and Lachie saying not a word about the best spots to catch them, about teaching Finn and Freya the feral ways of seawater. Nope. Nope. Nope. I cannot see any glitches there. No slipped words. I am sure of it. He thought I believed. He thought I knew he was a selkie.

The wind tries to take the letter from my hands but I have a tight hold on it. Never in one hundred years of vicissitude would I have imagined feeling grateful for my stupidity.

I walk back up to Effie's B&B with a smile. I must focus on Lachie now. I am not interested in that fool in the cells. I must do the right thing by Lachie.

I notice right away that the windows are not brightly lit and that is strange. I walk up the wide stone steps and past the pair of pots with their white geraniums. The sky is dark purple though it's still not late. Is Effie out? No.

I knock on the door. I stare at the door knocker, for the first time seeing the polish of the brass, I have never had a chance to notice before since the door is always flung open the minute you begin to walk up the steps.

I stand there wondering what to do and remember I have a key. I find it in the bottom of my bag and still no Effie opening the door.

I put the key in the lock and shove the door open. 'It's just me Effie' I say because I am sure she is in and anyway I don't want to startle her.

'Come away in Lorna, Thig a steach, come in.'

As I walk into the sitting room there she is in the chair. 'I didn't want to disturb her, you know, she's had a difficult time of it too.'

'Sula?' The cat is curled up fast asleep on Effie's broad lap. I laugh.

'Aye, poor wee peeshak. She's a bonny wee cat is she not?'

'I've never seen her so relaxed. Have you given her one of your scones and cream Effie?'

She chuckles. I don't think I've ever heard Effie chuckle before.

'I'm afraid I'll be a bit late with the scones today. I've been sitting here like this since I started my knitting and I haven't even been able to get up and get a new ball of wool. Will you pass it to me from the sideboard Lorna?'

I find the cream ball of wool and give it to her and put my hand on Sula's head. 'Sula, I thought you were going to come and live with me and Finn and Pearl?'

'Oh no, she'd not like that at all Lorna. You can see for yourself she's wanting to stay here with me. Poor wee pet. She's just wanting a bit of peace and quiet now so she is. Sure you can see that for yourself you being a vet and all.'

'Aye. Very good Effie. She'll be nice company for you when you don't have the B&B's staying.'

'Company for me? Wheesht. I don't need any

214

company. But the poor wee peeshak needs me. You can see that yourself can you not? Away and make us a cup of tea Lorna, there's a good girl. She's still not awake.'

Never before have I been allowed to lift so much as a spoon in this house but here I am off to make the proprietor a cup of tea.

I think I'll phone Johnny after this.

.

- 20 -

MALKY

Tuesday night

'What the …' What a fright I got in this quiet. Where the hell am I now? Oh, my head. Oh, my face is damned itchy. Oh Jesus my guts aren't good today at all, at all.

It's very bright in here. I better get up to pee. Am standing there for ages. I have to pee a lot now. It wakes me up all the time. I don't get more than a few hours sleep. No wonder I don't know where I am half the time. I don't get enough sleep for Christ's sake.

Christ, I've made a right mess of shaving. I can see that in the mirror. Is this the hostel I'm in or a motel or what? Oh, no, wait a minute … Aye. That's right. That's right. I'm at the police station in Oban. They've given me a room. Very good of them, me the worst for wear.

I'll just settle myself on this wee bench bed. Bit stingy with the blankets mind you. I'm a bit hot

217

anyway. Why did I come here? Something important.
Oh aye! The letter from Louisa. No, no. No! That's
not it. No. Not Louisa. She never sent me a letter.
Didn't even say goodbye. No, the letter's from Kirsty.
Kirsty! Aye, the letter from Kirsty. Now what was
that all about again?

Here it is. Now where are my glasses. Did I bring
my glasses? I'll just read this gus am bris an latha an
teach na sgàilean Minister, I will read this kind sir
until the day breaks and the shadows flee away as they
say on the gravestones of my ancestors. That's right
so it is boys.

Glasses on nose. Straight from top pocket.
Undamaged. All set to go.

Here we are. All neatly typed on fancy paper. Her
signature at the end. All faded.

JULY 1983

F.A.O. MR M. MCLAREN

I've no idea when you'll be reading this Malcolm and I get a certain satisfaction from the thought that it'll be a long time coming.

It's not just that I hope Lachie will live a long and happy life. While I am not naturally a cruel woman it gives me a great deal of pleasure to think of you labouring under your delusion that you sired Lachie. Your raging shame gives me such a warm glow. Ideally you will die in your purgatory. But if you're reading this it means Lachie has passed over to a heaven you'll never know.

I'll keep it as simple as possible for you Malcolm. I know your levels of concentration leave a lot to be desired. I'm writing this just after Lachie's 18th birthday. His coming of age. You are still not wanting Lorna to have anything to do with him, the devil's spawn as you refer to him, but I see you've failed in that as with so many things. Sure they love each other in a tender way. But that is not something you could ever understand.

I hope you burn in Hell.

I'm leaving this letter in the tin box in the bookcase of Tigh An Roin for you to collect should Lachie die before you. I've decided I'll give Dougal instructions and he'll tell you, you're far more likely to be up at the Hotel than anyway else, unless you get banned, in which case I'm sure Dougal will still pass on my instructions.

I prefer Dougal to do it. I don't want to put John-Mac in a difficult situation due to the content herein.

I could see you'd counted the weeks on your fingers after you first saw Lachie. I could see from the way you looked at him so full of fury and disgust that you thought he was your son. The seed of your evilness is what you thought he was.

That's why you didn't want him playing with Lorna. You thinking he might contaminate her, child of rape that he was.

You were so drunk and deluded you thought I was Louisa. Do you remember Malcolm? I remember it so very well. Do you remember how you offered me a lift? So kind of you. Do you remember any of it Malcolm? Let me refresh your memory for you – every detail is as clear to me now as the night it happened.

It suited me fine to have you so deluded. Better you thought him your son of disgrace than what he truly was. He was safer from you and your guns that way.

I thought you were so generous giving me a lift from the village. Me thinking what a poor soul you were having just lost Louisa. How broken-hearted you must be that she'd left you.

An easy walk from Struan home to Elleraig and my lovely new wee house. But something came over you in the car when I laughed, mistaking what you'd said for a joke, and I always wondered was it my laughter that set you off.

I knew right away something had clicked with you. Your eyes were blank like a shark's. I knew you could not hear a word I said or even see my face for who I was.

Do you remember me shouting "It's Kirsty Malky!"

Do you remember?

I cannot bear to think of your dirty hands upon me. You piece of ignorant filth. When I managed to drag myself away from you and back to the road I ran like a woman has never run that road before.

When I got to Elleraig I flew straight into the water, dark though it was, moonlight spilling onto my bare thighs. I didn't wonder what creatures were slithering past me in the midnight waters of Elleraig bay, sharks or dog fish or stingrays, none are near as foul a beast as you Malcolm McLaren. I washed your rank seed out of me in the salt water until my fingers were numb with the cold though there was fire inside of me.

You're a sad man Malcolm and that's all there is to it. No matter how much you believe it, or maybe if you've found any grace, want it to be, my Lachie is no son of yours.

Now I'm thinking that if you're reading this then my boy is dead. And so with his death comes your release from the little Hell I have colluded in creating for you.

Know now McLaren that it was not fear of you that stopped me reporting your raping of me to the police. Nor was it my sympathy for your grief-stricken state of mind and your mistaking me for Louisa that held me back.

No. I like a personal vengeance and I feel certain you will be haunted by the beauty of Lachie. I have already seen how afraid of him you are. This prison I am making for you; so much more effective than any jail on the mainland.

Why should I waste my time telling strangers what you did to me? Why should I have had to go to Oban for court appearances. No. There are better, more delicate, far deeper ways.

You raped me Malcolm McLaren and I will live
with that violation for the rest of my life.
You can live with the pain of it as well.

I hope you burn in Hell.

Kirsty Dunbar

I don't know what she's talking about 'rape' and burning in Hell and all the rest of it. That's not how I remember it at all. She came on to me. It was her did it to me. Her wanting my seed.

*

LORNA

Wednesday

'Don't say a word to the police Lorna. You didn't say anything did you? No. You can't have, you wouldn't be here.'

'What are you talking about Kirsty?'

'It was you wasn't it?'

'Me what?'

I'm just drawing a big flower on Freya's plaster cast with Effie's felt pens. 'What colour do you want the middle darling?' I ask her. She's a brave wee soul and loving her plaster cast and all the fuss over how to not get it wet.

'Pink' she says.

'They're all into pink. It's shocking marketing so it is' says Kirsty.

'I know, they even have a girl's aisle in the shops and it's all pink. We don't go now. I don't like it.'

'No. Course you don't. Look, come out to the garden when you're finished and we'll have a proper talk.'

'I see Auntie Kirsty's done a seal for you here' I say, raising my eyebrows at Kirsty.

'You know they're my favourite Lorna.' She turns to Freya and whispers very loudly to her, 'it's not a seal at all Freya. It's a selkie, like your cousin Lachie'.

'I thought he was my Uncle Lachie mammy?'

'Yes, uncle, cousin, same thing. 'Uncle' is fine Freya. But I suppose 'cousin' might be better. We were a bit like you and Finn Freya, which would make him your cousin, in a way, no, wait a minute, it would make him your uncle.'

I look to Kirsty who's nodding and smiling, 'Yes, let's make it 'Uncle Lachie' then' I say, 'Uncle Lachie the Selkie'.

'See you out the back?' she says wiggling a cigarette at me by way of temptation on her way towards the kitchen and the back door.

'I want to go out too' says Freya.

'No, you have to wait her and look after Sula.'

'But she's asleep on Mrs MacPhail's chair! Where is Pearl?'

'Pearl's at home with Rosa. Remember, Rosa from the surgery? Rosa's looking after everyone for us.'

'When are we going home mammy? I don't like it here. Are we going to Coll?'

'Not just now darling. Oh, look, there's Archie!' I

223

say pointing at the television. I go and turn it up a bit.

Poor wee plaster-legged Freya is instantly mesmerised. 'This'll be the last time I use Balamory as a babysitter.' I say to Effie as I pass through the kitchen and she's putting scones in the oven. 'I'm just doing another batch. Is Sula alright?' she says.

'Yes, she's fast asleep. I've never seen her sleep so much.'

'Aye, she's tired. As I said, it's been very difficult time for her. Slept all night in my bed. Purring away. Oh, I had the best night's sleep since my Iain died so I did. When is Johnny coming back with Finn?'

'I don't know. They're away down looking at the fishing boats.'

'I can't believe Sula is acting like I am not here. I am totally cold-shouldered and me the one that named her!' says Kirsty as I walk towards her.

I smile. I'm happy. Kirsty is here. Effie is here. Freya is here. Johnny and Finn are here … only one person missing, or maybe two, counting Kirsty's man, Alfie.

'Sit next to me here Lorna' she pats the space next to her on the wooden bench with its lion-headed cast iron sides. I was going to sit in the chair.

I sit next to her. 'So, it was you wasn't it?'

'What?'

'It was you shot Lachie?'

'Lachie?'

'Yes. It was you, wasn't it Lorna? You who shot him?'

'Shot him?'

'Yes. You. You shot him when you were all up at Easter did you not? But you must have known it wouldn't work. That's the bit I don't understand.

224

Why did you not use the skin?'

'What the hell are you talking about? What language are you actually talking here?'

'You don't need to pretend to me Lorna. Remember who I am. Give me some credit here!'

'Why are you saying you know Lachie was shot?'

'The police told me he was shot. That's why he's here. And also because you didn't put the skin on him.'

I stand up. The world is away off its axis again. I put my hands out in front of me, warding her off. 'Kirsty! I do not know what the hell you are talking about. Are you telling me you know Lachie was shot?'

'I don't need to tell you Lorna, you already know since you're the one that done it. What I'm annoyed about it the skin.'

'Wait. I don't understand. Explain to me why you think I would shoot Lachie?'

'Because that's what Lachie and me discussed.' She looks down at her hands, her fingers are clasped together ready for prayer. 'He wanted a way to get back if needs must when I was away. He felt things were changed and he didn't know for why. The sea was different he said. He'd found seals at Eilean Mhor dead and gutted.'

'Gutted? But I found seals gutted at Elleraig when I was up. And all the way along the skerries to Sorasdal. Five of them.'

'As far as Eilean Mhor?'

'Aye. I told John-Mac but he wasn't interested.'

'No. He probably already knew.'

'Do you think?'

'I do.'

'Now this is very strange. Were they shot too?'

'They were. Why did you think I would shoot Lachie?'

'Sorry. Yes. You were our back-up plan, you see. Lachie said to me that if he had to go, if he could stand it no more, being on the land you know, if the orca didn't take him, he'd have you shoot him.

'That you would understand. Mercy killing. Euthanasia, Lorna, you do it all the time with the animals. Put them out of their misery.'

'But that's …'

'Whatever. You've known Lachie was a selkie. Surely to God you'd help him in his hour of need?'

I am staring into Kirsty's eyes. I am just staring blankly.

'I thought you had shot him when you were up at Easter. You know the police in Glasgow interviewed Johnny about what you did when you were up there?'

'Eh? No. I did not know. He's not said a word.'

'Protecting you. He's a good man that one. Feeding you information as and when. Dash it!' she slaps her palms on her moleskin thighs. 'It's been the only thing holding me together. Knowing that when he wanted to go, it was you, his own sweetheart, that released him.'

She shakes her head, purses her lips and says something to some voice in her head. 'So did he not tell you about the skin? Did he tell you when you last saw him?'

I put my finger to my lips. There is something in the back of my mind. I cannot lift the covers to see what it is. 'Do you know, I think he did say something about a skin, but I thought he was talking about the otters …'

'OK' she takes in a deep breath and releases it in a

long sigh. 'Let's just go one step at a time.'

'But Kirsty, it's Malky that killed Lachie. The police were trying to get a confession out of him yesterday. They seem to have evidence or a witness or something.'

'The bullet' we both say it at the same time. I still have the bullet I found in the seal carcass in my pocket. I pull it out and show her.

'This is from one of the seals.'

As she's examining it I say, 'Why did the police not tell me about the bullet?'

'I suppose they thought you had enough on your plate already.'

'What do you mean? Did they say anything else to you?'

'They did.'

'About my mother?'

'Yes. One of the policemen; the other one, not McWilliams, it was McWilliams that phoned me in Sydney after John-Mac. No, it was the other one, the older one.'

She shakes her loose grey hair off her face. 'I met him before. Years ago. After your mother … disappeared. He wanted to ask me some more questions. To do with your father and Ruby.'

- 21 -

LORNA

Wednesday

'Right. You stay here with Freya 'til Johnny gets back with Finn and then come up to the police station. I'm going to go and get Lachie and take him home, proper home' says Kirsty and she's up and off the garden bench like she's leading an army.

'Where are you going?'

'I'm going to get my son, where do you think I'm going? We'll all be on the boat to Coll tomorrow come hell or high water.'

She splays her left hand out and counts us on her fingers with her right hand in a fist with one finger. 'You, me, Freya, Johnny, Finn and Lachie.'

I notice her nails are painted a fresh, pearly pink. 'I forgot to ask after Alfie? I can't believe I forgot to ask how he is.'

'You're forgiven. He's fine. Loves the light over

there. I'll be back with him in Sydney in no time. It'll do us good to have a wee break from each other. Sure we love it out there. I just need to sort out Lachie.'

She's headed back into the house when she stops and turns, ' … and you'.

'But they won't let you take Lachie, Kirsty. The detective was wanting to talk to me about the post-mortem. Obviously they saw … you know …"

'What? Saw what?'

'His … you know …' what I am to say? To his mother of all people?

Her eyes clear. 'Oh. Right. Not a problem. I know you're a vet and you're concerned about these things – science and facts and anatomy and all the rest of it.'

She looks for her hankie in the pocket of her chunky cardigan and wipes her nose. 'Maybe you should use your instincts for a change Lorna. You know, like you used to before you learned so much?'

I don't take offence. She means it kindly and it's what I've been thinking myself. Facts seem to be dragging me under.

'Right. I'm away' she says, 'Don't worry about the post-mortem. Or anything else. McWilliams is a good man. I could tell that on the phone. He's looking for someone to take the whole mess off his hands. That'll be me. Come and meet me up there when you're ready.'

*

MALKY

Wednesday

I've to pack up all my stuff. I'm being upgraded to better accommodation. I like it in here fine. Nice and simple. Very clean. Great room service.

I've had plenty of coffee and a bacon roll. I think there must have been a wee dash of the good stuff in the coffee. I'm feeling totally tickety-boo so I am. What more could a man ask for I ask you?

'Morning Detective' I say to the old yin as he opens the door and comes in.

'Morning Malky. I was just wondering … could I borrow your wee case for a minute?'

'My case?'

'Aye.'

'What d'you want my case for?' I've got in my hands now, pressed against my chest. It's all packed and everything. I'm not wanting him messing up my stuff.

'Give me your case for a minute Malky. I'll swap you for this mug of coffee.'

'It is as good as the last one I had?'

'Aye' he takes a sniff of it and sighs, 'even better I'd say.'

'Well, that's fine then. No problem at all.'

I hand him the case and I see he's looking at the corner that's got the old blood on it.

'What's this from Malky? Is it blood?'

'Aye. I was thinking that myself. It looks like old blood right enough.'

'Whose do you think it is Malky?'

'Must be mine.' I run my palm over my face and a couple of wee tissue wads I've stuck on the cuts fall off. 'I'm not very good at the shaving as you can see.'

'Whose case was it Malky? Was it Louisa's case?'

'Louisa? Aye. I think it's Louisa's right enough. Any word on where's she gone officer?'

'Not yet, Malky. Early days.'

'Aye. Early days so it is.'

He's away and next thing a young constable appears. 'Did you enjoy your coffee Mr McLaren, Sir?'

'Best coffee I ever had son. I'm recommending this motel to all my pals.'

'Very good Mr McLaren.'

Why is he smirking at me? Is it the cuts on my face he's smirking at?

'But I hear I'm being upgraded?'

'Aye. That's right.' he's looking under the bench bed and blanket.

'What you looking for there?'

'Just checking in case you've left anything. You're off now Mr McLaren. The, eh, manager - he's a doctor as well you know - is here to pick you up with a couple of his, eh, pals.'

'I even get taken there? I don't need to find my own way?'

'No. You won't be needing to find your own way again Mr McLaren. Isn't that a fine thing now?'

'So it is young man. So it is. Very shi-fine indeed.'

He gestures for me to go out the open door so off I go down the corridor. I see two men dressed in very fancy white trousers and jackets, like they're in the navy or something but without the silver buttons and falderals. They've very big fellas. The wee speccy guy in between them comes towards me with his hand out.

I take his hand and shake it and here's the two big

fellas on either side of me and I feel grand. I am like a king here getting escorted by these fellas, fine figures of men so they are.

We are quite the spectacular team in the reception. Everyone is stopping to look at us. Even the wee lassie at the desk. And no wonder. Me with my bodyguards and the smart-looking speccy guy chatting away to me about how nice my new accommodation will be. Own room. Sea view. Wee bits and pieces from home if I want them.

It's like they're all here to bid me farewell. Very nice.

God's truth! Even Kirsty's here, God love her.

'Kirsty!' I wave my arm at her, 'Thanks verra much for coming!'

'Hello Malky.' she says to me and she's flirting at me as usual with those big eyes.

'Just a wee minute boys' I whisper to my team and they nod at me. Very good at taking orders these ones, although I'm going to suggest they change their shoes, these white ones look a bit daft.

She's pulling something out of her jacket pocket and points it at me. 'Do you want a wee half to help you on your way Malky?' It's a wee brown leather hip flask she's offering me.

'No, no, no' I say, 'I don't touch the stuff.'

'Aye, very good' she says and smiles at me. Christ, now she looks like Ruby.

'Listen Kirsty, it's very good of you to come and see me off like this. I got the letter. Found it no problem. Bit hard to read. Faded, you know. But thanks all the same.' I've stumbled against one of my big fellas but he just props me back up vertical again.

'I gave it to the police. It's very important for them

to know that I was never Lachie's … Lachie's … you know.'

'That's right Malky. Good for you. You take care of yourself now big man.'

'Aye, you … who's that out there?' I hurl myself out the double doors and my team sprachle behind me. I'm very fast on my feet when I need to be.

'Louisa? Oh thank God you're here too Louisa!' I want to grab hold of her but decide against it. Anyway, there's a big fist curled round the muscles of my right arm.

'Listen! I've sorted it all out Louisa. Oh thank God you're here so's I can tell you!' I slap my forehead with my left hand.

'Listen, there's nothing to worry about at all. I shot the seals and I gutted them and made sure there wasn't a bit of you inside the bastards. So see, Louisa, see! I knew you wisnae dead. I knew you'd come back to me …'

No sooner are the words out of my mouth than my boys lift me right up in the air and into a white van. They strap me onto a seat with a very fancy seatbelt, plenty of straps on it. I am liking these boys looking after me so well.

One of my bodyguards on either side of me in the back of the van. I think it's a mini bus. when is Louisa getting in? Maybe she's going in the front with the driver. Very nice transport.

I lean over and crane my neck to see better out the tinted window. Make sure Louisa is OK. Excellent. There she is staring at the van and looking at Kirsty and at the van. Is she getting in then? She must be coming in her own car. I hope she can see me, 'Bye!' I wave to her, 'bye! see you soon!'

I relax into the comfy seat. I feel like I am on my boat. We're rolling about a bit but I am all neatly tied down so I won't fall out and drown. Well done Malky. You've done very well my son.

- 22 -

LORNA

Wednesday

'I knew fine he wouldn't take a drink in front of everyone. I know him better than he thinks. Course, he's not thinking much these days' says Kirsty on the pavement.

'Has he always taken you for your mother? Do you think you look like her?' She's looking at my face as though she drawing me.

'Only now and again. There was an old photo of them standing on the deck of the Columba in front of the lifeboat. They were smiling.' I catch myself looking at the empty street the white van disappeared down. 'It's hard to see her features in it.'

'I think you do look like her. Same hair for one thing.'

She puts her arm through mine, 'Come over here a minute ...' she nods and waves some kind of acknowledgement at the two Detective Inspectors standing near the front door of the police station as we walk away.

Two boys are pretending to look at something over the wall opposite. They'll be dying to tell their pals about the wild man getting thrown into the white van.

'Fire and water Lorna. That's what it's all about. None of your earthy nonsense. You Virgos are better off keeping your hands clean in the dirt. But me and the good Detective Inspector McWilliams there; we're old hands at the fire and water.'

'How did you get on?' I say sitting on the edge of the water and looking in my bag for my cigarette packet. She's handing me the hip flask, 'take a wee sip. Medicinal' she says.

I press the silver threaded rim of the worn hip flask to my lips and the firewater is like the seawater in a rockpool in the sun. 'Argh, that's disgusting Kirsty' I say, wiping my lips on my sleeve. 'Did you not think to put something decent in it?'

'Aye, well, there was always the chance he might take a sip right enough. Right …' she says slapping her thigh. Me and the good detective have sorted it all out.

'I accidentally left my lighter burning under the ream of papers he showed me and him being so damn slow he couldn't for the life of him remember where the nearest fire extinguisher was.'

'What?'

'Never mind. Look, here's a light.' She flashes her lighter but only a tiny flame appears before guttering out. 'Must be out of petrol' she laughs. I take mine out of my bag and light both our cigarettes. We both sigh a breath of smoke.

We contemplate the sea across the car park. Kirsty sits up straighter. 'So, yes. It's all done. The police have signed Lachie's body over to me for the funeral. "No suspicious circumstances" I believe was written somewhere. I've signed the form. The undertaker's putting him in a coffin – we can use that for someone else that's wanting it on Coll or whatever – and we pick it up tonight, put it in the back of my hire van and away we go on the boat tomorrow' she throws her fingers towards the sea. 'The police officer at the front desk has even booked us on the boat. I think they can't wait to see the back of us. In the nicest way possible, of course.'

'I don't understand. The post-mortem. They would have seen. Science. You know, discovery. It's important for discoveries to be shared. Someone would want to write up a paper … You need to share knowledge or else it dies.'

She laughs. She's actually laughing at me. 'Sorry Lorna dear. I don't mean to laugh at you. Really I don't.' She puts her hand on my arm and squeezes it.

'I for one am delighted you're a vet and can heal the sick. Plus, I get your services for free.' She plays with the filter of the cigarette between her long fingers. 'No. The thing is - can you imagine how people would react if the Daily Record had a front page tomorrow "Selkies are real! Proof from a dead one"

'What would it mean to people's minds? You can't just drop a thing like that on people. There'd be all kinds of repercussions. It would be an absolute nightmare.'

'But scientific proof …"

239

'So what? People are better off not knowing what they don't need to know. I for one don't want a whole lot of hippies coming to Elleraig and singing for the seals. Do you?'

'But you're an old hippy.'

'Ha. ha. Very funny. I'm wanting to move to the village in my old hippydom.'

She stands up. 'Now listen. Before Johnny comes up with Freya and Finn to collect you, Alan wants a wee word with you.'

'Alan? Who's Alan?'

'Keep up Lorna! Detective Inspector Alan Johnson. You know - the one who investigated your mother's disappearance.'

'Why's he wanting to see me?'

'Brace yourself Lorna' she pulls her own shoulders back. I remember she has lost her fairytale son. I remember Lachie will not be swimming at Elleraig again.

'With your father being here and certain folks happening to listen at key holes ...' she says, ' ... or more specifically, put tape recorder microphones in police cells – he's got all the answers about what really happened to your mother.'

'Has he?' I look at the door and then at the sea. 'I don't think I want to know.'

She looks at me with her head tilted, 'What? You, Lorna McEwan nee McLaren, but quite possibly nee some other name entirely, you Lorna, are not wanting to know?'

She takes a dramatic slug from the hip flask. 'Miracles will never cease' she says.

'He's wanting to speak with you. I think you should' she says.

240

I'm still looking at the sea. It is only Oban harbour which is not really the sea at all, just a bit of seawater captured by the land in a round bay. Even if there was an orca fin in that bay I would not see it from here. All I can see are the red funnels and black and white sides of the Cal Mac ferries, the ramshackle fishing boats abandoned next to the smaller pier, the pristine sleekness of vintage, varnished skiffs and fibreglass catamarans tied to bright bubbles of plastic in the middle of the bay. Furious tame seagulls screech over empty chip shop papers and shit from the top of streetlights.

'Sure you've got Johnny to keep you afloat. You can handle any heavy weather.' She holds my arms and leans back looking at me. 'You listen to me. You've also got Finn and Freya to think about. It's their history too remember. Go and speak with him. He's waiting. You've only got this chance Lorna.' She gives my arms a wee jiggle and rubs my jacket sleeves up and down them as though I am cold. 'Go on. he won't do it officially, only just the two of you over a cup of tea in the canteen.'

'OK.'

'Lorna?' she says as I turn away so I turn back towards her.

'It's not pretty, a gradh.' She nods at me, old woman to nearly old woman. 'But you know what they say; the back is made for the burden it takes.'

'Aye.'

*

I can't tell him anything yet. Not a word of it. I cannot form the words in my mouth. I don't want to speak them, these truths. If I say them aloud I will need to face the reverberations of them being spoken in the air. Blood and accident will bounce back on me with the vigour of a new life.

I don't want to talk to Johnny about what my father did to my mother. I don't want to taint him that way. I don't want him to see me as the child of a murderer. I was once just the child of a violent drunk, a molester of nature, an abuser of gentleness and touch. Now all that has been trumped. "Murderer" – it so neatly encompasses all his badness.

I am not just the child of a murderer I realise. No, no. I am the child of a, not matricidal killer, that's mother-killers. Is that a general term or can you only use that if you kill your own mother? Can it be applied to someone who kills any woman who is a mother?

I will have to look all this up. Or not. I'll not be labelled. I'll need to tell Johnny. When will I tell him? Will he still love me? God, I'm glad we're married already. He might not have married me had he known the truth of it. I'm not sure I'd love him if he told me his father had killed his mother. I mean - genes. Do these sorts of malevolent dispositions get handed down genetically?

Yet again I have a good rationale for a tribal system where you just take someone hunting and they don't come back. The tribe gets rid of the dangerous mutants. I've seen family pets behave this way in fact. Ostracising and bullying the odd ones to death.

I wonder will Kirsty tell him? No. She wouldn't. I

242

will tell him. What to say? Nothing to do with me what he did. Or is it? I was only weeks old. Was it the stress of a new baby? Did I cry a lot? Was I a difficult baby? Was it actually my fault? That makes sense. I've always known it was somehow my fault my mother had gone.

I'll tell him on the ferry on the way to Coll tomorrow. Damn, but it annoys me to talk - not just talk about Malky when I want to be focussing on Lachie - but also such horrific idyll-destroying facts to impart.

Nothing fazes Johnny. Take this week. Take any week. Freya is loving her plaster cast. And who's responsible for that joie de vivre? Certainly not me.

And Finn. Smiling Finn. So like his da. Thank God. He's getting so big. Here, look at this, he's managing to carry the hot casserole pot with oven mitts on and no spillage on the white embroidered tablecloth.

'Well done Finn. You make your mother proud.'

'Aye. Next we'll have you cooking it too' says Effie winking at me. Kirsty smiles and then the curve of her lip falters. She'll be remembering something about Lachie. Maybe how he ate basket after basket of oysters, couldn't eat enough fish. Just as well he swam and dived for his dinner.

'You alright Kirsty?' I say.

'Tired. Jet-lagged. It's all caught up with me.'

'You should go to bed early' says Johnny. 'Get some good rest.'

'I won't sleep. I tell you what, I had a good idea' she puts her fork down on her plate but keeps holding the knife in her left hand. 'You two take off for a wee drink at the Lorne Hotel and me and Effie'll look after the wee ones and put them to bed.'

'Yes!' pipes up Freya. 'Go away mammy. Go away daddy. We play with Auntie Kirsty and Effie!'

Finn is quiet. 'What do you think Finn? Would that suit? I'll spend a bit of quiet time with mammy?' says Johnny.

Finn shrugs his shoulders. 'Fine with me' he says.

'I just don't know which way is up' I say when we're out in the cool air. I'm remembering how much I dislike the smell of Oban and its fishiness. I cannot wait to get on the boat back to Coll.

'I feel like I haven't been to Coll for ages. But it's only, how many days? Two?'

'We could head up to McCaig's Tower. Gaze out at Kerrera' says Johnny. 'Instead of going to the pub?'

'I always think of vaginas when I see all these lancet arches' he says when we're pushing past the yellow-blooming gorse that's blocking the rambling path up to Oban's famous folly.

I notice he has a bead of sweat above his brown eye. He needs a haircut. He's wearing the green jersey Auntie Ruby knitted for him years ago. His jeans are all crumpled lines of folds. Some goose grass has stuck itself to his sock.

He smells of wild grass and acorns. The bristle of his unshaven cheek is like sand against my forehead. Rubbing away my frown. His mouth tastes of hops and oranges.

His weight on me keeps me from floating into the wisps of clouds above me. A dark grey cloud on the horizon. A storm coming and maybe it will pass.

There's a sharpness scratching at the back of my neck. It is a gnarled branch of purple heather. I move to one side, Johnny's hand is on my thigh, pressing, releasing, pressing more firmly.

I push his head away and see that his eyes are glassy and blank and I suppose mine are too. I smell sweat. I buck under him to loose him off me, fumble with the buttons of my jeans, still wearing Levi 501 button-flies after all these years. I push them down and right off my feet, my knickers roll up inside them.

'You are like a doll,' he says to me, 'a half-dressed doll' he manages to say as he pulls off the jersey from Auntie Ruby, 'might as well do the job properly' he says and his soft jeans are pushed to his knees, they will be padding against the wild heather moor. I can see a single arch of McCain's folly. We are only just off the path. I don't care.

'Did you see the two vets rutting like animals up at the folly?' they might say. 'They' - the ones that see but don't know.

I have my thumb pressed deep into the cleave of his shoulder, I am gripping his biceps in my fingers and now I have legs wrapped and my arms around him.

Into my arms he is and into my cunt and I am being driven into the earth beneath me, buried by the feel of his muscles and tendons and my skin and his hair and a droplet of his sweat falls on my face and I lick the salt and I think I am moaning. Yes. In the blackness I hear myself.

I open my eyes and he is looking at me and the power of eye-to-eye and breath-to-breath overwhelms me. For the first time it is like bearing a child – I am pushing through some kind of emotional pain barrier, I am throwing myself into the unknown and I am trusting to this building of waves inside me, waves that are building and coming in fast to the rocks of

245

my shore, they are growing ever taller and grander and I fear they will break before they even reach the shore and if that happens I will drown and the thoughts stop because I am the wave, giant and strong and primal and I will smash all in my path or glide gently beneath it and let it rise and fall, rise up my love and bow to me.

I don't care and if someone comes right now – a wee old lady in her plastic rain hat tied neatly under her chin and her good raincoat from Jenners in Edinburgh or a gang of young ones, wild and half-drunk, I don't care, for this is me here planted in the earth, pummelled, flesh on my flesh, bone to bone, semen rushing to my womb and all the science books I ever read never come in any way close to this feeling. This moment I am me in every smell and touch and taste and scream.

'Take my pulse! Take my pulse doctor! Am I here?' I say smiling and writhing when he has plopped off me, his cock hanging limp and loose with a tiny drip of semen trickling around the girth and down its length.

'I think you're still with us' he manages, feeling for my hand with his hand. The blood is thundering through my skull, pumping wildness into my brain.

We are on our backs and can only see the sky – shot with purple and peach, bruised it looks and here the storm cloud is nearly directly above us. It is looking down and wondering, will I let fall my water? Will I drench the earth today?

Sure enough there is a pitter-patter sound on leaves that makes me wonder is someone coming towards us? But it is the raindrops on the leaves of an old rowan tree and I notice the sound of rain is different on each tree and shrub it falls upon. Tickle-tickle on gorse thorns and flowers. Splish-splash on the old beech tree. Shhhhhh-Shhhhhhh on the narrow-trunked silver birch in their cluster.

Big spots of rain land on my hot, red thighs and run down between my legs. Before the feeling becomes not-heavenly I pull my knickers and jeans up together and fasten them lying down. Johnny puts on his jersey and lies back down. We are soaked already. We are used to being soaked. Not for us the running to shelter. We're Scottish after all. We know the rain and its ways. You just hang your clothes to dry on a nail near the stove. They will smell of woodsmoke for you next time and you will remember you are a beautiful beast of nature when you next put them on.

'She wasn't called Louisa. My mother.'

'Uh-huh.' he says, the perfect response.

'Her name was Jean Fleming and she was a runaway from Stirling.'

'A runaway?'

'"Wild-spirited" Alan said'.

'Yes' says Johnny, soft.

Giant storm tears push themselves out of my eyes and roll down into my hair and my ears. Tiny waves my big, round tears.

'She was only 19.'

'19.'

'Yes.'

'A wild child. Of the Sixties. You should be proud.'

'He killed her. Malky. With her case. But it was an accident.'

He turns towards me and gathers me up to his chest and in there I coorie up into the sweet smell of wet wool that reminds me of kissing orphan lambs in the byre at my Uncle James and his arms like the roots of an old tree that've surfaced wrap around me and I feel so small.

I do not worry about my tears making his jersey wet. My sides heave and I whine and I know why the sounds I make are like a border collie I once knew called Bob.

- 23 -

'… Malin and Hebrides: Gale warning. Easterly gale force 8 expected later. Southerly 6 in far west, otherwise variable 4 or 5, becoming cyclonic 5 to 7, occasionally gale 8 later. Moderate, occasionally rough later. Occasional rain or drizzle. Moderate or good, occasionally poor …' says the mellow, tenor voice on the radio.

'I could listen to the shipping forecast all day' says Kirsty.

'Not when it's a warning of gales and we're on the boat' says Johnny.

'I'm sure the boat'll still go. It takes a lot for them to not sail. They don't want the back-log, especially at this time of year' I say.

I'm glad of the good storms this week. They'll have cleared the seal carcasses off the beaches and taken them back into the sea.

'It better go' says Kirsty. 'I want Lachie in that coffin for as short a time as possible.'

'Got everything?' says Kirsty. 'Let's get going

down to the pier. You two are looking surprisingly fresh this morning.' She winks at us. 'Good on ya! As they say in Aussie. Good on ya mate!'

We all laugh at her lame Australian accent as we hug Effie and pat Sula. 'Traitor' says Kirsty. 'See you on Monday Effie. I'm flying back through to Sydney next week.'

'Very good my dear' says Effie, 'you just come any time that suits you. There's always a bed for you here.'

Kirsty gets in the van she's hired. I see her checking in the back, making sure no-one's stolen the coffin.

Johnny gets in the driving seat of our Legacy estate while I strap first Finn and then Freya in the back. Johnny helps manoeuvre Freya's plaster cast leg so it is propped between the front seats. 'I'm not comfortable' she says, rubbing her eyes.

'I think you're having it very comfortable' says Johnny. 'What with us all at your beck and call. Don't you be getting used to it now.'

My heart still skips a beat when I see the ferry in the early morning. No-one but passengers on the pier. It is 6.30am and we are ready to board.

When I was at school in Oban I would dread going back to Coll every holiday. The ferry would look to me like a kidnapper's carriage, the black funnel looking ominous, the smoke angry, the revving of the engines like the sound the Three Horsemen of the Apocalypse would make riding foaming-mouthed horses.

I would have enjoyed staying at the hostel instead of at Auntie Peggy and Uncle Charlie's. I could have spent the holidays at the hostel.

The only upside of going back to Coll for the

holidays was Lachie. And for a short time, Auntie Ruby. But as my high school years ran away from me so I ran further away from Coll.

Until I met Johnny.

It was Johnny brought me home. It was Johnny who gave me the strength to be home. And I suppose it I'm being honest it was Johnny I felt who would beat the crap out of Malky if there was any bother. So much for your educated womanhood Lorna I humph to myself.

'What?' says Johnny.

'Nothing - nothing at all. Where are the sweeties? I open the glove compartment. Licorice Allsorts? Who likes them?'

'Not me' says Freya.

'Not me' says Finn.

'Not me' says I.

'I do' says Johnny.

'Sure, we know that!' I say popping one in his mouth. 'There's a good boy!' I say ruffling his hair like he's Finn.

'Look, there's a packet of Dolly Mixtures here. That'll be Freya's. And oh, yes, Fruit Pastilles for Finn. And a nice wee baggie of Strawberry Bonbons for mammy. Perfect.'

The queue of vehicles starts to move and soon we're over the ramp and into the whale's mouth of the ferry. Men in bright yellow oilskins direct us where to park. "Switch off your engine!" says the sign directly in front of us. "No passengers allowed on car deck."

In the cafeteria there's a sense of a waiting place. A place of luxurious calm where there's nowhere to go. People sit with paperback novels and guidebooks.

Some stand at the windows with binoculars to their eyes.

A baby cries. A mother shouts. A boy falls off his chair and is told to 'sit properly and be quiet'.

The men serving the food wear neatly ironed white shirts with the sleeves rolled up, black trousers and thin black ties. Freya has to prop her leg on the seat next to us and after we have eaten breakfast – toast and jam, scrambled eggs and baked beans, coffee and more coffee - a little girl comes and stares at her without saying a word.

'Shall we take a walk on deck? See if we can see Tobermory coming up?' says Johnny.

'You mean Balamory' says Finn.

'Aye. Balamory. Come on, we'll have a look' says Johnny.

'I've seen it before' says Finn. He's spotted his third cousin Stewart at the other side of the cafeteria. 'I'm going to see Stewart. See you later' he says and he's off, shuffling between the screwed down tables and benches.

'I'm stuck here' says Freya, lips trembling.

'Is the novelty wearing off Freya? Ah, you poor wee birdy. We'll get comfy here and I'll read you a story' says Kirsty pulling one of her own books out of her leather bag. 'See, I've got one of my books here, you can look at the pictures while I tell you stories about fairies and witches and all kinds of enchanted creatures.

'How does that sound Freya?'

She slips down into her pink puffa jacket and the faux fur-trimmed hood is up so only her eyes can be seen now. She blinks yes.

'I think she'll be asleep in minutes' I whisper to

Kirsty as me and Johnny get up.

The blast of salt water and wild wind is furious when Johnny shoves the heavy wooden door open with his shoulder against the force that's keeping it closed.

'You better put your hood up' he says to me.

'Yes, daddy, it's already up, thanks very much' I say taking his already wet hand in my gloved one.

'I don't think they've replaced that lifeboat in thirty years' I say pointing at it as it rolls from side to side as if it's on the water and not on another boat.

'Do you think anyone's ever had sex in there?' says Johnny.

'How would you get the tarpaulin off?' I say. It's all hooked down.

'Patience.'

'I thought you said "patients"!' I laugh and the sea splashes into my mouth. I lick the salt off my lips. 'How do you think the locums are doing? Will we still have a practise to go back to do you think?'

'Oh aye. They're just great. They're married too, did I tell you? We should have them over for dinner once we're back and settled. Frank's great at phoning and letting me know what's going on.'

'Great,' I say, 'that's just great. Maybe we should sell it to them?'

'What?'

'Only joking. But I tell you what, let's start working towards retiring early. Move to Coll.'

'I'm happy with that plan.'

'Are you?' I'm surprised.

'Aye. I've been thinking the same thing. Do another 10-15 years of service then when the kids have finished school, we can bugger off up here.'

'Aye.' I look out over the water. It's like a piece of ruched satin fabric, folds upon folds. I wonder will a seal pop up or a porpoise. I look over the edge and my head is dizzy looking at the foaming green sea around the propellers of the boat, churning the waters of our wake. Lachie in the hold in a box.

- 24 -

Freya is wanting to see the first sight of Coll. Johnny carries her easily on the top deck of the boat where it is especially windy and wet. We all sit huddled in a group of oilskins and woollen hats, the hardy locals, salt on our faces and the skin of our hands red from the cold.

'I see it first!' she says and sure enough there is a sliver of darkness on the horizon. And the boat is like a telescope slowly magnifying the long, flat outcrop of rocks that is Coll.

'Will the waves ever wash over it and drown everyone?' says Finn and I laugh and tell him I used to lie awake in my bunk bed on stormy nights, waves lashing and battering on to the beach at Struan not far from the caravan, wondering the same thing.

Would a tidal wave break over the island, sitting so low as it did in the water, leaving only the tiny peak of Ben Feall.

'Yes' says Finn, 'surely a tsunami would put it under water?'

'No. I don't think so. Not in our time anyway' I say. I pull him into my side, 'The thing about Coll Finn is that it's precious piece of land in wild sea; an island we can cling to while the waters all around us change. That's why islands are so special.'

He rubs the end of his nose and sniffs.

'Is that a flock of crows on the pier?' says Freya. I squint my eyes.

'I've got my fancy binoculars here' says Kirsty pulling out a dinky, black and silver pair. 'I got a pair like this for Lachie, so he could see what was happening out at sea from the house. Keep up with the goings-on you know. They're very good.'

'Oh aye' she's looking through them and she runs her tongue over her the corners of her mouth, 'No, it's not crows Freya. It's some of our friends wearing black clothes on the pier. Mourning clothes. The old ways, wee birdy. They've come to meet Lachie off the boat.'

'Attention please. We are now approaching the Island of Coll. Island of Coll. Passengers with vehicles please make your way to the car deck now. We hope you have enjoyed your journey. Thank you for travelling with Caledonian Macbrayne' says the announcement over the ferry's tannoy system.

'We might as well take our time' says Johnny, 'Be last down there and avoid the rush' he nods at Freya and picks her up. 'You'll be enjoying all this carrying-about?' he says to her.

From the car we can see Kirsty's van behind us and to the left. There are wire containers on wheels holding boxes of spirits and beers and wines for the hotel. Another crate has what looks like a freezer for someone, plastic containers of sheep dip chemicals and bags of pig feed.

Whoomph and we're off the ferry at a gallop up the ramp and onto land. Johnny pulls over in the gravely car park and turns off the engine. 'There's John-Mac' he says. I look in the side mirror of the car. 'Oh, aye, I see him. He's looking for Kirsty to come off. Here she comes.'

We wait in the car, eating sweeties, until Kirsty parks the van and gets out. 'You wait here a minute with Freya, Finn' I say. He drops his head back and moans.

'Can I not go and see Stewart? He's just over there.'

'No, you can see him when we get to Rose Tree. Just wait here a minute.'

I see Kirsty stride towards the kelp forest of islanders in black. John-Mac steps forward to meet her. He shakes her hand. He'll be giving his deepest condolences. She'll be thanking him for everything he's done.

We walk up behind Kirsty so like her wee tribe come to back her up in this tribal ritual. The others, not all in black I see, but all the older ones are very much so, move as one towards Kirsty and she is gently encompassed in dark fronds of people.

The men shake her hand, the women hug her and whisper words of sympathy. Now John-Mac has moved to shake Johnny's hand and he nods at me, solemn and kind. I smile my thanks to him.

I shall remember this group of mourners. I take careful note of who is here, as I am sure they feel is fitting. It is partly why they came after all. To be accounted for, for Lachie.

Alec is here, his cheeks look so red from the sea

and it is odd to see him without his oilskin on. Dougal from the Hotel is here but is making a point of giving his condolences before collecting his supplies from the container coming off the boat. He is wearing a black jersey and trousers.

Big Brodie is here, is he up on holiday? He's standing behind Ruarhi who blusters blushing at Kirsty and God, if there are not real tears of sorrow coming from his eyes as he stammers for the right words.

Archie Achamore does not wear black. He lost his wife three years ago and even then he did not wear black. He'll have bad memories of the black crows and black dogs.

Fergus and Jordan are like two little boys up to mischief at the back of the group but they are here in their formal suits and I can see from the way Kirsty has leaned towards them that she is as touched as I.

We will acknowledge death and we will stand up and face it when it comes for it is the way of things and we honour the Reaper and his deadly scythe. Lead us not into temptation.

The curled ones in deepest black are like whelks clustered together in the car park. Agnes and Jack so frail and yet here, maybe Jordan gave them a lift down from the village. When was the last time they were ever at the pier?

But Agnes had Lachie dig peats for her, a job he hated more than anything, and collect a few clams now and again and he would see her right with seaweed for the little patch of potatoes Jack grew in their garden though the seaweed was there for them to collect themselves but several paces away from their garden.

With Agnes and Jack is Mrs Cuddy, no books in her arms today, but wearing her ancient black cat's eye glasses every day now. Jessie and Mrs Rohan are here and I see a space where Auntie Ruby would have stood.

Hughie slams the door of his new transit van that's just kicked up stone chips and pulls his black jacket sleeves down over his cuffs as he comes to Kirsty and takes both her hands in his huge grip.

Seumus from Sorasdal jumps out of the passenger seat of the van – this'll be why Hughie was running late; he's collected Seumus from Sorasdal. Even Seumus.

The doctor is here, she is very good at respecting and taking part in the old ways of doing things even though she is an incomer. Someone I don't know is with her. A woman with a fizz of hair rushing from her head.

The doctor shakes my hand. 'Lorna' she says, 'Here's someone I want you to meet' and she points to the frizzy-haired woman. She's about my age. I shake her hand, smiling.

'This is Margaret Paterson. She's our new teacher now that Janet has retired.'

'Pleased to meet you Margaret' I say and I am. She has a lovely face.

'Lorna. Do you remember the green car at Struan? Last Saturday?'

'Green car? oh, yes.'

'That was Margaret's car. It was Margaret that found Lachie.'

Margaret is looking at me so fondly, like I am a wee pupil in her class, that I find myself crying quick tears. Right there in front of everyone, I cry. Luckily I have a tissue stuck up my sleeve and it's that windy and misty my tears do not embarrass anyone.

'Thank you Margaret.' I smile at her. She's so nice. 'I am glad it was you that found him. Although - he would have laughed that it was a teacher who did. He was never one for ...' I trail off, not sure what I'm saying and instead I smile.

'I was glad too Lorna. If that doesn't sound too peculiar ... We can talk later if you like? Have a coffee some time? I hear you and your family are in every holiday?'

'Aye. That'd be great.' I'm thinking of putting her number on my mobile but for some reason the flashing of such modern technology would be disrespectful to the gathering.

*

We are an island funeral procession on the short single-lane road over rock to the village. Every time I see the gable end of the houses on Main Street, little white cottages rubbing up against each other, some conjoined, I think Auntie Ruby is in Rose Tree.

Once we're inside, the car left flung between the road and the tiny garden opposite, sloping side-ways towards the sea, Johnny gets the fire going in the stove and I put our bags in the back room. It is so dark in here, it is a womb, buried deep in the small hill at the back of the house. There's a small window at the side where this room juts out next to the scullery. I see the new wooden steps leading up to the toilet hut. No more climbing up steps slick with green water and moss roots when you're bursting for a pee having had too much tea or coffee and sliding down them on your backside when you're finished.

We've kept the toilet flush pull-chain with its china bauble at the end.

I get the table set with one of Auntie Ruby's tablecloths, the plain linen one with the pierced work in the corners. 'I'm going to see Stewart' says Finn.

'OK' I say, 'bring him back for something to eat if you want' but he's already away out the front door which is open. I go to close it as Johnny is carrying Freya out again.

'I'll take Freya for a wee walk down to the shop. Get out of your way' he says.

'We have brought her crutches haven't we?' I say.

'They're in the back somewhere' says Johnny looking at the car, 'at least I think they are!' He laughs and throws Freya over his shoulder so her plaster-cast points straight ahead.

Kirsty is coming in, she's carrying bags of milk and bread and I see a jar of bramble jelly at the top with a checked red and white cloth cover held tight with an elastic band. 'It's like Central Station in here' she says. 'Is the kettle on yet?' she says.

'Just about to. Johnny's lit the fire. Is that Jessie's jam you've got there? You're fast.'

'She'd left it at the shop for me. That's what she does.'

We're sitting at the table with our cups of tea and coffee when there's a noise in the scullery. It'll be a water rat under the floorboards, disturbed from its sleep by our arrival.

'Do you know, I always expect Ruby to come down those steps with an arm round a bowl and the other with a wooden spoon, beating' says Kirsty.

'Damn shame' she says watching the doorway that leads to the scullery. 'But you've kept everything exactly the way she had it. I like that' she says.

'Aye. And she kept it exactly like my granny. The same bedlinen and tablecloths and even china and cutlery.'

'There's a lot to be said for keeping things the same' says Kirsty. 'Not rushing around throwing good stuff out and getting the latest new thing just because so-and-so's got it. I see someone got a new freezer off the boat today.'

'Maybe the old one broke down.' I sip my coffee. It's the same brand of instant coffee Auntie Ruby used. 'I agree,' I say though Kirsty knows this already, this is one of our regular topics of conversation. 'Make do and mend. It's the best way. You know they're calling it upcycling now?'

'Yes. Upcycling. I like that. Sure I've done that my whole life' she rolls her woollen hat round her fingers. 'With so many changes and never knowing what's going to happen from one minute to the next, in the Seventies it was nuclear war we worried about you know ...' I do know, we've discussed this before.

We follow the happy conversational groove of this, one of our most favoured subjects, in the same way we trace the rows of piercing on the old tablecloth, the ribbing of our hand knitted woollen hats, the steamed pleats in our tweed skirts, the tidy rows of seed potatoes in fertile soil.

In a few minutes we will work our way around to Auntie Ruby and we will say how much we miss her. And when we get there it's as if all that comes before is a kind of pilgrimage to her, our list of traditional values like gifts we bring to her.

'Did I ever tell you your Auntie Ruby told me to look after you?'

'No.'

'Yes. When she was dying here. They should have left her to die in the back room. It was a sin that they took her to Glasgow.'

We have both said this before to one another. It irks us that she was taken away to die in the hospital in Glasgow. 'I don't want to die in Glasgow. Sure it was there I was supposed to live' she said to me as if I could do a thing about it.

What could I have said? The pain from the cancer'll be that bad Auntie Ruby that you'll need morphine all the time, big doses of it too? No.

'Will Lachie be alright in the van out there?' I say.

'Aye. He's home. Well, nearly.'

'It's funny how she told me to look after Lachie. I thought she meant Malky. But it's only recently when I've been thinking of it I realised she meant Lachie.' I say.

'You did a very good job Lorna. Of loving him. You'll know that from the letter.'

'Yes. I found it the other day.'

'I knew you'd find it at the right time. I told Lachie so when he showed to me years ago. He was thinking of posting it to you in Oban. I told him not to. Things get lost you know. Better to keep it at Tigh An Roin. Safe there.'

'Very safe.'

'Is it in your pocket there?' she says pointing at my waxed jacket.

'Yes.'

'Show it to me a minute. I only want to look at the

writing on the envelope just for a minute.'

I hand it to her. 'You knew I'd have it on me?'

'Of course you would' she says and traces the brown ink cursive letters Lorna. She takes a big breath and sighs.

'You'll make sure to pass that on to Freya when the time's right?'

'What do you mean?'

'Pass it on to her so's she'll pass it on to hers and maybe it'll go down the generations so the next time our descendants might be fore-warned.'

'Fore-warned?'

'Maybe I mean they'll have fore-knowledge. Not a warning.'

'Knowledge of the selkies?'

'Particularly that they'll be more likely to help with the next one.'

'The next one?'

'Lorna, I don't like it when you repeat everything I say like a parrot.'

'Sorry. You mean there'll be another one?'

'Apparently they come every ten generations or so - I mean human generations, not seal generations. So Lachie said. So it would be ideal if our descendants had a clue – although, maybe they'll be that bit more enlightened than us. Let's hope so anyway.'

'OK.' I say, sipping my coffee and wishing I had a bit of cake to go with it. 'I hate that Auntie Ruby died in Glasgow.'

'Well, at least she's buried here.'

'She told me a load of rubbish you know, about my mother's grave and all that'

'Course she did: protecting you.'

- 25 -

'I can't wait to get him out of that thing' says Kirsty as the coffin thumps gently after its tiny flight over the Windy Gap in the back of the van.

The graveyard is on our left as we crest down the wave of road towards Toraston beach and its fairy rock pool.

'Lachie came with me and Freya to put our pennies into the fairy well last summer' I say.

'Did he?'

There's a wide fairy path behind the graveyard from the machair over smooth, giant pebbles. The pebbles lie close together like the minke whales that stranded on Crossapol beach.

The path is marked by pale blue green lichen like paint on the dark Lewis gneiss rocks. 'Lachie told her one of your fairy stories before we put our shiny pennies in and made our wishes. I think he knew all your stories by heart.'

'Well, he should have done, it was him gave me most of the ideas for them' she laughs.

I turn to her, the seat belt hugging me close to the passenger seat and catching on my wax jacket. She's got just one hand on the steering wheel. The other is resting on top of the gear stick ready to change from third down to second at the black and white fences marking where the road goes over a pit with a burn at its bottom.

'Did he really?'

'Aye. Don't tell anyone.' She glances at me, 'be quiet now.'

We are coming to the Fishing Gate, so close to the sea I hear the waves sucking the sand, the wind moaning through the sand dunes.

I feel the need to touch the side of the back of the van with the flat of my hand as I walk past it to get back inside after closing the gate behind us.

'This is taking forever' she says and it's the first hint of grief I've seen from Lachie's mother.

'It's not like you to be impatient.'

'No. It's not.' She stops revving the engine and glances up towards Cornaig farm.

It is just me and Kirsty on this final part of Lachie's journey. Kirsty was adamant that Johnny and Finn and Freya were to stay in the village at Rose Tree.

'Only hags allowed at this funeral' she'd said.

'What about the others?' said Johnny. 'They'll need some kind of a wake. Something where they can shed tears together.'

'Yes' said Kirsty. 'Maybe we have a use for that coffin after all. We can bury the coffin empty at the graveyard. Sure John-Mac told me Jordan's already dug the grave when he heard. They'll need something to put in it.'

'So what are you and Lorna going to do … with Lachie?' Johnny had asked.

Kirsty had acted like she'd not heard him at all. Instead she got up and took the bottle of Whyte & MacKay from the top of the heavy wood sideboard and picked up three short whisky glasses between the fingers of her left hand, put them on the table and began to pour.

Neither of us says a word as we pass Cornaigmore and the sheep fank that's now decrepit but has a newly built house next to it. We say nothing as we pass the path to Bousd harbour.

But as we round the bend I see the gate that leads to Struan beach and I say, 'Stop here Kirsty. Stop now.'

The relief of knowing he was not curled up tight like a fist in his boat at Bousd gutting fish nor like a spring held in the too-weak hands of a child in the dank caravan had washed over me as we had walked into Rose Tree.

It was like some tiny, caged and frightened part of me had been released from the winding of an elastic band stopping her blood flow and had realised she was, at long last, at the age of 40 years, free.

Dark clouds looked less foreboding. The choppy seahorse waves in Arinagour bay were playful ponies instead of stallions frothing at the mouth. The machair grass offered visions of hula dancers instead of looking like it was being beaten to submission by the wind.

Kirsty pulls off the road onto the only flat bit of land, it's opposite the gate. She looks at me. 'You're not wanting to see where he was washed up are you? Not just now?'

'No. Something else.'

'To do with Malky? Do you want to get something from the caravans?'

I take my lighter out of my jacket pocket. I flick it to flame and stare at Kirsty.

'What? You want to get out and have a cigarette?'

'No.' My lighter is still holding a long flame like a candle long-burned. 'I'm wanting to torch them. The caravans.'

'What? Burn them down do you mean?'

'Yes, torch them to Hell. Fucking mother-killing, bastarding mother-fucking devil of Hell fucking bastard - and he shot Lachie!' It's all like verbal diarrhoea spewing from my lips. I have the image in my mind of a dog I once saw spewing shit all over the surgery when he had a foreign object stuck in his guts. He shat it out in the end. Unplugged.

'I see. Yes.' Kirsty turns off the engine and pats her fingers on the steering wheel between her legs. 'I see what you mean. Yes. And you'll need to get rid of all that anger before we ... uh-huh. Yes. Right. OK.' Who is she talking to?

I let the flame die and hold the plastic lighter up to the windscreen so I can see if there is plenty of petrol. I put my hand on the handle of the door.

'Wait' says Kirsty. 'Just wait a minute 'til I think. 'OK, let's take a walk down there.'

We step down out of the van. Kirsty doesn't lock it. I open the gate and let it slam against the wooden pole that stops it from going so far it'll come off its hinges. Kirsty gently pulls it shut behind us.

We start to walk the wildflower path towards the caravans in the sand dune gully. 'It's beautiful here isn't it?' says Kirsty.

I say nothing, I can't see much through the curtains of memories dropping one by one in front of me of all the times I've walked this way to the caravans, to home.

'It'll cause a lot of pollution. Burning all that plastic and paint. Toxic.' says Kirsty.

'Fucking right it's toxic. It's more toxic sitting there than if it was a pile of ashes.'

She grabs hold of my right arm stops walking and plants herself so I have to as well. She pulls my left shoulder towards her and hugs me as tight as she can through our bulky jackets.

She pushes me away and looks me in the eye. 'See here Lorna. You listen to me. You have a lot to learn about fire and water. I told you that already.'

I rush away from her. I am running with my feet kicking to the sides. I am aware that I am suddenly 8 years old and furious. Burn that fucking place down.

I stop at the top of the sand hillock and see wide, glorious Struan Bay. It is like the world right then. The tide is in. The rocks are submerged. The high tide mark is in the same place it was a week ago. I see the black lace of dried seaweed near the bottom of the graceful sweep of sand dunes. I see the water from the lochans and peat bogs seeping into a feathery estuary to the sea. There is no flotsam or jetsam I can see though now I look carefully for it.

'He was over there' I point towards the far end of the beach though I don't know if Kirsty is near enough to hear me.

'You'll not burn down the caravans Lorna. Look at them' she says turning me around to see the pale, sun-bleached blue shapes of them in the deep, soft palm of a gully.

A carpet of wild orchids and self heal flowers all around in the bowl that holds them. The sharp, thin grey pickets of a fence woven together with wire to stop the sheep rubbing against the caravans corners and making them roll like boats.

The little one has leaned in even closer to the bigger one so that in is pale blueness and its flighty wave of a darker blue decal that runs across its side it is so like a fledgling gull wanting under the wing of the bigger, green caravan that has moss all around the edge of its roof and stains of brown under the windows where rainwater has spilled like tears.

The ropes and tarpaulins holding the caravans down against the wild onshore winds have torn in great rips and snapped canvas. One rope from the wee caravan flicks like a whipping snake tongue in the air, whacking the big caravan. Whack. Whack.

Strong grass is long all around the wire and wood enclosure where the sheep, cows and other beasts cannot get to it except for a softly flattened path from the off-kilter gate to the front door. I see the silver groove next to the door. The rope hanging off to keep the door open has frayed so much it is useless.

'Aren't they beautiful?' says Kirsty.

I look from the caravans to the sea and back to the caravans. 'They have been here a long time' I say.

'Yes. They've weathered many a storm' says Kirsty. 'But they are still here. Bit like yourself?'

I take a huge breath. The salt is keen in my lungs. My cheeks tingle in the misty rain. I tilt my head back and some nerve in my neck releases.

I look at the caravans and see with Kirsty's eyes. It is a nice view.

Kirsty stamps her feet as though calling an

audience to quieten down. 'What we'll do is: we'll get a working party together and gut the caravans. Totally gut them. Keep all the good stuff you want to – the old cutlery, your mother's things, remember? We'll bleach the two of them within an inch of their lives. Then we'll scrub them clean with sand and seawater. Aye, fire is very cleansing but there's always a place for extra strong bleach. Although we'll need to make sure it doesn't get into the water …'

I smile as she talks. She's getting excited about the whole idea.

'After it's gutted and a new fence and gate – or not if you prefer – new curtains from Liberty of London, why not? - and lo and behold you'll have yourself the prettiest wee vintage-style caravans on one of the world's most beautiful beaches.

'Christ there's people in London'd give their back teeth to stay here for a week or two in the summer. And Finn and Freya, of course. Sure you have to think of them. The next generation. This can be theirs. Something to hand down Lorna …'

I walk down the slope, crushed shells and bits of dead grass and petals sticking to my wellies. I put my hand on the gate post and pat it and hold it firm and think about my father putting the rope from the gate over the gate post as he left to go to Oban and yes, sure enough, there is something scrawled in pencil that's gouged the rotting wood, GONE FISHING. NEVER COMING BACK!

' … and the boat Lorna!' Kirsty is shouting from the top of the grassy slope, ' … Johnny'll need to see to the boat and lift the creels. And him and Finn can get make the boat their wee project and get it all varnished and ship-shape for next summer …'

Her hair is blowing all over her face and some strands are flying straight up in the wind. She's in full flight. ' ... We'll burn those bloody creels – yes! We'll have a big bonfire on the beach and invite everyone over ... Lachie always loved a good bonfire on the beach ...'

'We'll put a wee sign up, give the place a name. It's never even had a name for God's sake! Get Finn to carve it into wood. I've got a set of chisels he can have, belonged to my grandfather in Edinburgh. Sure we'll see if Finn has inherited any carpentry skills. What about, "Tigh An Blàth"'

'House of the Wild Flowers?

'Aye. Something gentle. Pretty and wild.'

- 26 -

MALKY

'My name's Jean, not Louisa. Will you stop calling me Louisa? Here's your tea.'

'Aye, that's fine Louisa. Whatever you say darling. Fine by me.'

She shakes her head at me, 'What do you want for your dinner? Choice of - fish and chips or mince and tatties? Which d'ye want?'

'Whatever you feel up to making, Louisa darling. I'm just glad you're here. Sure I knew fine you weren't dead. All I ever wanted was to have you back. And here you are in flesh and blood looking after me so well.'

'Hey! Mr Malky! Wakey-wakey!' she's right in my face now. 'I said my name's Jean - not Louisa. Louisa is dead.'

'Is that him away again?' says the other woman who's also got a mug of tea in her hand, giving it to a crumpled old man - who are all these folk sitting about the place?

'Aye. I am so sick of it. Amn't I Mr Malky?'

'Why are you two wearing the same aprons?' I say. 'Have you joined that druggie cult Louisa?'

'We'll not have that language at Avonlea Mr Malky' she says to me. She taps the other woman on the arm, 'Can you believe he just called me a cunt Annie?'

'Oh aye, I believe that so I do.'

I feel a bump on my shoulder and a wetness between my legs.

'Would you look at that Annie? For God's sake – have you spilt your tea again Mr Malky? You're a right nuisance so you are.'

'It's you. You clumsy cow you. Hey, why don't you put that nice blouse on, you know, the orange one? Why you wearing that brown pinny thing?'

'Annie, did you hear that? More abuse I'm getting! I think we'll need to sort this yin out when the superviser goes for his break.'

I can feel the pressure of her grip on my shoulder. 'Aie! You're pressing a bit hard there Louisa!'

'Look at that Annie – he's gone and wet himself again.'

'Sure that's just appalling so it is.'

'Aye. He'll need a good shower and right good scrubbing down there. I think we'll need to start putting nappies on this one – won't we Mr Malky?!'

'Aye, whatever you say Louisa, whatever you say. Fine by me. I'm just glad you're here darling.'

'You just sit over here in front of the windae Mr Malky' she says and wheels me over to the sea view.

'No, I'm not wanting to see the sea. Take me away from the window Louisa, I don't like it.'

'It's not Louisa, it's Jean I'm telling you ya daft auld git ye. You just sit there and look out the windae. Give us all a bit of peace.' Her breast pushes into my face when she clips the brake on my chair.

'Aye. Sure you're wanting to see the sea Mr Malky. Course you are. Good fisherman like yourself. Course you'll want to see the waves and the wee boaties in the bay.'

'No. I'm not wanting to look at it. When can I go out in my boat?'

'Och, you'll never be going out in yer wee boatie again Mr Malky. I mean, you're not fit. What if you em, 'accidentally' fell over the side? No, that wouldnae do at all, no, no, no Mr Malky.'

She leans in to give me a kiss but just as I pucker up she whispers, 'Drowning's too good for the likes of you Mr Malky-man. We don't want you polluting the clear, blue sea, do we now?'

She's got that wee plastic cup in her hand again. I quite like those tablets. 'Definitely not a wee dram in there then?' I ask her again. I'm ever the optimist me.

'Just take your medicine like a good boy Mr Malky.'

The sea is choppy in the distance. It's too fresh for me to lift the creels today.

'Stop yer crying Mr Malky' says Louisa, whispering at me, I can hardly hear her, 'Remember how much I loved you' she wipes my face with a scratchy white tissue, 'And how you killed me.'

Her eyes are all wrinkly, watery pools staring at me. I don't like things staring at me. 'We've all the time in the world now to sort it out now, haven't we Malky my love?'

'I don't know Louisa' I say, 'I can't just now. I've

got the roof to tar and the wee caravan to tie down. But at least you're here at long last. I knew you'd come back.'

- 27 -

'It's all about transmutation, Lorna' says Kirsty when we're back in the van. 'It's perfectly natural for you to be furious. What you need to do is take that and turn it into something beneficial. Transmutation, see? You take one thing and turn it into another.'

'Oh God Kirsty.' I let my head fall backwards onto the headrest. 'You're not having one of your candle light and velvet scarves and incense ceremonies are you?'

'Don't you be so cheeky' she slaps me on my hand. 'What I'm telling you is you need to take the bad stuff and transmute it into the good stuff. Doesn't matter what it is. No point running around with lighters and not knowing what the hell you're doing. No. No. You got to think long-term, Lorna. Generations even. Sure only psychopaths have a short-term view. Did you know that? Aye. No long-term view whatsoever.'

She takes a deep breath and lets it free. 'There's plenty of psychopaths in folktales you know.

Bluebeard for one.'

'I hate the Bluebeard story.'

'I can see why' she nods towards the caravans hidden by the hills behind us. 'Ach. You've a lot to learn Lorna but sure I know you're gifted with the learning. It's just you've too much by the way of facts at the moment, you need to balance that out with your natural instincts.'

'Yes. I get that. Since last Friday anyway. Living by the skin of my teeth so I am.'

'That's right Lorna. Just so.' Kirsty pulls into the lay-by at Elleraig. It's tucked into a small cliff and only just wide enough to take the van.

It's less than a week since I was last here and already it seems the rushes are bushier and their rolled leaves longer. The bog that lies from the tiny road to Tigh An Roin looks bigger.

'What are we going to do?'

'I'll tell you as we do it. The first thing we need to do is get him out of that box.'

'Out of the coffin? Here?'

'Yes. Come on,' she's out of the van and walking round to the back doors. 'You watch in case there's anything coming. Let me know if you hear a car or see someone walking. The last thing we need is some idiot to come past and see us.'

I light a cigarette and stand on the road. The hum of quiet is thick all around us. My nerves are raw. I keep thinking I hear a car engine in the distance but it's the tide; the sound of an occasional big wave on the rocks sliding through the wedge of the cliff and hill that funnels the bog and all its run-off into the bay.

'How are you getting on?' I say, stamping on my

cigarette and looking in the back of the van. She's undoing the last fastening on the coffin.

'Perfect. Come in here now.'

I climb into the back of the van, at the narrow feet-end of the coffin. She lifts the lid and flips it over.

'Oh my God!' I pull my jersey neck up over my mouth and nose. I can't see a thing for the smell.

'Get a grip of yourself Lorna. You're professionally trained for this job.'

'What? Not bodies that've been decomposing for more than a week I'm not - *and* have been in the water. I deal with the freshly-dead.' I mutter through my woollen mask. 'I'm very good at carrying frozen bodies too.' I stop to retch under my jersey, my whole face under the wool now. I feel sweat beading between my breasts, my stomach is starting a slow death roll. Kirsty has started retching now too. She comes out of the van holding the back of her hand to her nose.

'Kirsty – Jesus - why does he smell so bad?'

'Why do you think? I thought you were a vet?'

I laugh at the two of us; the fairytale author and the veterinary surgeon at the back of a hired van taking a putrid dead body out of a coffin.

'Why don't we just carry the coffin to the house?'

'No. I want him out of it right away. I'm not carrying a coffin to the house of seals. We'll carry him ourselves as nature intended.

'But the smell?'

'Aye, Of course he stinks. I told the undertaker not to put a single chemical near him or I'd have his guts for garters.'

'I'll take the head end and you take the low road'

279

she says. 'Let's do it quick. No faffing about. In and out. One, Two, Three …'

We take a deep breath and rush into the darkness of the van. Lachie's face is luminous white. We have to lift together at the same moment because he's so rigid. He sits sidey-ways against our crouched legs and we move like two crabs out of the van. I listen for any car coming but all is quiet.

'Put him down here a minute' says Kirsty and we lay Lachie on the shrapnel stones of the lay-by. He is shining white, like the luminous underside of a mackerel.

I keep my hand on his flesh. I see the strange lesion he got from swimming in Oban harbour all those years ago never healed. I see the bullet hole with frayed edges just above it over his heart.

Kirsty shuts the coffin lid, "Remind me to fasten these things later' she says.

'OK' I say, my hand pressed on Lachie's shoulder. Kirsty locks up the van.

'Heave-ho then. You ready?'

'What are we going to do with him?'

'You'll see. Let's go.'

We lift Lachie like he's a ladder but he's a very heavy ladder so we need to hug both our arms around him and carry him against our hips on our right sides, lurching a bit.

'Sure it's just like carrying a baby on your hip' says Kirsty as we manage to navigate crossing the first tiny burn and small peat ledges without tripping over ourselves.

'Don't make me laugh Kirsty!' I say.

'Quite right. Let's just get the rhythm of our feet in step.'

We are both exhausted by the time we get to Tigh An Roin. 'Did you leave the gate open? says Kirsty.

'No. I'm sure I shut it.'

'Maybe the fairies opened it for us. Look, the front door is open too.'

'So it is. That's odd.'

'Lorna, please don't say, 'that's odd' again today. You'll get very repetitious so you will.'

'Aye. OK.' I laugh to myself and wonder am I already mildly hysterical? No, I've never been the hysterical sort and I can't see myself starting to be now.

'Stop here a minute' says Kirsty.

She raises her hand to her eyebrows, 'Can you see any seals on the island'

I squint into the pale sunshine, it's hard to spot seals against the rocks but we are both well practised at seal-watching.

'Yes. There they are. Good.' says Kirsty.

'Oh yes, I see them. Two and a pup?'

'OK, let's head down to the water.'

'The water?'

'Just to let them have a proper look-see.'

'OK. Can we change arms again?'

We have Lachie repositioned on the other side of us and my shoulders are aching. Kirsty catches my smirky expression, 'I know what I am doing Lorna. You just follow me and try not to comment.'

'Fair enough.'

We carry Lachie down to the water. I am looking around to make sure no-one is watching. I check the high hill on the right and the low rocks on the other side of the small bay past the sea cliff.

We're over the difficult part; the boorach of

smooth stones with their sparkling minerals and veins of white quartz. Now we're on the white sand. 'No! Don't put him down here. Just wait a minute, bring his feet up next to me so we're level and they can see the full length of him. Right, good. That's us. Back to the house … Do *not* giggle Lorna.'

'I'm sorry, I really am Kirsty. It's just …'

'Don't say it.'

The sun disappears. Clouds are racing across the sky. I feel sea swell on my face. No, it's rain. Torrential rain. 'Hold him steady Lorna.'

'God, you're strong for an old caileach Kirsty.'

'Aye, you've good muscles yourself. That's perfect' she looks at the rain and the purple sky, 'Do you remember that song about the rain washing you clean so you'll know?'

'Yes. I do' and as I watch the rain pummel down onto Lachie's body, collecting in puddles and making his hair like deep sea kelp and his long whiskers flatten to his skin, even the ones above his eyes, I am not only serious but suddenly reverent.

'Turn him over before we head back. Get the other side done. Wash away all those hands touching him and poking about and footering with him'

I have his ankles in my hands now. His heels are like old boots washed up on the shore. They are grey. I never noticed that before. Kirsty has her arms locked under his armpits.

'Yes' I say, 'he'll have residual chemicals from the trolleys and tables and just from the air in the mortuary. Maybe even from inside the coffin too – all that polyester lining.'

'Exactly so. Like I said, you're a quick study Lorna.'

By the time we get Lachie into the house and lay him down on the floor between the kitchen table and the sitting room we are both panting.

'I'll get the fire going' says Kirsty. You sit a minute and then go and get the box of groceries and our bags out of the van. Then I want you to collect some self-heal flowers and whatever other wild flowers are out there. Take the bucket from next to the oyster shell midden and fill it with sea water and bring it all in here.'

I close my eyes. 'OK'

'I'll get the kettle on and some hot water.'

'Wake-up, I said wake-up Lorna.' I must have nodded off for a minute or two. I'm feeling quite refreshed. 'The sofa sucked me in again. Power nap' I say rubbing my face, 'I've even learned to do them between clients now and again'.

'Up you get and go get the flowers and seawater.'

'Do you want me to put the flowers in the seawater?'

'Yes please.'

I deliver the box of groceries to the kitchen table. Already the house is warm from the fire in the stove. I see Kirsty has the big pot out ready.

I take the bucket down to the shore. The tide is on the turn. It will be coming in soon. I fill it three-quarters full of sandy seawater and veer left away from the house to start collecting the flowers. Self-heal is LachieLorna's flower. I pick plenty of it.

A bumblebee breezes past, the sun is out again. It is as if it didn't rain at all. The light is shimmering, the colour of the petals of all the flowers are vivid against the green and brown mat of their leaves and the grasses and the mosses. Wildflowers of the machair and peat bog.

'Oh, you got bog cotton too – that's ideal' says Kirsty as she peers into my bucket. 'Pour it all into the big pot' she gestures to it sitting on the floor next to Lachie.

'Wild Flower Soup' I say as the leaves, heads and petal flow into the pot. Kirsty lifts the pot onto the stove.

'It's like a cauldron that thing' I say.

'I've made poached eggs and toast for us, here' says Kirsty, pulling a plate off the stove' hotplate.

'Thanks.'

'The coffee'll be ready in a minute. I see you've been having that instant rubbish.'

'I like it.'

'Push the plunger down now, there's a good girl.' Kirsty sits opposite me at the table. Lachie is behind her. We both take a moment.

'It doesn't feel like he's dead any more does it?' I say because it is so very normal to be sitting here eating poached eggs next to a putrid dead body, against all my veterinary science training. 'I've gotten used to the smell already.'

'It seems to be leaving him.' She finishes chewing her toast. 'It is a cauldron, you know.'

'I'm not surprised.'

'Given to me by a coven down near Roseneath.'

'Oh.' I say.

'It's a shame Freya's just that bit too young.'

'Too young?'

'Yes, to do it with us. We'd have the three generations then see? The old hag, the young maiden and you, the fertile mother.'

'Right.'

'You think I'm joking?'

'No. Not at all.'

'Well, he made it to his fortieth birthday and that's something.'

'He had a good birthday too.'

'Aye, I heard; an oyster feast.'

'It was great. And he taught Finn and Freya to swim.'

'To swim? You mean to be at one with the sea do you not?'

'Same thing, apparently.'

'Lorna, there's something I wanted to ask you.'

'Yes?'

'It's an idea me and Alfie have been talking about. We're having fun doing our books in Sydney. Alfie loves how pure the light is there and we've been very inspired by the Aboriginal dreaming artworks and whatnot. Stories in the pictures. But it's not home and we're not getting any younger.'

'Do you want a biscuit?' she says running a knife along the plastic wrap of a packet of chocolate digestives.

'OK.'

'We reckon we'll come back home for good in maybe a year. Time to retire. I'll be sixty-seven years of age this September. Alfie is seventy-two already. We'll want to come back to Coll. But ... I'm not sure why, but I'm feeling we'd be better off in the village in our old age. More people around us, safer you know when we get a bit frail, and a blether with the neighbours and so on...'

'You? Frail?' I laugh. 'I can't imagine that. It sounds like a great idea.' I say, 'I can see why you're thinking that.'

'Aye' she pauses. 'Do you like Tigh An Roin Lorna?' she glances around the kitchen, her eyes resting on the pans hanging from nails on the beam neat the stove.

'You know I've always loved it Lorna.'

'Yes. I should really tell you now. With Lachie gone … the house'll go to you, naturally. And Finn and Freya.'

'Really?' I am a bit winded. I put my coffee mug down carefully.

'Yes, of course. Who else should have it but you? I won't have it rented out to strangers no matter how pleasant they are. But that's not the point anyway. It needs to be kept in the family not just for the descendants but the selkies too.'

I hang my head down and pick at my fingernails; bits of grass fibres are caught there. When I look up our eyes meet and I nod.

'It would mean a lot to me if Finn and Freya had their holidays here at Elleraig and swam in the bay and remembered their Uncle Lachie' says Kirsty.

'It would mean a lot to me too. They can roam free here, like LachieLorna did. It's too busy now in the village – the cars and all the rest of it.'

She looks at me expectantly. I am supposed to join-the-dots here. 'And you and Alfie take Rose Tree until you die.'

'My thoughts exactly. We'll do a wee swap. Eventually there'll be a house in the village, a house at Elleraig and the pretty wee caravans at Struan: a wee empire for the wee ones.'

I smile.

'OK. That's settled. You can see what Johnny thinks. Listen, he'll need to get out and lift the safe as well. Smash it if the sea hasn't taken it already in the storm and release any lobsters or crabs still alive in it.'

'I will. I'll go out with him too. You can maybe take Finn and Freya for the morning.'

'I'd like that very much' she says. 'Will you be going to Stirling when you get back?'

'Stirling? Why would I be going to Stirling?'

'Alan told you. Have you forgotten? He told me he gave you her address and everything.'

'Oh. That.'

'Yes, that. You'll need to go and see her right away. The poor woman's been waiting more than forty years for her lost daughter to come back.'

'God. I never thought of that.'

'No. I'm sure she'll be delighted to see her great-grandchildren. And they're very lucky. Most children don't even have grandparents. But a great-grandparent that's been longing for her child for nearly half a century? That is a very fine thing indeed.'

'Yes.'

'She's not even very old. She's ages with myself. What's her name again? Oh, yes, Pearl, isn't it?' she chortles. 'Same as your wee cat? Funny that, eh? Makes you think about how real the fairytales are, doesn't it now Lorna?'

I laugh. It would be nice to bring Pearl to Elleraig. Pearl, my granny.

'Right!' says Kirsty. 'Let's stop dawdling. Let's wash the dishes. Have our coffees and you have a cigarette if you like and then the water'll have boiled good and we can start washing him down.'

'Where will we do it?'

'I think just here. The floor'll absorb any moisture. I want to wash his body in Tigh An Roin.'

'We're not doing it naked or anything like that are we?'

Kirsty laughs, 'No, a gradh.'

'I got these for you. They're in full bloom over near the road.' I give Kirsty the bundle of yellow irises tied with one of their leaves I'd hidden under my chair.

And there are the tears in her pale blue eyes. One or two spill over quickly and the rest ebb away. She holds me in her gaze, it's as if she's pouring wisdom directly into my soul, then we are in each other arms and my body feels as big as a beast's and hers like a little bird.

'Tapadh leat, a gradh, thank you a gradh.'

'Tha gaol agam ort' I say, I love you.

'Tha goal agam ort-fhèin' I love you yourself, she says to me.

- 28 -

'We'll use the bog cotton flowers and just swish the water all over like this' Kirsty takes a fistful of the fluffy white heads, dips them in the water and spills it over Lachie's chest, letting her hand linger on his hard skin.

'Sure it's already quite leathery-feeling' she says.

I have my hand on his thigh. 'He's like a waxwork figure of himself. I think he's more waxy than leathery' I say.

She catches me looking at his penile opening. 'Have you not seen that before?'

'Yes, I have. You know, when we ran about the place.'

'And?'

'You're asking me did we ever have carnal relations?'

'I am.'

'No. It was never like that with us. But I did see. I asked him about it once when he was peeing' I hesitate.

289

'Uh-huh?'

'Well, you know, I'd seen my father's many times.'

'I suspected that.'

'So I knew Lachie's was different. Like maybe he didn't have one. Maybe I thought I'd mistaken it for his belly-button. I was only about ten.'

I sit up on my hunkers. I am still looking carefully at the opening, the slight rise of something muscular underneath.

It is clear to me now that I can study it that it is a seal's penis he has; sheathed internally for protection the same way as dogs.

'I suppose I didn't really think about it at all. But I remember once thinking maybe he was ... deformed'

'Always the scientist eh Lorna?'

'Yes.'

'When it doesn't fit your facts, it doesn't exist. Well, I'm glad you never thought of him as a freak of nature. Even though he is, of course. But not in that horrible, scientific way.'

'That's what was worrying me about the post-mortem. That they'd want to study him and suspend him in formaldehyde.'

We both shiver and rub our hands.

'No. They'd not want to do that. No money in it for them. Freak shows are different things altogether nowadays. All done behind closed doors.'

'Like us just now you mean?'

She laughs. 'Well, now you come to mention it. It is a bit freakish right enough to have him cleansed by this lovely marriage of you with your science and me with my art.'

When we've finished washing Lachie's body in silence and unuttered our private reveries of remembrances Kirsty stands up, stretches and leans down to see through the kitchen window.

'We'll need to wait for dusk' she says.

'OK.'

'The tide is coming in beautifully. It'll be a nice high tide for us by dusk and then it'll be on the turn. It could not be more perfect.'

She looks down at Lachie's body, 'Perfect like himself. Do you know, I've always loved those wild whiskers of his' she says. 'Aye' she grips her lips together and releases them, 'I've always loved him. My boy.' She looks out of the window and I can see she is seeing him walking up from the water and waving at her, his arms full of a string bag of oysters for dinner.

*

The sun is away down the back of the hill but it is still technically daylight. It is a Friday in 2005 and me and my best friend's mother sitting vigil over his dead body. The shell-encrusted table light is on near the sofa and so is the driftwood hanging lamp in the kitchen.

I hear a sheep baaing for its lamb in the distance.

'We'd usually be having our shellfish pasta about now' says Kirsty.

'I'll make us some dinner. I'll do some damper bread and tomato and basil pasta. Do you want garlic on the damper?'

'No. Keep it plain tonight. And don't make too much.'

'I can take the leftovers down to the village for the cawing gannets at Rose Tree.'

'Aye. OK. Thanks.'

When we've finished our meal and washed and dried the dishes, put the plates away in their rack and the cutlery is restored to its order in the felt-lined drawer, I am determined not to ask Kirsty what we are going to do with Lachie. I'm like a gun with its safety catch off trying to keep the question held tight in my chest so it doesn't explode out.

'Do you have something to wear into the sea?' she says.

'I think so. I've got my thermal top and leggings under this.'

'That'll do. I've got my thermals too. We'll need to both have a hot shower and stay warm before we go in. You go first. It'll be cold in the sea. We'll need to go in warm. You go have a shower first.'

I want to say how odd it is for me to be bossed about this way. But I've remembered about not using that word for today. And as I come out of the shower, all pink-skinned, I think about how much I'm enjoying this going-with-the-flow; how easy it is to let things unfold instead of trying to control events, how surprisingly comforting it can be to live with uncertainty.

There's a frisson of thrill at my unknowing. Me, the paragon of knowledge so at peace with not knowing. We are to go into the sea Kirsty and I. And Lachie I am guessing. And will we all return?

I feel an excitement I have not felt since I was half of LachieLorna and he was half of a seal. It's a wildness in my belly, a twist of possibilities in my guts, an abandonment to opportunities in my womb.

I spread my arms wide and close my eyes and breathe.

I have my wax jacket over my thermals when Kirsty comes in dressed in similar fashion. 'No hats' she says.

'No.'

'OK. I'll just go and get it.'

'OK' I say not knowing what she's referring to.

As she comes back in through the back door from the outhouse she is holding a grey scarf in both hands in front of her.

'Here it is now. It looks perfect. I was worried about the mice since Sula left.'

'You're wearing a scarf?' I say.

'A scarf?' she laughs and bends over snorting, 'No. It's not a scarf Lorna. It's his seal skin.'

'His seal skin?'

'You're doing that repeating-parrot thing again,' she says. 'This is why he came ashore before. When the teacher found him. He wasn't in his skin.'

I get up off the chair at the kitchen table and move towards her. The skin looks like nano-felted wool, hand-dyed in every shade of grey and black, blotched and splattered and exquisite. Closer, I see there are hairs on it, fur of a kind.

'His seal skin?' I say 'Can I touch it?'

She smiles, 'See, there you are again, needing to touch things to make sure they are real. Of course, hold it yourself.'

I take the soft, hairy skin and a cloud of sea air and salt surrounds me. It's different from the seal carcasses on the shore. The inside of this seal skin is more smooth than anything I've ever touched, more smooth than a rose petal, more soft than angora or chinchilla fur, more supple than a spider's web. My fingers don't seem to touch it at all, it is so light and delicate, I run my index finger along the inside. It is a skin right enough.

'So beautiful' I say, releasing my breath.

On the other side of the skin is rough fur, grey, black, grey like the rocks around Elleraig, the colour of clouds before rain.

'They all have different patterns, you know' says Kirsty. 'Individuals, of course. Lachie's was quite dark, quite black you see? Safer for him in the water to be more invisible.'

I hand it back to her, holding it on both of my palms, upwards in an intuitive gesture of respectful supplication.

'Let's have one last look at him this way' says Kirsty. I see her lips move and she is canting a murmur of words over him. I see a film on Super 8 of LachieLorna running wild and laughing, drinking freshwater shrimps and him spitting them out and me swallowing them whole with bits of peat.

'It might not be easy to get it on. I'm not exactly sure how it …' Kirsty is moving the seal skin about, looking for inspiration.

'I think we just let it float down upon him.'

'*Upon* him, eh?'

'Yes, just let it float down.'

She lifts the seal skin up high, arms reaching to the wooden ceiling and lets it go.

It hangs in the air like a piece of silk in a gentle wind. It drifts feather-like, moving from side to side over Lachie's body like an empty hammock swinging. It turns in the air, rolls upside down and right way up and suddenly surges down, a rogue wave from nowhere spiriting downwards and there on the floor of Tigh An Roin is a lifeless, beautiful seal.

    'See the magic there Lorna?'

    'I do. I see the magic Kirsty.'

    'That's a good girl, a gradh.'

- 29 -

'Are you nervous?' says Kirsty as we stop outside the house and look down to the murky well that is the bay.

'No. Not a bit. I feel … dreamy.'

'We need to take him at dusk. He came in on the tide at dawn. He needs to go with the tide at dusk. There's an onshore breeze. It's all just as it should be.'

I'm holding his tail end in the circle of my arms. Kirsty is grasping him above his tiny flippers. I see a child's hand limp in the flipper, narrow finger bones sheathed in leather. I see his claws.

We're walking barefoot through the marram grass, then the flat machair, then the pebbles, then the powder sand and now the damp sand. As my feet feel the cold of the wet sand I see lumps in the water.

Lumps like raised cysts on the film of the bay. The light is fading, or is it my eyesight? There are numerous bumps of darkness across the bay; shadows that are heavy and deft.

A quiet wave tickles my toes and rushes over my

feet. The water splashes up my calves. I feel tiny flounders slip away under my soles.

I want to tell Kirsty how much flatfish freak me out but I keep quiet because I am hushed by awe in an oceanic cathedral. Kirsty is leading the way, one foot in front of the other, determined. We are pall-bearers.

I feel a slick of seaweed or is it an eel lick my calves and I flinch but grit my teeth. The water around my knees has an electric feel of air bubbles and turbulence under water as though there is a giant propeller somewhere past the island that forces the water through the two narrow channels on either side.

The whole bay is full of movement, flickers of shapes rising and falling above the lapping waves. I am so relieved it is not stormy. But I am beginning to feel afraid. Out of my depth, I am close to being right out of my depth. I clasp Lachie's skin and sucker my finger tips to it.

A head right in front of Kirsty. Huge eyes, corners sloping downwards. It dives. I see the arched back slip down. I feel it coming to me in the pull of the water but even so I gasp as it rears up in front of me, to my left, looking. I fall into the eyes. So close. So familiar. The seal's head turns, whiskers catch the moonlight though the sun is still in the sky where we can't see it, away. He turns towards Lachie's body and briskly dives under, back arched again and now there are hundreds of seals filling the bay, I see more flowing through the firths on both sides of the island. Streaming towards us. Kirsty keeps walking, she has not hesitated and I suddenly remember, panic, that we must be nearing the sand shelf where the land surrenders entirely and quickly to the sea and the ocean is deep and fathomless. I want to keep moving, with confident steps like Kirsty, but I falter, my feet wanting to grow roots into the sea bed but I feel Lachie move in my hands and I cannot let him go, the force to want to hold him and do this thing for him is stronger in me. A child's determination.

My hands win-out, my feet release and I am floating with Lachie as my buoyancy aid … and wasn't it always the way?

Kirsty is floating ahead, she turns to see am I OK and I can feel my eyes widening. We are both afraid. I can see she is afraid and she is somehow telling me we would be fools to not be afraid for look, she says nothing but I follow her gaze and see a small fin, tar black and curved like a sickle and Holy Mother of God it is an orca, carving its way through the frog spawn of seals, it is coming as slow as death creeps in the night stealthily smooth along the channel on the right of the island and the seals are dipping and diving, dipping and diving and I have my fingers on the top of Lachie as he floats, a boat, an imagining, my dearest, sweetest friend, and Kirsty is on the other side of him to me and her fingers reach for mine and together our hands clasp over Lachie as he floats.

Two seals, females I think, surface one on either side of us and push us away with their necks. I feel wet whiskers and a barking moan as my feet start to kick, find strong stroke, killer whale bait our four legs are dancing and luring underwater.

Elleraig Bay is full of sea mammals coming to take Lachie back to where he came from. The returning of the gift.

But the orca has not come closer, she, I feel the orca is a she, how do I know, it does not matter, she is cruising in wide circles, keeping the crowd of seals back, stopping more of them from entering the channels and whoosh comes the water in front of him as she swims towards us and leaps from the ocean, not too high, and the seals clear away from where she will land, in front of Lachie and his two seal companions, and crash lands the black and white majesty of a beast and I go under water where there are bubbles and tiny bits of fish and kelp but the water pulls me back up to the surface when the orca glides away and I see she is carving a channel for the seals who nudge Lachie. More seals join them until he is but one in a flotsam of seals, he is bobbing on the surface, rolling now and again as if in play. They are all of them moving as one, they are taking him home, far out to sea.

As the seals around us become fewer, joining the main herd, Kirsty gestures with her finger pointing towards the left channel which is almost empty of seals now as they all rush through the right with Lachie. Small fins and leaping luminescences of delight – dolphins.

I look questioningly at Kirsty.

She sprays away salt water from her mouth. All I can see is her head, detached from any earthly body. 'I'm surprised to see the dolphins. They must have come all the way from Arnamurachan.' she says, spluttering at the ripples lapping her lips.

I look back again, the pod must be ten or more strong.

'It's you' she says, 'they're coming to you.'

Indeed they are swimming towards us. I realise my beating arms, out by my sides, in close to my breast, that are keeping me afloat, are also a signal of welcome to them.

'Are you pregnant Lorna?' She rubs at her nose causing salt water to trickle over her mouth. 'Sure they're very curious about pregnant women. I think it's the foetus floating in the amniotic fluid that attracts them. Are you pregnant?'

'Quite possibly' I smile. But I stop smiling when they begin to rub against me, three or four of them are swimming across my skin, bustling at me. I put my hand on their flanks and feel the strength of silver moonshine under my hands.

'For God's sake don't hold onto their fins or they'll think you want to go out with Lachie!' says Kirsty.

They swim around us like a shoal of joy. I am swimming with dolphins. I am communing with dolphins in Elleraig Bay. Bam. They are off after the orca-led seal flotilla, bringing up the rear. Rushing so fast and leaping friskily over the waves. Whoosh-whoosh-whoosh spit their blowholes; snatches of maritime music.

We are left with only the lapping of the waves on our chins.

We are not so far from the beach. As we breast-stroke slowly alongside one another, I can see the house with its dim lights glimmering. I never knew how beautiful it looked from the sea. How wholesome and welcoming.

I let my legs drift down and my feet fumble to where the shelf of sand is, a small sandbar cliff breaks off under my toes. A slippery-something swims away. It tickles. I like it. 'Imagine that now' I say aloud. Gone is my fear of seaweed, eels and flounders under my sole.

Kirsty turns around and looks out to sea, where it seems there is nothing but blackness and the thickness of water. 'Aye. Imagine that indeed' she says.

'Well Lorna,' she says as we walk through the water, making rivulets of splashing sea foam, our bodies heavy, leaden and lumbering with wetness, 'as Lachie would say: all things are possible; it's only our beliefs that restrain us.

'Let's away into the warmth now. Sure, I have a belief a wee dram is in order.'

ABOUT THE AUTHOR

Flora Kennedy was born in Glasgow, Scotland in 1965 and grew up in Stirlingshire and Argyll. She trained as a journalist in Glasgow before her career as an advertising writer took her to London, Sydney and Auckland for the next 25 years. She is a published poet as well as a novelist. Her short story *Tenderness* was included in the Bloody Scotland International Crime Writing Festival *Worth the Wait* anthology. After living overseas for two decades she returned home to Scotland as a New Zealand citizen in 2007 and now lives in the Outer Hebrides.

33043526R00176

Made in the USA
Charleston, SC
03 September 2014